MW01073537

Girl: Repurposed
A Novel

Meaghan Curley

Cosmic Teapot Publishing

Hanmer, ON

Girl: Repurposed

Copyright © 2017 by Meaghan Curley

ISBN: 9781988762081

All rights reserved. No part of this publication may be reproduced, distributed, or transmitted in any form or by any means, including photocopying, recording, or other electronic or mechanical methods, without the prior written permission of the publisher, except in the case of brief quotations embodied in critical reviews and certain other noncommercial uses permitted by copyright law. For permission requests, write to the publisher, addressed "Attention: Permissions Coordinator," at dylan@cosmicteapot.net.

Published by Cosmic Teapot Publishing
Hanmer, ON, Canada
www.cosmicteapot.net

Ordering Information:
Quantity sales. Special discounts are available on quantity purchases by corporations, associations, and others. For details, contact the publisher at the email address above.

"Rebirth: that's God stuff...Or, but, thenagain...not always. There's secular reincarnation too."

Salman Rushdie *The Satanic Verses*

"If there's a prize for rotten judgment/I guess I've already won that"

Megara, Disney's *Hercules* (1997)

Dedication pages are formal and weird, so I'm doing shout outs instead:

Shout out to my grandma Sharon and my two former coworkers Jeanette Barlett and Darla Krull for inspiring major scenes/ characters/ or themes for the book.
Shout out to Tina Williams (of Tina William's Editing Services) and Dylan Callens (of Cosmic Teapot Publishing) for sifting through the crap that was my first several rough drafts.

Shout out to Sal, the love of my life, and for a long time this novel's only reader.

Shout out to my sister Alice for supporting the fuck out of me and for coming up with my dope as fuck author picture idea.

Shout out to my mom for wanting a lawyer, or at least a painter, and getting my punk ass instead.
Shout out to my brother Larry (you didn't do anything I just know how much you hate books and thought this would annoy you).

Shout out to Alyson Kaltak (of Nordisla's Blacksmithing) for taking my author picture and Jessica Poczatek of Nevermore Tattoo Shop for creating the cover art.

I love you all!

TABLE OF CONTENTS

LESS PRIDE, MORE PREJUDICE

"Which one are you?"

"I'm Tranquila, Grandma." Just as she was yesterday and the day before when she asked.

"Oh. Well—why the hell are you home, then? Don't you have a job yet?"

"I can't, Grandma," she said with a drawl, not even bothering to point to her ankle bracelet this time.

Grandma Sobriquet, a French name for a woman older than France, shook her head, judging. "Such indolence. Christ, how old are you anyway?"

"I'm eighteen, Grandma."

"Eighteen!" Any age with only two digits appalled her. "And you still don't have a job? You should be on your third job and raising a family by now."

"Why?"

"Why?!" Grandma Sobriquet sputtered, "Because life's depressing and we like to keep it that way. Now go out there and don't come back until you either have a seventy-hour work week or a newborn."

Keenly aware that she should not argue with Grandma Sobriquet while she's going through her *forget-me-whats*, Tranquila retreated upstairs into her bedroom. There was nothing of interest for her. The most advanced gadget in her entire room was wrapped around her ankle like a tattle-tale troll. A laptop sat fallow on a chair full of clothes and Tranquila hoisted herself to grab it. But once she'd logged on she remembered why there was dust on the top: Mom had paid the neighborhood nerd twenty bucks to make it so they were only allowed the basics like Wikipedia: "Might as well learn something since you're gonna act like Boo Boo the fool" or WebMD: "When Grandma Sobriquet starts pussing and oozing randomly." Tranquila slammed the laptop in half and exhaled.

Boredom never hurt this much.

She lifted her head and looked around. How she wished she could sew or knit or do origami. Anything to take the itching away from her idle hands. Suicide was tempting but she stashed the thought away as being pointless, *what could be more boring than death?* she reasoned.

Half a minute of boredom later, she opened the laptop once more and went to Google. She started with Louis XVI, who she sensed was a fellow compatriot also locked in a position without pursuit or direction. Of course, she was only on the internet ten minutes before she clicked on a regrettable link and was left traumatized after looking up the meaning of 'phimosis'.

And so the fate of all who dwell on the internet...

Frustrated and half-insane, Tranquila yanked the laptop until it released from its charger. She tossed it onto her bed, flopping along with it, and screamed everything she could into a ladybug-shaped pillow. All of this on day four of her house arrest.

The ensuing boredom made her consider tasks that she would never have done otherwise: binge-watching courtroom dramas and cleaning. Even talking to her Grandma Sobriquet, whom her mother had appointed to watch Tranquila, to ensure no 'pot smoking and munchy crunching' was going on whilst she was at work. As if she could, when a burly woman with a clipboard watched her pee in a cup three times a month.

It was why a defeated Tranquila plodded back downstairs in hopes that daytime courtroom dramas would ease her crippling indisposition. She skidded into the living room like a depressed cross-skier.

"What's wrong with you?"

"Nothing, Grandma. I'm just so bored," she sighed.

"Oh," said Grandma Sobriquet. "Well—try being good at something."

"I wish I was," she replied. "I'd give *anything* to be good at *anything*."

Her grandma rolled her eyes after that and went back to partaking in her favorite form of inactivity: watching exaggerated people trying to become viral-famous on a petty showroom court. Tranquila plopped onto a loveseat beside her, finally willing to submit to the mental succumb that is daytime television. They maintained a dead silence for a good couple of hours. Then, during the first commercial of *Who Wants to Be a Celebrity Judge*, Grandma Sobriquet made a casual suggestion.

"You can always ask Hades."

At first, Tranquila misheard her: "Why would I ask Haiti for help? Don't they have their own problems?"

"No, you ignoramus, I said *Hades*." She exaggerated the name by pushing her dry lips up and revealing her front wooden-looking teeth. Tranquila's slowness angered her. "You don't know who Hades is?"

She did, but she remembered the flaming-blue-man reject that Disney created out of commercial spite to the Greeks and Graecomanics. "I know who he is. He's that Greek…dude— god of…bad jokes?"

Grandma Sobriquet could feel her left foot start to die but she ignored the psychosomatics to tell her ignorant kin,

"He's the one that rules the dead. When Zeus and Poseidon were too good to deal with the dead, he took a throne and controlled more than both his brothers combined." She paused, waiting for her granddaughter to engage, which turned out to be futile, "He's got the three-headed dog! Lives underground?"

She nodded but wasn't convinced or interested. "Thanks for the suggestion, but you aren't gonna see my funeral anytime soon." *Sketchy old bitch.*

"I'm not saying you're bored, go kill yourself. *I'm saying*, if you want to talk to someone about the circumstance you're in, *talk to him*," she stressed, the cracked-out wobbly voice she garnered from senility now levelled and wise.

Tranquila was not swayed. "Sure, Grandma, I'll go right out and ask the ancient Greek dude that lives underground with his three-headed bitch."

Her sarcasm didn't generate an insult or the creative new curse word that she expected. Instead, Grandma Sobriquet just gave her a squinty grin before turning her head back to the full attention of the television. Tranquila dismissed the thought as another one of her demented moments.

"Up next on Who Wants to Be a Celebrity Judge—"

"Your honor, she used me for a set of snow tires."

"Now that's a whole 'nother level of hoe."

The fake courtroom burst into hoots and hollers.

The screen lulled momentarily while a commercial about online cosmetology courses switched on. Her grandmother's waiting face peered at her from just out of vision.

"A dollar says you're full of shit," said Tranquila.

The withered husk gave her a smug, lopsided smile. "Help me up so I can show *you* up."

*

Apparently, everything you need to make communication with a god of the Underworld can be found right in your cabinets. Supported by Tranquila's arm, Grandma Sobriquet directed them to the side yard with an armful of gas-station merlot, tap water, some milk and a bear-shaped honey bottle. They wobbled over to a patchy part of the yard where—using Tranquila for balance—Grandma Sobriquet slipped off her prescribed shoes and used a thick bunion as a spade to make a golf-ball-sized hole in the earth.

"Okay," she breathed, signaling Tranquila to let her go. Tranquila did, taking one step sideways as her grandmother raised her elbows. Tranquila watched her flick off the honey bottle's yellow nip and tilt it downwards. She chanted in a language dead and fallowed. Her haughty but shaky voice growled unpleasantly until Tranquila was convinced that underneath the afternoon sun in the treeless backyard lurked shadows and whispers of oblivion.

Sunlight illuminated the thick golden strain that hung from the bottle. Grandma Sobriquet flung it aside and snagged the cup of water, not losing place in her recital, not even to take breath. Once the plastic cup was drained, she tossed it over her shoulder and extended two shaky arms before herself with the bottle of merlot and the milk still in her grasp, continuing without pause or inhale. Only when her incantation was done did Grandma Sobriquet rotate her wrists and let the third and fourth liquids fall with the rest of the libation. It took several seconds for the bottle of wine and the quarter gallon of milk to empty.

Tranquila waited one second more after the sacrifice for something to happen.

"Give me a dollar," she demanded, finally.

Grandma Sobriquet didn't argue. Two heartbeats later, a blackness materialized from the sticky mixture, transforming into a shadowy man with a white spotted face and yellow lid-less eyes.

"No, give *me* a dollar."

Tranquila had no time to react, let alone give her a dollar—for the Dirt Monster had already strong-armed the unsuspecting female.

A swift breeze later, they were descending far and fast from the surface of the yard, like hopeless beings thrown from a cliff. Tranquila screamed until she felt her heart turn to ash. With one final gust of consciousness, like a man passing out after torture, she berated herself wildly for listening to that soulless bitch.

WAR ON DRUGS

Doesn't it always start out with someone young doing something stupid?

In this case it does.

It was sometime in the summer at a party of a friend of a friend's when Tranquila was searching for a bathroom in her green Airmax shoes and her faded green and dark roots. Eventually, she found a bathroom in which kids weren't doing drugs or each other. However, she opened the door to find a man on the toilet around her age. He was slumped against the wall with a needle hanging out of the crook of his elbow like a Christmas decoration.

Being half-buzzed and three-quarters of the way stoned, Tranquila Obiit was dulled to the seriousness of the situation.

"Fina-fucking-ly!" She exclaimed as she dug into her strappy purse, pulled out her cellphone, and a bright blue zipped-up bag.

Tranquila recently became Naloxone administration certified, due to the ever growing increase of heroin and opiate related overdoses in her city. Much like anyone who just learned CPR, she was eager to put her new skill to use. Unlike most, however, Tranquila was pumped and prepared. Kneeling in front of the young man, she dialed 9-1-1 and put the phone on speaker while placing it on the edge of a nearby sink. "9-1-1 what is your emergency?"

"Hi, so I'm at a party and I just found this guy in the bathroom and I'm like nine hundred percent sure he OD'd."

"You're nine hundred percent sure?"

"Yeah. His lips are blue, he's not moving and there's a needle sticking out of his arm," she replied, as she unzipped the bag, took out the gloves and began filling the syringe she had with Naloxone.

"Oh yeah, he OD'd," the operator confirmed.

"Yeah, so anyway, I'm giving the guy Narcan. Just letting you know," she informed as she administered the shot into his other arm.

"What's your location, so we can send an ambulance?"

"I'm at 600 Plant Street in Utica, NY. Second floor," she answered.

"Okay. Please stay on the line while the EMTs arrive."

Tranquila reached over and tapped the phone to be put on speaker. She listened to the 911 operator as she made commands in the background. Tranquila watched the young man, staring at his pale face for a change to occur. She tapped him on the shoulder, trying to coax a response out of him. Nothing changed. She waited and waited.

Then, his eyes fluttered. The dead man on the toilet let out a stuffy-smoker's-like cough.

Tranquila almost threw-up from absolute joy. She saved a life.

*

Another half-a-minute went by until the EMTs arrived to the party. By then, the entirety of the party heard that some guy OD'd in the bathroom and had flocked around the open door, only to be disappointed. "Wow…he's not even dead!" "This is lame. "Come on guys let's go find someone with alcohol poisoning."

After the EMTs came the cops. Once they found out she was the person who saved the heroin user they started quizzing her, "How did you find him? Do you know what he's on? Are you on the same thing? Did you guys use together? Did you share a needle?"

Tranquila was bewildered. She had never been accused of being a junkie before. "I was trying to take a shit when I found him like this."

"Why do you carry Narcan on you if you don't use?"

"Because when I worked at Dunkin Donuts last year I walked in on mad people OD'ing in the bathrooms and I wanted to be prepared."

The cops sensed she was lying. In-part because who carries an opiate overdose prevention kit in their purse unless they're around heroin users frequently. But mostly they didn't trust anybody with stupid hair not to be a junky. Regardless, they didn't ask anything else. They remained silent as the paramedics carried the toilet guy into the hallway and down the stairs into the first floor where a stretcher awaited him. They strapped him in, carrying him off with a crowd of gawkers before they loaded him into the back of the ambulance. They drove off, leaving Tranquila to stand on top of the stairs of the second floor. Looking down upon the waves of parties, she thrust her arms into the air and cried,

"U-S-A! U-S-A! U-S-A! U-S-A!"

The remaining partiers cheered and clapped for her, which caused Tranquila to jump up and down. Something fell out of her hoodie's pocket and smacked against the floor. She heard this and froze.

An eighth of weed fell out. Right in front of the police. They didn't hesitate. "Ma'am, you're under arrest."

"What?!" she blurted out, as they twisted her arms behind her back and slapped handcuffs around her wrist with absurd speed.

"Lame!" one partier bravely declared.

"W-what?!" she squeaked out as they lead her down the stairs. "This is fucking insane! I saved a guy's life! What about the Good Samaritan Law?"

"That only counts when there's unintended consequences from your assistance," replied one of the cops without sympathy.

"Besides," began the second officer, "there are more important things to worry about right now and that's making sure people with drug problems are locked away and segregated from law-abiding society."

With that being said, Tranquila Obiit was lead past the under-aged alcoholics, twenty-one-year old men lurking for fourteen-year old girlfriends, and the group of huddled teenagers salivating over an involuntary nude picture, into the back of a cop car.

So began Tranquila's six month house arrest sentence, the decline of her mother's respect for her daughter, and the even more nightmarish sentence of Grandma Sobriquet as her live-in babysitter.

MAS SABE EL DIABLO POR VIEJO QUE POR DIABLO

Like the moments that perforate a car crash, flashes of her certain death came but were followed by the sounds of breath. The shaky focus and electric heart attacks signified that she cheated death. In between checking her pulse and her pants, she found out that she was standing. Opening her eyes, she saw the dirt monster was gone and the patch of earth they dug was far from view. She was standing in what felt like a massive cave.

She looked down and saw with paralyzing vertigo that she was trembling precariously on a small aerie. And just below her elevated plot stood legions upon legions of face-bearing skeletons steeped in gook, soot and hand-given suffering. These were the insensible shadows she'd felt during her grandmother's libation—had the old lady called them out to traumatize her granddaughter? So she could witness men and women endlessly melting in waist-deep magma? Or watch as identifiable souls were victimized by the leaders of this world? She watched as Disease whipped criminal doctors; almost went into cardiac arrest listening to the ear-gouging screams as Old Age nail-gunned fear-mongering journalists; and gagged on air soaked with the freshly spilt blood of the recently re-decapitated.

Thus was the Underworld.

Tranquila stood there, steeled and ensnared by doom, when a sonorous voice bashed against the walls and jagged crags, sending her heart into her ass, "Where's this mortal who has summoned me?"

She gasped violently, instinctively clutching at her chest as she searched for the owner of the voice. Tranquila could feel her ghost slipping out of her as she beheld reality. Hades was real and Hades stood before her. Tranquila was so trifling a creature that he did not see her at first—in the same way a lightning storm isn't aware of a mouse until it unintentionally strikes it down.

In her ignorance, she thought how Hades looked like he had fought the Earth just to be here. How was she to know that his skin was comprised of the ashes of a volcano that had almost stomped out life epochs ago? And that his eyes saw the inside of his own father's stomach, which explained why they had deep, rutted valleys around the eyelids. And how Earth was just a rumor to him when he was already a millennium old. She knew none of this. To her, he stood like a tree burdened by a hefty tire swing. When his eyes beheld her for the first time they were inexplicably human. She could recognize the annoyance they possessed.

"Oh, for the love of—*another Goth kid*?" Hades let out irritably, referring to her wild hair and piercings. Cupping his hands for stereo, he shouted at her like a nurse in a geriatric unit: "I—CAN'T—TURN—YOU—INTO—A—VAMPIRE. STOP CONTACTING ME ABOUT IT. Jesus Christ!" Hades turned to the figure who had kidnapped this girl and lambasted him, "Stop sending me the weird kids."

"Sir," his courier said, repressively, "she was sent by Jeanette."

The ancient god stopped at the name. Hades turned to address the mortal, "Jeanette Sobriquet?"

Tranquila nodded vigorously and explained in-between squeaks and pants, "I'm...I'm...her granddaughter."

The god blinked. "She begat?" He felt as though he might cry, then to himself he mused, "Hmph, I always assumed she hated children."

"S-she does."

He laughed. "True in any species: those that should never reproduce, always do."

Tranquila tried laughing with him but she was too busy weaning herself off the heart attacks.

"Don't overexert yourself," Hades replied, patiently. "Many mortals have died trying to laugh at my jokes when they should've been trying to give themselves CPR. I am patient. Prepare yourself."

She nodded in thanks, bending over with her hands on her knees to take giant breaths before easing herself back into the conversation, still breathless, "Holy shit! Holy fucking shit! I can't believe this. All those long-ass poems they made us read in school were true."

Hades scoffed, "You mortals. You'll accept our gyros and our togas, but tell them how the world works and they call it mythology."

"Wow," she gasped, captivated. "God *is* real!"

Hades shook his head. "I forget how far behind you mortals are. And yes there is a god, a whole super team, actually."

"Wow. The Greeks were right." Who would have guessed the bankrupt country of Socrates would turn out to be right on the money? She asked innocently, "Doesn't it bother you that you guys are called *myths* while everyone is giving all the love to some fake, single God?"

Hades didn't ponder long. "In the end," he replied, "the Greeks were right and that's all that matters. But tell me, my American maiden, why did Jeanette send you to me?"

Tranquila thought it was funny how a fourteen-billion-year-old deity knew her grandmother's name and she promised herself if she were to ever return home, the first thing she'd do would be to call her out for being so damn old.

"I was complaining about boredom," she admitted sheepishly, before quickly adding, "But I've learned my lesson. I promise I will never call bullshit on you again."

"Now, now, mortal. I was not summoned because your grandmother wanted to prove you wrong. I was notified because I was under the impression you were in need of a favor," he said, the depth of his voice sounded more colossal than it truly was. "Now, tell me, what is it you seek?"

"Um…" she hesitated. A god, an all-powerful underground wizard, essentially, was asking her what she needed. She had asked for her grandmother's help and—while twisted—why waste a resource when it's given? It's not like she was trying to make a deal with the devil, just Hades. "I just need some purpose. That's all I need. Something to do, to keep me from killing myself for a couple of months. That's it."

"That's it?"

"That's it. I just want to be good at something. Keep my mind busy. Keep me busy."

"You came all the way to the Underworld to find purpose?"

"Is that what they call it now?"

He smiled at her. "You're ambitious, I'll give you that. Most mortals would rather agonize over that problem than face risk and ask."

She didn't argue but thought him wrong. Had mortals and English grads only took the *Odyssey* seriously, Hades would have seen more and more of her kind coming down, just to be pointed in the right direction.

"So what say you then, my American maiden? I give you purpose and you give me something onus?" asked Hades, his voice airy like a man trying to proposition.

'Onus'? Dammit, why is everyone trying to make me learn lately? "I thought this was a *free* consultation," said Tranquila.

"Listen, maiden, you're in the Underworld. Free advice will get you the standard 'go back to school, read some books, learn a skill, get married or something if you're bored' da da da da da—BUT, for an ordinal fee, you can get what you actually need."

A whiny groan escaped her but once the groan was born it begat an epiphany. "I want a job," she said. The simplicity of it made Hades laugh, until she added, "here."

He made the same noise a man would make if they were laughing with a mouthful of chicken wings and in their jubilation started choking. "You want me to give you a job?"

She nodded vigorously, while he stared at her, truly shocked. He hadn't been this dumbfounded since he watched the glorious, seemingly-expansive Ottoman Empire get their ass handed to them by a bunch of potato farmers on a boat.

"Maiden, are you in perfect possession of your faculties?"

She mentally translated that as: bitch are you cray-cray? Nonetheless, she stood by her statement.

Hades was not the blue-haired Disney reject many knew him to be. He was not keen on enslaving the soul of a young woman, especially after his separation. He was too cautious to be making half-assed deals.

"You…want to trade your soul…for a job?" he asked. "You realize you could have done that by getting a job in the mortal world?"

Shaking her head, she explained, "Nobody wants to hire a green-haired kid on probation." Unless she came out with a fire mixtape, her options were slim.

"Maiden, I respect the situation you're presently in, but what job could I give you that would be worth becoming an eternal serf in the Underworld once you die?"

Good question, she thought, the internal argument visible in her eyes. A sparkle flashed as she pleaded, "I can be your dog-sitter!"

"What?"

"C'mon, let me take care of your dog. I know you have one."

"You want to take care of my three-headed guard dog whom I use to strike fear into the hearts of all those who dwell here, for all eternity?" asked Hades, incredulous. He thought this over. His altruistic side convinced him it would only be fair to let her see what she was up against. Jerking his head, he led the way down the Flaming River and past the Vale of Rejected Crybabies.

Alas, they found the giant guard dog perched on an island of its own. One head gave a blink-less stare at his approaching master and follower; the other chewed on a conscious man's body, the man screaming until one sweet crunch on the skull silenced him abruptly. Naturally, the third head was chewing on its groin because a dog's a dog no matter what dimension it's in.

Hades flourished a long, beefy arm at his demonic canine and asked again, "You want to take care of this foul, loathsome creature for all eternity?"

Staring into the six eyes of a giant mutated puppy, Tranquila squealed, "Take care of a three-headed pitbull forever? Hell, yeah!"

Initially slack-jawed, Hades' mouth eased into a grin. Lowering his arm, he rotated the wrist and stuck out a flat hand. "Is this what you wish, my bodacious maiden?"

She looked at his surprisingly smooth, obsidian fingers. The longer she stared, the more sculpted they appeared. These were the final moments of being the sole owner of her soul. But her thinking was done, as a new bastard cancer spread inside her heart and mind that made the prospect of returning back to the monotony, back to the purposelessness, back to daytime courtroom television, more hellish than Hades. Recklessly, she announced, "Yes."

Hades' grin grew into a full teeth-baring smile. While nothing supernatural happened, Tranquila felt a soft tingling in her palms.

"Deal," the god of the Underworld breathed. His eyelids lowered and his chest puffed. Was her imagination already taking flight or was he growing? Her hand pulsated as Hades inched closer and closer to her body. Her wrist adjusted so he could gently feel the tops of her knuckles instead of her palm. He was already another two feet taller when he lowered himself to meet her horrified stares.

A cold frost creeped up her hand. She snapped it back, releasing from his crusted touch. But before she could tug or even flinch, Hades raised one hand perpendicular to his shoulder and promised, "Starting tomorrow, you will never be bored again."

With her hand still in his, he swung both of his tree-trunk arms until the three hands met and produced a loud crack.

Within that clap, everything turned black, airless, and unbearably warm. Panic overrode her as one truth screamed in her blood that she was dead—she was dead, and—worse—she knew it. No doubt she was dead. Hades was dark; Hades was hot; Hades was—soft? Jerking around like a seal in a fishnet, she realized she wasn't dead, flopping around until she untangled herself from the blankets and dropped to the ground.

Bruised and frightened, she twisted around until she freed her feet, and stood up to find—her room. "What the..." she said through a barely audible whisper, bewildered and panting.

A noise from behind made her jump. Turning around she found Grandma Sobriquet stood in the doorway, nudging the door so it would creek loud enough to get Tranquila's attention.

Tranquila's reckless mind berated its owner for the deleterious decision she'd just made—delivering a thousand insults per second in an internalized diatribe—interrupted by Grandma Sobriquet's hobbled voice, "Where's my dollar, bitch?"

LOL@ WOMEN'S RIGHTS

Sitting in a bed, too hot for blankets, Tranquila trembled. She didn't know but it was 3:42 in the morning, a full fifteen hours since she had made her reckless decision with Hades. Worse than the bad decision was the fact that she had no one with whom to confide.

She recalled her conversation with Grandma Sobriquet, barking at the old biddy, "I can't believe you sent me to Hades for a dollar!"

"I know—I should have done it for a dollar and eight cents; I forgot everything's got a tax now."

And how Mama Sobriquet had returned home from work but she said nothing about what transpired, knowing she probably shouldn't share the good news. What could she say anyway? *"Guess what mom? I traded my soul, to a cave wizard, for a job. You proud of me?"*

It wasn't even the fact that she was too afraid to explain to her mother that her new job involved working with an antiquated ruler of the dead—it was the fact that technically she wasn't allowed to be respectable yet; she was still on house arrest for another six months. The thought of this made her look down at her ankle, rubbing it, as if she could scrape away the stupidity. Would she ever learn to make good decisions?

*

In a plane of existence just a car accident away, sitting upon a throne crystallized by the volcanic ashes of a Siberian eruption long extinct, Hades asked himself the very same question. Time didn't move as fast for him as it did for mortals. Whereas Tranquila measured her confinement in hours because humans based time on how fast it took for the Earth to circle the sun, it would be asinine for Hades to try and measure time that way. He was in the center of an event horizon on the very outskirts of a black hole. Tranquila's 'tomorrow' was his next week, so understandably he had forgotten about the nearsighted maiden already. Regardless, his lamentations ran as deep as hers, only he thought of another morally ambiguous female.

Basaltic lava once ran through the carvings of the floodplains where Hades held his meetings. It was here, while in the midst of a PowerPoint presentation with his Department of Creative Punishments on the logistics of making an edible spider bomb, a bomb they planned to force-feed to rapists and judges who gave predators light sentences when he received the news.

"So, as we see here," Hades lectured, pointing to a slide that showcased a nasty arachnid devouring the belly of a camel, "we would need to use the giant camel spider for this task since they are one of the few spiders that can eat through flesh."

One of his crew members, Agony, raised an eager hand. "How many spiders should we put in each of these explosives?"

"Generally speaking, in order for the bomb to be most effective we're going to need to stuff eight to ten spiders inside the bomb so that they can adequately feast on the human's limbs, face, torso, chest and genitals." He paused, allowing his team members to scribble away. "Now, Aeacus from Inferno Support," Hades stretched an affable arm to the said crew member, an angry-looking Oriental spirit with an overgrown unibrow that somehow morphed into a beard and sideburns as well. Aeacus gave the room a silent nod as Hades continued, "is here to offer training on how to properly assemble the bombs and to—"

The sound of tiny, rapid footsteps distracted him. Hades knew in the millisecond before they arrived that his cosmic courier was coming with a delivery. Hades kept himself from being impatient with his messenger or from berating him to come back after the project at hand was completed. His built-in managerial instincts kicked in and he knew better than to dismiss a worker.

"What is it, Hermes?"

Possessing no eyelids made Hermes perpetually alert and laser-eyed. When the intercessor who sped through worlds faster than light emerged into the room, even some of Hades' employees felt the nervousness vape off Hermes. He simply stood in the dank boardroom with his hands behind his back with his blink-less eyes averted.

"Sir—" he began.

"Hey Hermes!"

"Oh, hey Old Age!" he coughed and readdressed Hades in a deeper tone: "Sir, I'm sorry to interrupt—"

"As you should, Hermes," Hades said, half-scolding. "We were in the process of developing time-sensitive spider bombs."

The members of the meeting burst into applause at their beloved spider bomb, which was already dubbed a god in their eyes and was even given a holiday, December twenty-fifth, as a birthday to celebrate its arrival.

"I'm sorry, sir. I know how excited you are about the ESB's but I was just summoned by the queen…"

Hades' entire body tightened. Even now, decades after she had fled, he still couldn't hear her name mentioned. "She is no longer your queen," replied Hades, coolly. "You do not have to address her as such."

Even Aeacus, who held the same pissed-off countenance since he'd found out Pangea broke up, grew visibly uncomfortable for Hermes. It was a reflex anyone would have made. She was their queen for twelve thousand eras. It would be like someone being told their entire lifetime that their name is Jane, only to find out it is actually Liliuokalani.

Aeacus looked to the minor entities of the Underworld. They tacitly agreed that they'd rather be the test subjects for the ESBs than be made any more uncomfortable.

"Um, Hades, we're…going to go to lunch," Aeacus lied, as he and his coworkers edged out of the boardroom.

"Since when do abstracts eat?" Hades began, but when he turned they were already gone. He let out a frustrated sigh. Rounding back on Hermes, he demanded wildly, "What does that ungrateful wench want?"

Trembling, Hermes merely handed him a scroll he had tucked away in his garment which looked like a modern track student's running skirt. Hades unfurled the scroll without touching it, letting it dangle midair far enough away for him to read. He, like many old people, became nearsighted with age. After a few quick skims, both the document and his face dropped.

"Ye gods, no," he groaned.

*

The Olympians didn't spend eternity bumming around on the clouds like an inferior Christian icon. They preferred to live above the stars on a mountain made from a nebula that hovered above the perimeter of the universe.

Hades traveled back to Olympus, spending the whole journey already regretting his homecoming. On his arrival, he softly groaned at the sight of the sun god languishing before him on a lounge chair comprised of the diamond rains of Jupiter. With nothing else to do but screw around and just plain screw...was Zeus.

"Hey, handsome," Zeus greeted incestuously. "You come here often?"

Hades shuddered in disgust. Outwardly he implored, "Zeus, please. You know why I'm here and yet you cannot change your baseless ways in light of the circumstance?"

Zeus sighed, annoyed. "You could never fake pleasantries, Hades."

Probably hasn't moved in centuries, Hades thought bitterly as Zeus sat up then swiveled himself so his bare feet would brush against a nimbus cloud.

"I was just trying to *lighten* the mood."

Hades glared. Zeus lived in perpetual sunshine and thus found sun puns endlessly hysterical. Seeing his brother sulk, Zeus groaned, pulling himself from his chaise longue throne with a stretch and a lazy yawn. "Brother, please. This is only a formality. It will not take long. Do not let your mood turn foul."

It was too late for that. Incredible forbearance permitted Hades from relating this to his brother who, even as they walked side by side, led him through Olympus as if he were a newcomer.

Beside one another, the siblings' striking differences stood out like blue against orange. They, along with Poseidon, shared the features passed down by their cannibalistic father: same thick hair; same enormous size; same virile beauty instilled by firm jawlines, bold eyes and broad lips. But there were discrepancies between the oldest and the youngest. Zeus aged beautifully while Hades looked like one giant scar. The sky god beamed with optimism while the lord of the dead kept his lips sealed with a frown. Zeus who looked like life was kind; Hades wore death for a uniform. Zeus smelled of fresh wine, clean water and sex; Hades reeked of bureaucracy, old dirt and lonesomeness.

Olympus was grand but gilded. There wasn't much a god or goddess could do anymore; science had taken all the fun out of everything—environmental catastrophes, disease, even war. Back in the day, gods would make a hurricane, terrifying the mortals into loving them again. Now, people blamed low-pressure areas. They blamed climate change. They blamed Republicans. Back then, Aries and Hera had to start trouble just to get the mortals to battle. Today, man domesticated death in the forms of hydrogen bombs and assault rifles. With so much turmoil and bloodshed in the world, Olympus had a thousand channels and nothing to watch.

"Magistrate. Magistrate!" Zeus ordered those who watched their contemporaries with disdain and lethargy. When they didn't move fast enough, he picked examples: "C'mon everybody…Ares, stop instigating ISIS and North Korea. Hephaestus, stop harassing all those home improvement TV hosts. Aphrodite—*Stop being so damn sexy*."

Normally, Hades would have scolded Zeus for hitting on his son's bride/his own daughter, but as the deities stirred from their mental wasting and made for the tribunal table, he noticed the way many of their eyes re-shaped as they passed him. No longer hooded from limitless boredom or narrowed as they usually would upon sight of his visage. No—they rounded—made malleable by pity. It irked him to the point where he clenched his hands hard enough that if he were human, his fingernails would have torn through his palms and he would have bled.

"This—is—humiliating," he hissed.

"It'll be over with soon," replied Zeus. It was the best he could offer.

"Why does this have to be done at all? Down on Earth, your spouse can leave you by text message now," Hades hissed furiously in his brother's ear.

"You and I both know that's only true for Las Vegas," said Zeus, trying to be funny. "Just be glad you're not in New York. Breaking out of jail is easier than breaking out of a marriage contract."

Hades' tight lips strained to restrain himself. He wanted to open his mouth to unleash a diatribe against their outdated systems, against tradition, against his asinine brother who upheld them. Then he saw her.

Out of every color that they knew to exist, she had to choose green.

Lavished in an emerald dress one could only find on a wet pasture in the middle of an Irish July, there she stood— lovelier than ever. As if gliding over water, her bare legs weakened him. Hades had to stifle his own thoughts—berating himself for not grooming before he came, for not knowing that she was going to do something like this, for not using this as a chance to make her want him the way he desperately wanted her.

She came with her mother. Her clingy, lackadaisical, thoughtless, butyraceous *mother*, to whom Persephone clung like a hungry newborn. They—Demeter and Hades—made eye contact first. It took Demeter a full five seconds to make the connection of who he was. In fairness, it had been a good dozen millennia. Demeter burst into giggles and turned her neckless head into her daughter's ear. He watched Persephone's eyes (sometimes blue, sometimes green, depending on the light) widen immediately. She pinned him with cruel sharp green eyes. They held contact for the first time in half a century.

Gone within a standard blink, she took that from him as well. Persephone sauntered over as fast as she could tug Mother Girth, Hades' secret nickname for his mother-in-law. He was smart enough to never, ever say aloud.

Zeus stole a glance at his brother's wilted face. Zeus' eyes softened with empathy, which he shook off before placing a hand on his brother's shoulder to ask, "Ready?"

Hades searched the swirls of gold orbiting the dilated irises of Zeus's hazel eyes, unrounded and cloudy with hedonistic thoughts. Hades felt like touching his brother's hand but then a lachrymose feeling forced him to avoid that potential tenderness for fear of looking soft.

"You and I both know I'm not ready," Hades sighed, after which he turned and walked into the tribunal anyway. Because that's what one does when they have to get over their feelings and get back to work.

Fashioned in the absolute center of the skies, the Magistrate all presided—an audience of peers seated in a circle upon their designated thrones. Every god was in attendance, but two thrones once conjoined and now separated were left empty.

Persephone already stood in the circle, arms folded tight against her chest. Hades did his best to walk slow and proud. He wanted to show her she could never knock the crown off his head. This turned increasingly difficult the second he walked past Hera and Zeus and Hades saw the enormous distance between him and Persephone. If he had a heart, it would have shot straight to his throat. But he made his paces and took his spot and ignored the hot stinging in his eyes and stomped out the sadness because there is a meeting coming up and a new virus that has to be signed off on.

"Alright," the ultimate god began, his penetrating voice buffeted the empty skies like thunder, "the Magistrate has come to order. Persephone, since thou hast summoned the council, what you want girl?"

"Council," began Persephone, her inherently sweet voice heated with personal injustice, "I desire to end my woeful marriage."

Persephone's announcement sparked a derisive uproar, unheard of in their time-resistant realm. *Wives* leaving husbands? Women *thinking* they should be happy? Not to mention, since when did men give their wives permission to be happy?

Zeus burst out laughing at the absurdity. "Woeful marriage? Persephone, you're a wo-man. Your sex should be accustomed to woe. It's in thine title."

Needless to say, only half the tribune laughed at his joke. The other half remained silent, except Hera, who almost ground her back molars into talcum powder.

"Well I don't want to be full of woe anymore," Persephone insisted. "I deserve to be happy." Edgy with rancor, she extended a bony finger at her husband and sneered, "And I can never be happy living with him."

Such a powerful statement left the council waiting in uncomfortable anticipation of Hades' reaction. Alas, for a god who ruled from the base of a primordial volcano, he didn't explode with unsightly rage at his wife's damning statement. Instead, he glanced at the finger she still pointed at him, as if it were a sword too close to the eye. The most spiteful thing he could do was deny her the eye contact she wanted.

"Brother?" Zeus called, not pressed by nosiness, but concern. He was astutely aware of the humiliation that his brother faced. Hades would be the first one in their family to get divorced if he conceded. Even he—arguably the universe's worst spouse—was still joined together with Hera. Not out of undying love or some sanctimonious respect for matrimony—the Greeks barely understood monogamy, let alone the premise that two people would contractually obligate each other to keep such a promise. They remained together because marriage was a business pact and one could do worse than being partners with the king of the universe.

Hades and Persephone's marriage was unique, though, and Zeus's heart stung for the heartbreak in which his older brother must have been drowning. *It's always the faithful that get fucked over*, Zeus thought sadly as he still waited for Hades to respond.

"What say you?"

What could say he? Hades, first tight-lipped then resigned, said to Persephone, "If you are unhappy, you are unhappy." Addressing the Magistrate, but mostly his younger brother who bashed him with sad eyes to the point where it made Hades sick: "Whatever I must do to let her be free of this marriage, I will do. Whatever I must sign, I'll sign."

A few members of the council slumped in their thrones with disinterest. *How unfair*, they said to themselves. The first congregation they'd held since Ares proposed to start shit in the Middle East, and it wasn't even funny. They were Greek…and, damn it all, they wanted some drama! They wanted to listen to Persephone complain about Hades' copulation skills. They wanted Hades to bequeath Persephone a bumptious whore. They wanted secrets and lies, not respect and dignity. Since when did divorce proceedings end without both parties cursing each other out? Did cable television teach them nothing?

"Alright," said Zeus once the grumblings of petty deities had ceased, "since this is what you both agree to, let's talk about redistribution—"

"Oh no," Persephone interjected, "I'm not interested in partaking in my ex's thirst for avarice. Attachment to material things kills the soul, man."

If Hades were given any consolation, it was hearing the agitated groans of his contemporaries at his wife's hippie ways.

"Oh blah blah blah! Get back to your bong, you dirty hippie," beautiful Aphrodite cried out.

"Don't you have a mortal to fuck?" interjected Queen Demeter.

"Hey," crippled Hephaestus shouted. "Don't talk to my wife like that."

"Why? You think kissing her ass will stop her from sticking her tongue in Ares's?" Demeter jabbed.

"You better pop, lock and drop the fucking attitude, Demeter!" angry Ares snapped, his face already red. "I know she's your daughter but if you don't close your fucking pie-hole, I'll...I'll..."

"You'll what?" Demeter drawled. "You ain't going to do shit. You haven't started a war since your boy Hannibal pussied out and killed himself."

"DON'T YOU DARE TAKE HANNIBAL'S NAME IN VAIN."

"Oh, fuck off, you crusty cuckolder."

"Hmm, classy," muttered wise Athena, examining her fingernails.

"Not as classy as punishing your brother's rape victim for having the audacity to be assaulted in your temple," Aphrodite snarled, giving Athena a look of pure loathing that Medusa would have thanked her for. "Heartless bitch."

Zeus looked to his wife, thinking perhaps he had forgotten about one of his conquests, but she shook her head and pointed to guilty Poseidon.

After this, all went ill. Hades watched quietly as his extended family squabbled and cursed each other for their depravities. Everyone except drunk Dionysus who passed out in his throne before the meeting had even started, his hand still clasped around a cup that never runneth over. Like most people, Hades could not be bothered with the family drama. He walked away from the humiliating circle, bent to Zeus's lap to sign the divorce papers and left Olympus as invisible as his name. Only he, faithful efficient Hades, would think monotonous work could pound out the grief that made him raw and shameful instead of just sticking around to watch his sisters and sister-in-law gang up on his ex and ex-in-law.

SUCK IT, HOMER

After two consecutive nightmares about being burnt alive like a package of hotdogs in a lava storm, Tranquila determined she could no longer do the adult thing of 'toughing it out'. Instead, she crept downstairs and repeated a sad regressive mantra of "Mom…?" until she was granted access into the little space in her mother's bed that was cleft with security. By 4:30 in the morning, she finally made peace with sleep.

Midmorning came. An August sun magnified through window glass, burning into Tranquila's closed eyes, blinding her awake. With a face matted in old drool and hair, she opened her eyes to discover Mama Sobriquet gone, replaced by the man who had dragged her to Hades perched on a nightstand, staring her down with his uncovered jaundiced eyes. "Hey."

He didn't receive a greeting in return, which he expected. What he didn't expect was for Tranquila to chuck a pillow at his head, then use that pathetic delay to jump from the bed in an attempt for the door. But she didn't make it to the door. Instead, her foot caught in the bedsheets, tripping her chest first on the hard floor, severely winding herself. Breathless and wheezing in pain, she yanked her foot free only to see that the demon hadn't moved from his sedentary position.

Believing herself to be half-doomed, her thoughts preened terrible visions. "Where's my mom?" she asked at once.

When the apostate didn't answer fast enough, she broke into screams, "MOM! MO...M!"

"Holy shit, mortal, de-stress yourself. It's 10 a.m. Your mom's been at work for four hours now," informed the blink-less thing.

"So. So sh...she's fine?"

"Well, she's a single mother working sixty-hour work weeks, but yes, from a physical standpoint, she is fine."

Tranquila, mollified, took this time to catch her breath. After a pause, she looked up into the yellow-eyed creature's face and panic reabsorbed her. "GRANDMA!"

"Jeanette, it is just me—Hermes," the creature called out for reassurance. "I'm just retrieving her for her first day of work."

"I DON'T GIVE A SHIT IF YOU'RE DRAGGING HER DOWN TO BE THE CERBERUS' CHEW TOY!" Grandma Sobriquet's voice screeched from the nearby living room. "TRAN! YOUR LASSITUDE IS GONNA GET YOUR ASS BRUISED!"

Tranquila growled at her grandmother's apathy; no doubt she was angry that Tranquila was screaming for help during her TV programs. Tranquila took the hint and calmed down. In a calmer voice she asked, "You're taking me to the Underworld?"

"For today," he replied. "Tomorrow, you're going to find your own way. I'm a deity, not your taxi."

"Okay," she said, slowly rising to her feet. "Can I get changed?"

He looked at her with his uncomfortable stare for a short moment but consented. "I'd put your hair up too, while you groom." When she turned to leave the room, he added, "But not too high. Marie Antoinette made that mistake. On the way down she got scalped. She had to walk around holding her own bald head like it was a baby."

Tranquila winced at the imagery as she left for the bathroom. She brushed her teeth while crying.

When she was ready, she walked up to Hermes, who chose to perch on top of a nightstand, to be a creepy asshole. Stepping down, he led Tranquila through the living room. Grandma Sobriquet was already in her chair, eyes glued on a commercial for teeth whitener named I-Can't-Believe-It's-Not-Bleach. The salesman, who must have been a vegan, told the viewers, "It'll take that savage wasteland of animal carcasses the majority of you call a mouth and it will kill one hundred and twenty percent of the bacteria that lives there! And then, using time-activated molecules, it'll bleach your orifice, taking away years and years off the blood of innocents while making your teeth shine!"

"Um, can I say goodbye first?" Tranquila inquired timidly.

"You know, he has no intention of keeping you," Hermes said with all seriousness.

Grandma Sobriquet snorted indelicately. "You sure about that?"

"Silent, you bitter creation," Hermes scowled.

"What?" Grandma Sobriquet asked in mock innocence. "Oh, I'm just joking. That's the kind of relationship we have. I call her names, she asks why I'm not dead yet, we laugh, then watch TV together without talking."

Hermes secretly found it hard to believe that this decrepit beast could form relationships. He looked to Tranquila and, with a nod, gave her the gesture to do what she must. Tranquila, finding it harder and harder to get the images from last night's lava-themed dreams out of her head, stepped closer to her grandmother and asked, "Okay, just in case I don't get back before Mom gets home, will you cover for me?"

Grandma Sobriquet smirked. Without looking away, she said, "What makes you think you'll get home even when your mother gets out of work?"

"Grandma, I'm not in the mood for your salty-bitch ways. Will you please just make up a story for Mom, in case I come home late?"

The bitter creature agreed, then gave a half-assed insult before drowning herself in dissipation.

Tranquila exhaled in relief, "Thank you."

With that, they exited the living room, passed through the kitchen to the back door and out into the backyard, same as yesterday. Once they stood on top of the votive pit where Grandma Sobriquet had performed her paganisms, Hermes held a pale arm out towards her. She took it, swallowed as much fresh air as she could and tensed herself as Hermes began a charnel exhortation.

Like yesterday, the earth opened its mouth and swallowed them whole. Like yesterday, Hermes' ears were pierced by Tranquila's screams. Unlike yesterday, they did not collide with the cavernous floor like a hapless meteorite. Instead—PLUNK—they plopped like a raindrop into what Tranquila figured was a boat of some sort; once they landed, the force of their collision caused the boat to rock. Before she could gasp for breath she spat up sewage water. She threw up on herself.

"Damn, maiden," Hermes remarked, helping her sit up. "You're a mess."

All she could do was nod, too sore and sick to speak. She was barely able to stretch her head over the side of the boat to spit up the remaining bile. She shuddered, while letting her chin rest on the edge and her fingertips dipped into the dirty water. It took a few seconds for her blurry, tear-filled eyes to see that in the reflective waters there was a new monster towering over her with fire in his hollow eyes.

She looked over her shoulder to find a scraggy skeleton standing with an oar. She would have screamed had a second bout of vomit not spewed forth.

"Man, this mortal pukes a lot," said the oarsman in a deep, throaty voice that often made people think he didn't speak much, which was a false notion. Just because he didn't possess proper vocal cords didn't mean he was thoughtful or quiet. To Hermes he asked, "She die during one of those hotdog eating contests?"

"Nah, she's just frightened," Hermes replied, as he used a flat hand to scrape the vomit from her lap.

"Ah, I see."

"Dude," she groaned to the oarsman, "I'm sorry about your boat."

"It's fine, mortal. It's fine," insisted the oarsman, dipping his ancient paddle into the waters, propelling them down the murky waters. "You aren't the first and you won't be the last."

As the boat glided down a dank, sulfuric river, an almost magnetic pull against her skin warned her not to go down any further. Panic shot down into her nerves alerting her that this was a devoid realm, a place that existed only in the wet dreams of nihilists, an insipid cave-like existence where hopelessness roared and the inevitability of death was nigh. Going down this river, in this boat, with these creatures, went against all primal instincts—like suicide or eating Thai.

Something fluttered too close to her head, causing Tranquila to jump backwards within the boat. She turned to Hermes and the oarsman and asked, "What is this place?"

"This is the River Styx," Hermes replied, not taking his eyes from the destiny head. "It's the largest river in the known universe."

"Yeah," snorted the oarsman, "it makes your Amazonian look like a drunkard's piss stream."

"W-why are we taking this way?" Tranquila asked, afraid this river was gnawing away at her soul.

"Because this is your first day and it's customary to give you a long, drawn-out tour so we can kill some time," Hermes explained. Opening his arms, he announced, "Anyway, this…is the River Styx. And like Charon said, this river could kick all of your oceans' collective asses."

"Damn straight," said Charon, proud.

"And as I mentioned before, this is Charon."

"Hey."

"Hey."

"He's the…what are you again?" Hermes inquired.

"I'm the skeletal-psychopomp slash demon slash boating enthusiast."

Pause. "So, yes, Charon is the Head of our Soul Transport Department. Charon, this is Tranquila. She's going to be working in Hades."

"Working?" Charon blurted out, incredulous. "Wow, we haven't had a live one down here since that punk-ass Orpheus didn't know how to follow simple instructions."

Great, Tranquila thought, *I'm gonna have to go home and Google that now.*

"So, what shoddy decision-making skills landed you in such a predicament? Sell your soul to be rich only to get killed by greedy relatives?"

"Nope."

"Sell your soul to save your boyfriend's life but he turned out to be a jerk and now you're stuck here for all eternity to lament your bad romances?"

"Ew, no! I wouldn't sell my soul for some asshole that I'm dating. Shit, I won't even let them make me watch their shitty TV shows, let alone trade my soul for them," Tranquila said, repulsed by the memory of an ex trying to make her watch *The Walking Dead*, and their immediate break-up afterwards.

"Well if you're not down here because of wealth or because of love, what else would possess a young woman to dwell in the Underworld?" Charon inquired, dumbstruck.

Hermes spoke up to exhibit a limited amount of affection, "She sold her soul to find purpose."

The sense of emotion in the inhuman thing made Tranquila uncommonly proud. She turned to look at him but saw his gaze was squarely set on the river. Charon continued with his monotonous strokes.

They traveled down the River Styx in silence for several hundred rows, weaving down seven different bends with the ease of a lazy river but the speed of a water slide. After the seventh pass along the bend, Tranquila noticed how the cave walls no longer had a zenith where they and the top met. Instead, the sides seemed to expand outward in length, and when Tranquila tilted her chin to find the roof of the cave she saw only limitless black. Returning her gaze to the river, she saw that the width of the waters had grown too. They were no longer riding in a medium-sized boat on an extra-large river but in an extra-small boat coasting along the Pacific Ocean.

Don't—go—crazy, Tran, she said to herself. *If you get a mental illness now then all your teachers will think they were right about you, and we can't let that pompous turd dragon Mrs. Mullen think she was actually right for once.* But then the small amount of natural light that was left available to them could no

longer cover the ever-expanding universe. All at once darkness
toppled over them.

With her useless human eyesight, Tranquila was
rendered blind. She tried not to panic. She thought of smug Mrs.
Mullen and tried to be spitefully calm; then, the air became
sulfuric and unbreathable. Before she could even worry about
suffocating, a horrible noise came, like the roaring sound of a
thousand snowplows hurtling down a solitary night road.
Grandma Sobriquet was right, she thought as she held onto her
juddering chest and screamed silently, *she knew I was going to
Hades to die.*

She was too busy being traumatized to realize that the
boat had stopped or to notice that the deafening roar had ceased.
It wasn't until something cold tapped her nose did she stop being
afraid enough to open her eyes to find Hermes holding out a
stone that had been carved into a bowl.

Dazed, half-hyperventilating and fully crying, Hermes
had to repeat himself three times before Tranquila was aware she
was being spoken to.

"What?"

"Drink this," he said.

She looked down into the carved rock to see it held a
milky-white substance similar to the almond milk her mom had
once tried to push onto the family. She stared at it with the same
distrust.

"Why?"

"It's like those tetanus shots you get back on Earth,"
Hermes replied with the same casual authority. "It's just so you
don't catch anything once you get into Hades."

"Why? Are we almost there?" she asked, finally able to
spit out more than vomit or a single syllable.

"Almost there?" Charon interjected with dismay.
"Mortal, we are here!"

His announcement was emphasized by a husky echo. Tranquila turned herself to see—with instant recognition and slight heart arrhythmia—the Gates of Hades. Their unrelenting presence occupied an entire ocean's length. She could see from her position in the boat that the bars were not made from steel with their earth-weathered texture and infernal blackness. She would never have guessed, though, that those bars were made from the bones of slain Titans.

Something didn't sit right with her and she let it be known. Turning to Charon she said, "You said this was the longest river in the known universe."

"And?" Charon asked, not following.

"And we've only been in this boat for, like, an hour. How is this the longest river in the universe if we're already at Hades?"

Charon gave her an odd look as if the answer was more than clear. He opened his barren mouth. "Physics."

Tranquila grimaced, but having never taken physics she accepted the answer. She turned her attention back to the beastly barrier. Even at several arm-lengths away she could tell it was emitting energy. When she took her first step out of the boat and touched the concrete-like ground, her feet could feel the vibrations. It was pulsing like a microwave, only alive and far more dangerous to her DNA. Staring into the gate, seeing eons of crusted earth etched into its bars, made her think of gamma rays—something she wasn't aware she knew until this moment.

If she possessed a dog's hearing, she heard little cruel whispers reciting the exact time and date of her death.

A light touch snapped her out of dreadful hypnosis. She saw it was Hermes, gesturing towards Charon who remained in the boat, patiently.

"What?" she asked, realizing yet again Hermes had been trying to speak to her but she was too stupid with fear to hear him.

"Give him a dollar," he murmured through his teeth.

She obeyed. Walking over to the skeletal boat dude, she dug into her jeans and generously gave him the last three dollars she possessed.

The oarsman's eye sockets twitched.

"What's the rest for?"

"I dunno," she replied. "For not getting mad at me for puking in your boat?" Even without eyes, the incomprehension in his fleshless expression was obvious. "It's a tip."

"A...tip?"

"Yeah."

Pause. "Is this a mortal custom?"

"I...guess?" She thought about the wait-staff industry and knew that this wasn't true but didn't have the heart to explain to the bony boat guy that Earth was brimming with cheapskates.

Charon continued to look at the excess money. He made a small grunt before tossing the change into his boat, digging the oar into the waters and pulling away without saying much else. She watched him for a moment before going back to stand with Hermes, who was still holding the primitive cup. She took it without being asked and chugged the substance within two gulps. The second it touched her throat she almost barfed for a third time.

"Jesus Christ!" she gagged, dropping the cup so she could keel over and spit. To the ground, she cried, "It tastes like I just drank rust."

Hermes allowed a short time of recovery before squatting down beside Tranquila, turning his head so she would be forced to look into his frightening yellow eyes, "Are you done complaining?"

Giving a weak grunt, she replied, "It's hard to complain when your throat's melting."

Hermes gave her a small pat on the back. "Good."

Straightening up, he wheeled himself over to the Gates. Tranquila followed. Up close, the verve from the Gates was unnerving. Sensing intruders made the power within them intensify, and the gentle hum—the warping noises Tranquila had felt earlier—grew more condensed, urgent, threatening and deafening. The Gates were aware that they—or maybe just she—could not be trusted.

They stood there for so long the chemical make-up of Tranquila's brain was starting to change. She felt intensely hot. Her vision was racy and dulled. Hearing was tricky.

Hermes tapped her shoulder to get her attention. In the drowning babel of a thousand hateful voices she saw his hand. She had to grab it or else be doomed forever as a schizophrenic. With the ferocity of a baby, she squeezed his hand as he led her through the Gates. Her body slid past the bars like she was wind. She looked down at her long-sleeved shirt that had tacos at the cuffs and a chest that read 'mano off the taco' and saw her fleshy solid pass between the barriers of Hades, glitching like a videogame. But with Hermes coaxing her along, she was able to make it through.

The ringing stopped. The wonkiness in her eyesight stopped. The voices that made very convincing arguments to blow up Florida stopped.

"You should blow up Florida."

"No! I'm not gonna blow up Florida"

"...Please?"

"Okay I'll think about it."

Tranquila tossed her head back towards the Gates of Hades which were no longer buzzing with distrust, no longer instigating insanity, and she laughed. "Fuck you, Gates! You ain't shit!" she taunted, pointing and mocking the barrier that two Earth seconds ago almost persuaded her to start a war with America's favorite peninsula.

"Don't taunt the Gates, mortal," Hermes heeded. "Trust me. Those Gates are all about the ABC's."

"ABC's?"

"Always Breaking Psyches."

"Uh…psyches starts with a 'p'…?"

"Regardless, keep acting like an asshole to the Gates and you will see which of ye 'ain't shit'."

She glanced back, sighed, then apologized aloud, "Sorry, Gates."

"Good, you have no pride," Hermes observed. "That'll come in handy working in Hades."

Tranquila looked about. Yesterday, on arrival, she was instantly submerged into scores of the wicked and unfortunates languishing before her, being tortured, whipped or judiciously raped, but today—there was nothing. Not even the familiar smell of sulfuric shit filled the air, just the same stuffy, stale air found in an attic.

"This…is Hades?" she asked. "Where's the dead?"

"The dead arrive by a different river. Charon went back to retrieve them," Hermes explained. "River Styx is for employees only."

"Damn. How many rivers do you guys have down here?"

Pause. "They don't delve much into Greek mythology in American schools, do they?"

"Nah. I mean, kids now have those *Percy Jackson* books to read but when I was in school all we had was the *Odyssey* and sometimes if a sub came in we just watched that *Hercules* movie, but that's about it."

"Ugh," Hermes shuddered in disgust. "The *Odyssey*!"

Tranquila burrowed one of her eyebrows, confused. "You guys can't stand that book either? I thought you Greeks would geek out over that shit."

"Believe me, mortal, even us ancient Greeks couldn't get through that dribble when it first came out." He drew in closer and whispered, "Most of us preferred the *Aeneid*, to be quite frank."

"Really?" Tranquila asked, feigning surprise. She was not about to confess that she had no idea what the *Aeneid* was.

"Oh yes. Even your employer. We're all, as you saw, team Virgil."

Tranquila laughed.

"You have no idea who Virgil is, do you?"

"Nope."

Hermes made a face that might constitute a grin. Sadly to her, the expression only made his unblinking traffic-light eyes even creepier.

"Come now, I think we've wasted enough time. I'll show you to your post," he said, beginning to walk into the dimness that was the Outlier of Hades.

SHAVE THY HEAD AND START ANEW

Traveling into the dimness, the solitary sounds of Tranquila's footfalls began to get increasingly louder. She glanced up to see that while they were not walking at an angle, the walls slanted upward, drawing further and further away with each step. As if Hermes continued to lead her through a fat cone that yielded no light, just the continuation of half-darkness. *No wonder he's got those freaky yellow eyes*, she thought, feeling her pupils strain to adjust to the drabness, *he needs them just to see where the fuck he's going.* Her eyes were beginning to blur from farsightedness until something caught her attention that turned them bug-eyed instead.

While she could accept the Gates standing at an immeasurable height and the river swelling to fill an excessive space, Tranquila's mind could not come to grips with the cavernous chamber she stood within.

Laid out before her was nothing short of a tunnel system for the Grand Canyons. She gawked with the realization that any or all walls and ceilings were gone, absorbing the fact that they were probably miles upon miles away. She nearly snapped her neck trying to catch the dizzying emptiness at every angle. It was sickening, frightening, exhilarating, exasperating—and strangely calming—to think she was like a sesame seed fallen from a hamburger bun that landed in a swimming pool.

"Jesus," she murmured.

She heard Hermes laugh, which snapped her out of her imagination and back to his incredulous face. He waited for her to continue.

"As if that pussy Christ could create something this monumental," he chuckled.

Tranquila didn't feel like explaining Jesus was just a curse word to her, she instead went back to following his lead while they continued past the gargantuan tunnels. Passing them, he explained, "I'm just giving you a quick rundown so you won't get lost tomorrow. This tunnel is where the souls are taken to be judged." A quarter-mile down, a second tunnel came into view. "This is where those judged 'bad' go—this is where you were yesterday." To punctuate this, an ear-shattering scream followed by a burp of fire erupted from the tunnel. Tranquila hurried to meet Hermes who had stopped in front of a sharp, shadowy-looking valley. "And we don't have what you humans call a 'break room' per se, but we do have this lovely spot just beyond the Valley of the Shadow of Death that has a microwave."

Tranquila made an attempt to see what lovely spot Hermes could be referring to, but all she could see were some menacing-looking rocks and mountainsides molded out of living worms. "Okay," she gulped, as she caught sight of the valley-side coiling and recoiling.

"We don't have a refrigerator, so if you pack a lunch in the future try to bring something that won't spoil easily."

She wanted to puke—not consume—but she okay'd him to death, nonetheless, just to shut him up.

"Now, breaks are whenever you feel you need one. No one is going to be watching over you but I wouldn't exactly abuse the honor system, if I were you," Hermes went on, seemingly ignoring Tranquila's distress. As if passing by the

Land of the Damned instilled in her any idea that she could get away with anything here.

"As for your shift, time here is…well, complicated. For example, an hour to you is three weeks for us but three weeks in Hades is only five minutes on Earth, but five minutes in Hades still runs for five minutes."

Pause. "Okay…So…how long have I really been here?"

"Hmm, about two weeks."

"Earth time?!"

"Hades time."

"Okay, so-o…how long is my shift for today supposed to last?"

"Eight hours."

"Does that mean I'll be gone eight hours on Earth?"

"No. That just means you'll be here for eight Earth hours."

A longer pause. "…Okay."

"It'll get easier the longer you're down here," Hermes reassured.

Tranquila figured that was a lie, but she thought of all the daytime television and forced interactions with Grandma Sobriquet she was missing and accepted the lie.

Hermes and Tranquila continued down for, she guessed, a mile. *Do they use miles down here?* She thought. A small panic hit, as the possibility of having to learn the metric system crossed her mind; she thought about how she'd rather get schizophrenia again.

Through the canyon, Hermes spoke to her like a professional tour guide, exhibiting the many plains that existed in Hades: past the beleaguered plains where Grief, Old Age and Anxiety prospered; over the barren valley where Hunger and Disease flourished as they pleased; quickly skirting the tunnel where all the collective monsters of past fables gathered in troves to discuss new and exciting ways to mess with the wicked. Alas, it wasn't until Hermes introduced her to the familiar Vale of Wailing. "More like Vale of Bitching." she joked.

"Well said, maiden," Hermes commented, as they finally approach Tranquila's workstation.

Isolated on the edge of the dead's entrance stood the three-headed Hound of Hades. Tranquila peered in wonder at the features she didn't noticed yesterday: the mane of cobras that hissed and writhed against its tripled-throat; the lion claws the dog used to scratch its underbelly, which contained far more nipples than Tranquila had ever seen on a canine before. While her eyes traveled down its belly in an attempt to count how many teats it possessed, she was alarmed to learn, "Cerberus is a female?"

Hermes nodded. "Only a mighty bitch can keep the innumerable souls of Hades in check."

"Hmm." She turned to Hermes and asked with excitement, "So what do I do? Take her for a walk? Teach her some tricks? Give her a bath?"

"Give her a bath?" Hermes echoed in disgust. "Mortal, does this ghastly beast of yon look like it can use a bath?"

Judging by the cobwebs, flakes of old snake skin and a slight case of mange, she would have said yes but kept this answer to herself.

"Mortal, I know you are enthused but do not be mistaken that because Cerberus is a dog she is like the dogs on Earth. She is the literal Hound of Hell," Hermes warned, his voice cold and disapproving.

Tranquila shrank a little. It was misguided of her to think that a demonic dog currently using two of its heads to devour five corpses at once could be the same as the dogs back home.

"So, what do I do then?"

Without saying anything, Hermes handed her an oversized inoculator which she had to carry with both arms.

"You have two hours to administer her rabies shot," Hermes informed. "After which, your first shift will be concluded."

Hermes turned away to leave when he was called back, "Wait!" Tranquila cried, "What do I do if I finish-up sooner?"

Hermes glanced over his shoulder at her. In that second, Tranquila could feel the hot, tire-melting breath of three dogs all at once frying her skin. She looked up to see reflected in each pair of eyes that no help or hope of help existed within that canine. Instead, she saw only a vague minimized mirror image of herself multiplied six-fold as if those eyes were six murderer's blades.

Hermes vanished within a clap of white mist as the sound of Tranquila's high-pitched screams rang out.

*

Back on Earth, five minutes after Tranquila left, Grandma Sobriquet's eyes hadn't wandered from the glowing radiation box; not even when a noise from the backyard overpowered the rambunctious laughter of the audience/jury members on *Who Wants to Be a Celebrity Judge*. Seconds later, she heard the alarmed barks of several neighborhood dogs sounding off at once, in response, no doubt, to their Satan senses sending them into fits. Grandma Sobriquet, who couldn't be bothered, retrieved a dog whistle from underneath the seat cushion. Her crusty lips gave the whistle one solid blow. She didn't stop until she succeeded in hurting their delicate ears. She was still cackling at their pain when her granddaughter came in through the backdoor.

Covered in thick drool, banged-up and shirt stained with old puke, Tranquila looked like a defeated butterfly fighting its way out of a nasty crystallization.

"How was your first day?" Grandma Sobriquet asked with a taunting, salty laugh.

Tranquila shot her a piercing glare before her face cracked underneath the weight of despair. She bolted upstairs, waiting until she was protected by the sounds of a running shower before bursting into sobs.

*

Six hours later, Earth time, Mama Sobriquet returned from another ten-hour shift to find her wrinkly mother in the same spot as always.

"You're like a freaking house cat," she remarked, half-joking, half-envious.

Grandma Sobriquet grunted a hello.

With an armful of groceries, Mama Sobriquet lugged the bags by herself into the kitchen, dropping half of them onto the floor. She started putting the perishables in the fridge when a barely audible noise caught her attention. Even with the blaring noise of Grandma Sobriquet's programs playing in the background, Mama Sobriquet's maternal powers of hearing were not hindered. Within seconds, she was able to decipher that her only daughter was crying.

Mama stopped what she was doing to walk back into the living room and stand at the bottom of the stairs to strain and confirm that yes, Tranquila was crying.

"What's wrong with Tranny?" she asked her mother.

"How should I know?" Grandma Sobriquet mumbled.

"How should you know? You've been with her all day!" her daughter snapped.

"How *the hell* should I know?" Grandma Sobriquet snapped back, her eyes never averting the screen. "Maybe she's just realizing how stupid her hair is."

Mama Sobriquet glared at her mother, but then the sound of soft crying caught her attention again. Ascending the stairs, she said to her mother defiantly, "I like her hair."

The second floor wasn't large. Half a step, then a left turn, and she was already in Tranquila's bedroom. Two steps to the right led her inside the bathroom. Nearing the closed door, Mama Sobriquet could hear the crying more clearly. She opened the door without knocking. Peering in, she found Tranquila, in a towel, on the toilet, trying to wipe away her tears.

"Tranny? Tranny, what's wrong?" she asked, fully opening the door.

Tranquila's face was scrunched up and pink but she jerked herself on the closed toilet as if that would make her mother leave. Mama Sobriquet cooed sadly before stepping into the bathroom, closing the door behind her.

The bathroom was only big enough for a stand-in shower, a sink and the toilet. Piles of clothes, baskets of makeup and hair care products, and various jars of coconut oil pushed the two together until they were nearly on top of each other. Still, Tranquila refused to look at her.

"Tranny?"

Tranquila hiccupped a few times, chased by a couple of sniffles. Mama Sobriquet waited. Then, "Mo...m?" her daughter's little voice croaked out at last.

"Yeah, Tran?"

With a sharp sniffle, she turned to her mother revealing an onslaught of new tears and a face, tomato red. She squeaked, "Why can't I make good decisions?"

"Oh, oh sweetheart," she said with sad sighs, kneeling down so that she could touch her daughter's hand and try to look her in the eyes. "Everyone makes bad decisions when they're young, sweetheart." She held onto her daughter's left hand and smoothed out a patch of hair with the other. "Everyone does."

Tranquila cried a little longer before wailing, "Yeah, but…not everyone keeps making the same shitty ones."

"Yes they do, Tranquila. You won't believe the same mistakes people will make," she argued gently. In a lower voice she said, "Look at me, for instance."

"What about *you*?" Tranquila asked bitterly. "You provide for your family all by yourself. You got this house on your own. You don't have to wear a plastic bag on your ankle when you take a shower."

"Yeah but I'm the idiot who didn't listen to reason and let your grandmother back into my life."

The bluntness in her mother's voice made Tranquila laugh which in turn made her laugh. They laughed for a solid moment before Tranquila said, "Your mom's such a bitch."

Mama Sobriquet sighed. "Yeah, no arguments there."

"Can we *please* put her in a home?"

Mama Sobriquet grinned hard at that request. "Oh Tranny, you know we could never do that. She'd either burn it down or get charged with trying to build a meth lab."

"Yeah, no arguments there," Tranquila chuckled, then exhaled deeply as she cast her gaze to the tiles at her mother's feet.

Mama Sobriquet studied her child's face. "Is that why you're so upset?" she asked in an honest whisper; the same whisper parents use when asking their children if their uncles are doing inappropriate activities when they're not around. "Is she being that mean to you?"

Tranquila shook her head. It wasn't all Grandma's fault she felt this low. "No…No…"

Her mother waited for an explanation but didn't receive one. This didn't bother her, as it would other mothers. She was wise enough to know that what can be said will be said. Picking herself up, Mama commented, "Tran, I know you feel like you've made the worst decision in the world and that it will follow you for the rest of your life. But like I told you when you said you wanted green hair: if you want your real hair back, you're going to have to shave your head."

With that, she bent down, kissed her child's vibrant hair, went to the door, announced she was making enchiladas for dinner and left.

COMPASSIONATE, SERENE, TRAMPOLINE

The following morning, Tranquila went downstairs, set on going into Hades prepared. She wore old painting clothes with her hair up in two high pigtails. She had with her a bike chain and four pages full of notes she had taken from the internet on dog training. She slept decent, even packed leftover enchiladas for lunch. She was as determined as ever.

But as she stormed downstairs to set off anew, the salty wench that was her grandmother sidelined her.

Upon seeing her, Grandma Sobriquet cackled, "Holy shit, kid. A notebook and a bike chain? Jesus, are you going to the Underworld or community college?" she cackled.

Well, that dream died, Tranquila thought bitterly, as she felt all her confidence deplete from her soul.

"What makes you such the expert?" Tranquila demanded suspiciously. "You know, you never told me how come you know Hades is real. Or why Hades knows you personally. You sell your soul for an easy retirement and unlimited saltiness?"

Grandma Sobriquet scoffed, "Okay, first off, *saltiness* describes food *not people*. So stop using it and learn some real adjectives, for fuck's sake. And second, it doesn't take a genius to tell you a Walmart chain made in Mexico isn't going to hold down the two-ton fury that is the Hell Hound of Hades."

Tranquila grudgingly found her words to be true and dropped the chain onto the living room floor.

"And third, those dog training notes you got from the internet aren't going to do shit for that dog," she added, noticing the folded-up wad of paper tucked into her elastic pants. "Christ, didn't that creepy bastard Hermes explain that to you? Cerberus isn't like real dogs. You can't just kick it until it does what you want."

Tranquila frowned. "Well, I have no idea what I'm doing. Today I gotta go down and deal with that monster and they didn't teach me shit. I've got no training! I don't have any coworkers! And I don't want to—"

"Tran. Tran. Tran!" Grandma Sobriquet shouted, cutting her off. When she calmed down, she explained slowly: "Take your lunch. Go to work. And face that damn dog."

She waited, thinking more advice would follow, but nothing else came from Grandma Sobriquet's sunken, severely chapped lips.

"That's it?"

"Yep." She averted her attention back to the glowing box of mental decay. "Now, shut up. You're interrupting my stories."

Tranquila balked, "You're watching the news."

"—a fatal motorcycle accident in New Hartford leaves two dead and one victim without a leg today—"

Grandma Sobriquet burst out laughing at the tragedy, a signal that their moment of kinship had dried up.

Tranquila grumbled as she exited the backdoor, dropping her notes onto the ground. Her grandmother may be heartless, possibly soulless, but it was all the more reason to listen to her when it came to the facts.

Stepping onto the mound, she prepared herself to descend by squeezing the little blue plastic container to her chest and holding her breath. In that plunge, where her body disconnected from the comfort of gravity and hurtled at breakneck speed, she was brave for an eighth of a second.

"AHHHHHHHHHHHHHHHHHHHHHHHHH"

Her pansy screams didn't last as long as yesterday or the day before. One second she was tumbling, the next she could feel her feet again. The leftovers were still pressed against her person as she raised a trembling eyelid to discover she had not, as yesterday, landed in Charon's little boat.

"What the?"

She looked down to discover she was smack dab on a very tall, grassless mound that bore a narrow zenith and a long, seemingly endless drop. One step in either direction would have sent her entire being downwards—but down where, she couldn't discern. She tried to bend, to lean forward without disrupting the delicate balance that allowed her to see better, but when she did all she saw was the continuation of a downward slope.

"How the hell did this happen?" she cried, instantly pissed off. Her anger resonated trifold, bouncing off walls she couldn't see. Soon, her echoes were interrupted, not by the call of another voice, but by the low, thick, indisputable sound of rolling.

At first, she couldn't make out which direction it was coming from. She twisted her neck left to right to left to differentiate, but as the object in motion continued—its presence made known by the heart-stopping sounds of its crescendo—she soon didn't care. All at once, the heavy rumbles were upon her and she saw, in horror, a perfectly rounded giant stone bowling its way upward, towards her.

Once again she screamed, but to be fair, many would if they were seconds from being steamrolled by a vengeful rock. Without another delay, she cannonballed for dear life, off the thin ledge. Though her ears were immediately flogged by rushing winds, she still caught the voice of a man complaining from above:

"NO-O! WHY DID YOU LEAP? I WOULD HAVE STOPPED! I COULD HAVE USED A BREAK!"

Alarmed, Tranquila used all the strength in her neck to turn back, checking if schizophrenia stalked her again. Rejoice! Not this time. Falling further and further from the mountainous slopes, Tranquila was amazed to see a man, at least what was left of a man. He had the body mass of a soup can. His skin hung off of him like cotton rags and he possessed a natty, bird's nest of a beard that only Rasputin and hipsters would find appealing. He stood before her with his hands flat against the rock that had threatened to turn her into pita bread.

She laughed, happy she wasn't going insane, but that happiness didn't last when she remembered—*oh yeah, I'm falling to my death*. Rearing her neck back to face the impending ground, she watched as veering blackness rushed to liquefy her feeble human vessel. She sighed, disappointed. *Why did I even bother bringing lunch?*

*

While Tranquila was on her fifth near-death experience in three days, Hades was in the recesses of his domain; a place where the dead, who arguably have the least to lose, feared to tread.

Off the coast of the River Lethe—to ensure no one dead, half-dead or alive would know where Hades lies—stood a powerful fortress cleft from the rock of ageless ages. It was a dense, unwelcoming base that held no windows, no doors. Just a single entrance which bore three pillars, each forged from the solidified magma of an underground volcano that made the one sitting in Yellowstone look like a dormant burp. Look closer and one would find evidence that each pillar contained the disintegrated bodies of a hundred species, species extinct before man was even conceived.

In this home, befitting the immortal king of the dead, Hades completed his employment taxes. Sitting at a big, black office desk that he had partially repaired using the hide of a T-rex, Hades stared at piles and piles of receipts, documents and dreaded Social Security information—a cautionary tale for Greece: even Hades couldn't escape the clutches of his creditors.

"Jesus Christ," he cursed aloud. "Not the labor of my hands can fulfill the IRS's demands."

His struggle was interrupted by a page from his intercom: "Hades, call on extension two six four, please. Hades, call on two six four—"

In a maddening rush, he snatched up his phone and snapped into the receiver: "What? What? What?"

"Sir, we're having issues here," the familiar voice of Panic rang out, needless to say in a panic.

"Ugh, how many times have I told you? 'Thieves gets beats.' Tell those Wall Street wolves they are no exception," Hades said sternly.

"No, sir, it's far worse than that," Panic explained. "Sisyphus has stopped rolling the rock."

Hades' hearthstone-brown face went impurely black at such a statement. "How can that possibly be?" he almost screeched, then cringed to say: "*Persephone* implemented that punishment herself. No man can ever escape a woman's sentence so easily."

"That's the worst part, my Lord! He did so saving that maiden you just hired!"

Hades' brow furrowed with perplexity. "What maiden? I didn't hire anybody new."

Panic stuttered stupidly, trying to think of the aforementioned's name. Hades could hear him have a side conversation with the other entities, asking, "What's her ridiculous name again?"

"Trampoline?" guessed Agony.

"No, no, I think it was Serenity," thought Fear.

"It was some stupid white-mom-trying-to-make-their-white-kid-more-unique name," scoffed Panic.

If Hades had a heart, it would have stopped. He completely forgot. "Tranquila!"

*

"What is the name of this ambrosia again?"

"Enchiladas."

The starved creature used his hand as a bony spatula to serve the hardened flour tortilla straight into his mouth. He gulped it down entirely, making an orgasmic sound in between chews. "I haven't eaten anything this good in over three thousand years."

Tranquila served him another. "Man, you'd love Tex-Mex then."

The pair were sitting at the top of his rock which now rested at the base of his thousand upon thousand hills. Somehow, Sisyphus was able to roll his mighty boulder expertly to where she should have been steamrolled, caught her instead and controlled it so the boulder eased into a gentle stop. However he did it, be it through kinetic energies, centuries of bicep blasting, or by simply possessing the spirit of a geologist, Tranquila used leftover enchiladas as a way of showing gratitude.

"Agh," he gasped with a satisfied breath, once he was done swallowing the second helping. "I cannot relay my appreciation enough, generous maiden. You have no idea how long it's been since I have had…well…food."

"Dude, you're the one who saved me from being steamrolled," she thanked, giving his homicidal boulder a pat. "How can you even control this thing? It looks like it weighs a shit-ton."

"Three shit tons, to be exact," Sisyphus corrected.

"Damn." She looked over to the side to see the continuous stretch of high-reaching slopes and narrow peaks in the distance. "And you've been rolling that heavy-ass thing up and down for all this time?"

"I have," he said miserably. "It is my fate."

"Damn, what did you do to piss off Hades?"

"Hades didn't give me this punishment. Persephone did," Sisyphus admitted. Seeing her eyes go blank, he informed in a lower voice, "His ex-wife."

"Oh," Tranquila said, trying to recount the only reference to Greek mythology most American young adults had claim to: an anachronous Disney film she hadn't seen in over seven years. "Was she that really skinny one that Hercules stole?"

Pause. "What?"

Sisyphus's brief time to explain the many inaccuracies in that sentence were cut short. Heavy gray smoke filtered into the air, and out of nothing appeared dreaded Hades, his face burning with rage.

At once, Sisyphus submitted to groveling, holding up two peach-colored hands as his only source of white flags. He prayed vehemently: "Sir. Terrible, black Lord Hades. Spare me!"

"YOU STOPPED YOUR OWN ETERNAL TORMENT AND EXPECT REPRIEVE?" Hades bellowed, growing larger as Sisyphus shook and cried. Hades opened his mouth to howl again when in his farthest sight he saw Tranquila, herself paralyzed by fear, still cradling the plastic container bearing last night's dinner. What he saw enraged him more. "AND YOU USED AN UNDESERVING TONGUE TO EAT MEXICAN?"

"PLEASE, SIR!" Sisyphus cried, cowering on his brittle knees.

Full of guilt and sadness to see a bearded dead man cry, Tranquila found bravery in the moment. Getting to her feet, she stood and called to Hades: "Boss?"

Hades had already crooked his elbows and unhinged his jaw in preparation for grabbing the condemned man with his bare hands and swallowing him whole, when Tranquila's tender voice tamed him. She took that small abeyance as a chance to speak, "Boss, it wasn't Sissy's fault for not doing his job. He only stopped so he could save me. I somehow came in the wrong entrance and landed here. He used his rock to save my life. The only reason he ate was because I gave him my lunch to say thank you."

Hades stared at the grassy-haired maiden, his deep brown eyes bayed by strong emotion. He then turned to the sniveling Sisyphus. "Oh, Syphilis," he said with a startling sigh.

"Sisyphus."

"*Whatev*er. Do you even remember what you have done to incur the gods' wrath?"

"N-no," the man admitted, lifting his head up slightly. "I think I killed some people… Or…seduced my niece into bearing my children so they would grow up and kill my brother king…I'm not sure anymore."

Hades sighed. "It has been so long." He glanced over at Tranquila and ordered, "Take him with you to Cerberus and see to it he gets past."

"You mean?"

The undertaker nodded solemnly. "You have fulfilled your debt. You may rest with the dead."

Sisyphus's hollowed, pruned eyes unleashed a full stream of tears. He thanked the god a hundred times, before Hades, bored with his groveling, turned away and disappeared within a cloak of smoke. When he left, an overjoyed Sisyphus leapt to his withered feet, praising Zeus and Hades.

He then reared on Tranquila, his masticated body barely able to wrap himself around her, and exalted her, as if she were a goddess. "Compassionate, serene, Trampoline! I will forever praise thee!" Tranquila accepted the gratitude as graciously as one could while suffocating on the repugnant smell of two thousand years' worth of body odor.

"You're welcome! You're welcome! Jesus Christ, stop hugging me," Tranquila shouted, unable to withstand the miasma any longer. Choking on the lingering fumes, she asked, "Do you know how to get to the Acheron River?"

Sisyphus nodded vigorously. "I've dwelt so long in this realm I could draw a map of it blind."

"Good," she panted. "Lead the way."

He shook his head with excitement. "Good ol' Back Breaker will get us there!"

With that, he plopped back down on the boulder and waited for her to take a seat. With a good pat, the rock automatically zoomed down the beaten slopes that it had known so well and raced away in the opposite direction from those hellish hills for the last time.

They whipped through Hades at tremendous speed, the winds yanking Tranquila's hair to the point where she lost the overstretched hair-tie that tried to tame her thick collection of tresses. Her long St. Patrick's Day hair flapped loosely behind, making souls that caught a glimpse of them think Sisyphus was streaming a banner throughout Hades as he cried with unconcealed joy: "I AM FREE! I AM FREE! I AM FREE!"

His boulder, the massive curator of torment, skidded through the dingy waters of Acheron as if it were a mere road, and almost drowned Charon who was unloading a set of souls onto the banks.

"HEY! I'M WORKING HERE!"

But Sisyphus who was dry, defiant of physics and free, continued in his jubilation: "I am free! I am free!"

When they made it to the entrance, they dropped the rock to the ground while dozens of new arrivals gawked. Sisyphus strode confidently past them, to become the only man ever to walk up to the Hell Hound with a smile on his decayed face.

Cerberus watched this spectacle with all six eyes and bowed her three heads, growling at the man. Her vicious barks sent terror into the hearts of the newcomers, but Sisyphus didn't flinch. He smiled at the dog, as if he wished to pet the mutant. Cerberus, innately aware of her master's new rule, didn't charge or snap at Sisyphus with its monstrous jaw. Instead, Cerberus turned herself, making room for entry. The fresh souls, and even Charon, watched in amazement as the scraggy subject of torture swaggered through the opening, as if walking into a country club and not the inescapable nightmare that was Hades.

"Ye gods," Charon's rattling voice sounded off. "Is that Sisyphus?"

"Yep."

"Why isn't he pushing the rock?" Charon demanded. Looking to the rock, he yelled at it, "You didn't do your job, Back Breaker. You were supposed to break his spirit."

Tranquila was about to explain to Charon why Sisyphus' rock rolling days were over when she caught sight of the stunned, bewildered and scared faces of the dead. An empath's need to comfort them welled in her.

"Hey," she said gently, to catch their attention. The group of shadows gave a startled turn in her direction, assuming her a demon. With her many piercings and dark makeup, many living people made that assumption as well. "Um…Welcome? Welcome, I guess, to the Underworld."

A couple of them made audible gasps.

"So, this is Hell?" a frightened man's voice rang out.

"Not…really. This is Hades," she corrected.

"Hell's a Christian and Coptic concept," Charon interjected.

"Wait. So the Greeks were right?" another soul shouted, sounding appropriately alarmed.

"Sucks to know doesn't it, cocky mortals? Ha ha ha ha ha ha ha ha," harked Charon's obnoxious laughter. It shook the dim atmosphere with its malice, but still the mortals were having trouble believing the skeleton's words.

"So, wait. There's no Anyanwu?" piped up an unsure soul.

"Nope," Tranquila replied.

"No Allah?"

"Nuh-uh."

"What about almighty Ra?"

"Sorry, man. Just Zeus and his crew."

Needless to say, this invoked many to swear and curse their choice in religion.

"I can't believe I gave up masturbating," cried a Muslim Imani and a Catholic priest simultaneously.

"I can't believe I said 'no' to birth control," shouted a woman with an irate brogue. "I was freaking pregnant for twelve years in a row."

Their regrets and resentments began to overlap in a loud babel. Tranquila shouted over them until they went silent again,

"Hey. HEY! Why does any of that matter? Aren't you a little glad you were wrong?"

"NO!" they yelled back, disgruntled.

"Well, you should be," Charon scolded, once again drawing their attention with his gravely unpleasant voice. Leaning on his oar, he addressed the souls: "In your respective hells, one thing is certain: follow thy tedious rules or be screwed; be on your best behavior and hope, pray even, that you are spared from eternal torture. We Greeks, as silly and archaic as we seem, do not believe in that. In Hades, you have to really, really piss off the gods to ensure wrath. To the rest, you live as shadows and you reflect. You spend your time in Hades understanding your mistakes; you get to the core of how and why you did as you did on Earth and hopefully you can find peace in that enlightenment.

"Now, I don't know about you, but I would rather be dead wrong in Hades than be 'right' in Hell."

With his speech finished, Charon maneuvered his boat back into the waters and veered down the river. He had a job to do and it wasn't to comfort dead assholes.

Still, their anxiety was noticeable to her, so Tranquila tried rationalizing with the souls, "Hey," she spoke up. "You saw that guy that walked in?"

"The manorexic that smelled like turd noodles?"

"Yeah. *He* incurred the wrath of the gods. But he did his time and now he freaking runs into Hades." She made a small pause to smile at the souls. "Could be worse, right?"

Her simplistic words eased the woeful new arrivals. They each shared nervous glances, but eventually all of those with the same death-day went together and passed by Cerberus. They would never leave, and it was understood.

Tranquila lagged behind them, waiting for Cerberus' growl and distrusting eye contact. Like dogs on Earth, the Hell

Hound searched for Tranquila's eyes and they held an unblinking gaze for a full minute. The bloodlust that she saw yesterday had disappeared in those six eyes, but weren't exactly replaced by excitement or interest either.

The remainder of Tranquila's shift were spent on the banks of Acheron, keeping a safe distance from the sharp-tempered dog. The untouchable coat of luscious black fur that mocked her dog-loving urge to pet the beast. Hourly, she rose to greet the new souls that Charon ferried in.

It wasn't until she was back home, listening to the howls of her grandmother's amusement at an Utican family's house fire, that she realized she had a coworker.

ZEUS'S SOLUTION TO EVERY PROBLEM EVER

Working in the Underworld became more routine than her weekly drug screenings. Though she had seen neither Hades nor Hermes in almost two weeks, and while Cerberus still regarded her with the same distrustful disdain as a house cat, and despite the mind-numbing repetitiveness she endured during those low-mortality days of September, Tranquila was content.

Of course, she was lucky. Many mortals, even gods, found themselves without purpose, lazily wasting their days transfixed on favorite vices or acts of mental decay. For Zeus, companion to the cosmos, king of almost-everything, his favorite way to spend time was being insatiably horny. And unfortunately for many, Zeus was very, very, very horny.

Coasting along the curve of the ionosphere, Zeus fortified his celestial powers. Not to absolve humans of suffering, poverty or disease, but to scan the world to find a new booty call.

Surveying the world's population with eyesight superior to raptors and hawks, Zeus weighed up his options—because if he was going to invoke Hera's fury, it better be for a booty that's worth it: "No. No. No…Ooh!" Zeus cried, excited. "A lonely college student walking late at night," But Zeus shook his head. "No. Female students have enough problems with over-excited, uncontrollable males without me adding to it." He cast his eyes down again and squealed with delight, "Ooh, a men's prison."

As he searched for a male prisoner who didn't have shank wounds, another heavenly body appeared alongside him, as if a supernova exploded next to him. Out of the blinding light appeared a woman with pupil-less, pearly-white eyes. She harked in a voice drained of femininity and volume control, "Zeus, to whom we call God of gods, I have come to thee bearing a message of great importance."

Zeus regarded the oracle informally, "Oh hey, Pythia. How's the kids?"

"One's annoyingly going through puberty and the other one is entering the terrible two's, *but that is not important right now*. What is important is that you stop what you are doing and heed." The Oracle of Delphi's voice boomed with an ominous and androgynous voice, "HEED, I SAY!"

"Jesus! I'm heeding, I'm heeding," Zeus stated, exasperated by her sudden loudness. "Now, what am I heeding?"

"Son of Cronus, you must not continue with your philandering ways. You must remember your vows and from this moment forward retain monogamy with Hera."

Zeus let out a hearty laugh. "Nice try, Pythia. Who put you up to this? Hestia? Was it Hestia? She's always getting on my case about 'being a homewrecker' and 'tearing this family apart'."

"No," the Oracle asserted. "I speak only with the knowledge of what will surely be. Think of your brother, Zeus. Think of the heartbreak that consumes him."

"Oh, Hades," Zeus said, sighing sadly at the reminder of his brother's pain. "I had no idea he was still taking it hard."

"The man was married for sixteen million years and the divorce took place only three weeks ago," Pythia informed, irked by his ignorance.

Zeus sighed, shaking his head. "You're right. Poor Hades. I should go visit him."

"Th-that's not what I wanted you to get out of this…"

"My brother needs me," Zeus determined, ignoring the oracle and the message she was presenting to him.

"No, he doesn't," the oracle half-shouted. "Hades will be fine. What YOU need to do is—"

"I need to stop being selfish," Zeus finished.

"Exactly. You—"

"I need to remember that I have a duty."

"To your wife—"

"To my brother."

"NO!" the Oracle screamed.

"Yes!" Zeus exclaimed, slamming his fist into his palm triumphantly. "I'm going to go to the Underworld, get my brother out of his funk, and I'm going to score with some dead people."

The oracle was left speechless, Zeus took her hand and thanked her for reminding him of the importance of family before transforming himself into lightning and striking down into the Earth's Underworld at a fantastic speed.

The oracle punched herself in the head and cried, "How did I not see that coming?"

*

Twenty miles below the Earth's core and forty miles west of where Tranquila was stationed, Hades was busy preparing for the surge of births that were expected in the nine months that followed Valentine's Day and St. Patrick's Day. Standing on the Pool of Lethe with a few of his employees, he read aloud from a clipboard, "Elizabeth Keckley?"

A broad-faced, mix-raced and classically dressed soul walked ahead to meet the undertaker at the edge of Forgetfulness. She held a strong stride for several steps. As she crossed, nearly reaching the assisting hand of Hades, the courage from within her dissipated. The hand that Hades held out for her to grab no longer seemed compassionate. The proud woman nearly ran back, but one of the harpies grabbed her by the elbows and heaved her headfirst into the waters. At first, she made frenzied splashes; soon waters absorbed into the woman's light skin. She became placid and full of bliss.

Harpies at the deep end scooped up the emptied vessel and sent the former slave on her merry way, to be reincarnated into a scarlet macaw, born out of captivity and free to be colorful.

"Okay. Joshua Morinitti?"

As the lord of the dead went through the names, there arose a stir in the line. A wild-eyed man with a beard down to his knees was actually skipped ahead of people. He had rushed through the masses like a drunk close to sobering up in the middle of a liquor store until he recognized a familiar face.

"Mister Doctor King! Mister Doctor King! You must let me take cutsies," the soul begged in a thick, troubled, Russian accent.

"Of course you can, comrade," mused the Reverend, giving Rasputin space to go in front of him. Rasputin practically jumped in line, dunking behind the spirit of the woman ahead. Noticing his apprehension, the former pastor and African-American civil rights leader commanded, "Fear not, Grigori. Soon you will be wiped clean of your past debaucheries and in that birth anew you will rediscover lost values."

Rasputin looked at him as if he were crazy. "Are you kidding? I regret nothing from my life. The only thing I regret is not going to more orgies!"

"Then why are you shaking?" Dr. King inquired, confused.

"Because Zeus is here!" Rasputin's once commanding voice carried across the dreaded field of Hades, shrill with fear.

Everyone in line heard. Immediately men, women and skeletons took proactive steps to dissuade the ill-famed god. Women ruffled their hair into unkempt knots, tore at their cheeks and bit their lips. Men tucked themselves in, to flatten any flattering bulges and ripped out facial hair to make luscious beards look patchy and unappealing. Rasputin and Martin Luther King Jr. resorted to enfolding themselves into each other's bodies. Quaking and close to tears—the trauma of Zeus's last excursion weighed heavily in their hearts.

Hades, distracted with his duties, didn't know what was going on until it was too late. He heard his brother's heavy footsteps and looked up to find glorious Zeus basking in his own divinity. With his marvelous blend of rich hickory skin, Zeus strode forth, shimmering in his glow, blinding those who stood too close. He smiled at the dead, who were forced to their knees. Not in reverence but in fear, Zeus flashed a lecherous grin at those he found desirable. "Hey, Rasputin…"

The mad monk let out a devastated squeal, while Dr. King stroked his greasy friend's head, whispering, "It will be okay, it'll be okay."

Zeus, surprisingly, distracted himself from his lechery and turned to his brother. He held out his arms, expecting a hug, proclaimed, "Brother. It has been too long."

Not for Hades. Concentrating on the litany in his hands, Hades made a small effort of a hello. Zeus, lacking omniscience, didn't get the hint. He took it upon himself to give his brother an insufferable hug that would have squeezed any mortal's skeleton right out of their bodies. Hades, who was just as strong as his little brother, used his clipboard to pry himself off him.

When they were apart, Hades let out a groan, turned to one of the harpies and ordered, "Do a few dozen more. We'll do the rest next week."

The harpy nodded in understanding, took the clipboard in one claw and squawked out, "GAWWWWK! Medgar Evers?"

Hades returned his attention to his brother. In a voice devoid of enthusiasm, he said, "Hey Zeus. What brings you to my secret compartment of the world?"

"Oh, you know, I was just scouring the regions for a mortal to tend to my nether regions—" Zeus began, as they strolled down the archives of the Underworld.

"You were always gay for wordplay, brother," Hades said in a monotone voice.

"—when I realized that I haven't been there for you as of late," Zeus finished, punctuating the sentence by placing a hand on Hades' shoulder. In a gentle voice, emptied of promiscuity, he asked, "How are you, brother?"

Hades didn't look at Zeus, or the hand which always seemed to find a way onto his shoulder. With his eyes to the soot-filled ground, he answered, "I am fine."

Zeus's fine lips pressed into a worrisome line which Hades poignantly ignored.

In a brighter tone, Zeus stated, "How busy the Underworld seems. You must have your hands full."

"No more than usual. Although that Syrian revolution is keeping us pretty steady for August and September," Hades replied earnestly.

Zeus smiled. "I have no idea how you keep up so efficiently. Then again, you were always the hard worker."

The compliment melted him. Hades reverted his gaze to meet Zeus' hazel eyes that never ceased to beam with warmth, even during rapacious moods. He could feel his lips curl despite himself, but they also trembled under reoccurring thoughts.

While sex-obsessed and clueless, Zeus had one redeeming quality that was never scribed in Ovid's tales or Homer's epics: he was a good little brother. Especially to a melancholy-prone Hades who found himself needing comfort and fraternal love more times than he cared to admit.

Even if he did come all this way to violate a corpse, Hades thought, looking over his shoulder to find that Rasputin and Martin Luther King Jr. were still cowering in each other's arms, *he's still the only one who's come down to visit since the divorce.*

With a grudging sigh, Hades whispered, "May we speak privately?"

In a true sign of respect, Zeus resisted the urge to make a sex pun out of the word 'private' and simply nodded. With a snap, Zeus and Hades dissolved into a gray gas cloud, which curled into a wisp that rose to the cavernous ceiling before evanescing entirely.

When Zeus was gone, the dead men and women erupted into fanatical cheers, praising benevolent Hades for sparing them from 'thirsty' Zeus.

*

Relocated within the confines of his castle, Hades unloaded all his apprehension to Zeus.

"The truth is, brother, I am not keeping up with everything. Ebola, the crisis in the Middle East, those weekly mass shootings in America...ugh, don't even get me started on the shootings! Every punk-ass with a weak constitution wants to be infamous and now I gotta deal with the fallout. I have more in Tartarus than ever. And I can barely keep up with new and cruel punishments. That was always something Persephone was good at. She...She could make rolling a rock up and down a hill a fate worse than Christian Hell. But me? Me? What do I think of? Spider bombs…Unending thirst in the lake of fires…Common core homework. My punishments suck and I'm running out of ideas. And lately, lately, I've been having such a hard time concentrating. Do you know what I did? Two weeks ago, I harvested a soul—I actually got someone to sell me their soul! Do you know how long it's been since I collected a soul? And what? What happens? I *completely* forgot about it. That's how you know this divorce has gotten me all out of whack. Normally, collecting a maiden's soul would make my whole week but I—"

Zeus's forbearance ended the second a maiden was mentioned.

"A maiden!" Zeus interjected. "You didn't tell me you had a new soul walking around here."

Damn my diction, Hades cursed to himself. Out loud, he lambasted his brother: "Five seconds! Five *Earth* seconds you went without thinking with your dick. I knew you wouldn't listen."

"Who said I wasn't listening? You said you're having trouble concentrating, you're overwhelmed, you're feeling burnt out. Well, through dialogue we have found truth. Your answer lies in *lying* with thy maiden," Zeus reasoned, not without a sensual chuckle for emphasis.

"Zeus, not every solution to man's problems is lying with woman."

"Oh, c'mon Hades! Yes it is," Zeus argued. "Besides, have you ever copulated with a mortal? They're a riot! Half of them have never felt a proper orgasm before. Unlike our goddesses who think anything under thirty climaxes barely constitutes a first date. Besides, it might do you some good to do someone. Sex relieves anxiety, depression, crankiness—"

"Zeus!" Hades cut in, getting cranky. "For one, I don't sleep with my employees. That's employer-employee rule number one. And two, I don't need sex—I *need* help."

"She works here?" Zeus choked, surprised. "Is she working here now?" When Hades nodded, Zeus nearly imploded with curiosity. "No way! No way! Show me what she looks like."

Irked, but needing to change the subject, Hades rolled his wrists in the air. A cloud, that conjured high-definition images of whatever he desired, appeared. Speaking directly to the cloud, he ordered, "Tranquila."

Instantly the cloud reformed, showing Tranquila stationed on the riverbank of Acheron trying to comfort a group of Amish who just realized they had forsaken a life without the internet for naught.

Zeus emitted a noise that signified lusty desire, "Ooh! She's one of those *Suicide Girls*? Damn, well, if you're not interested Hades…"

"I wouldn't get too ambitious, brother," Hades crooned smugly. "That's Jeanette's kin."

"Ah," Zeus flinched from fear the way most men, women, children and land animals did when Jeanette's name was mentioned. "Jesus, no wonder you have no interest."

"And since when are you so easily derailed from putting your dick into something?" Hades demanded, bemused. "Hera has laid waste to nearly all your demi-gods and not even that deters you."

"Yeah, but Hera just goes after my lovers and my offspring. Jeanette would try to kill *me*. And when she didn't succeed, she'd just bully me until I ended up killing myself," Zeus insisted, edging away from the floating image of Tranquila, as if she were contagious.

"So you see now, brother? My problems cannot be resolved as easily as you would assume," said Hades.

Zeus paused, looking pensively at the vision of Tranquila. "Maybe not. But maybe, just maybe, the company of a lady can assuage you, brother."

"I don't understand."

Turning his attention away from the maiden, Zeus beamed at Hades, not with salaciousness but sagacity, "I sense new truth, Hades," he proclaimed. "The truth being that this lady can be the solution you seek." Hades' silence revealed that he didn't understand. Thus, Zeus spoke again, "Train her. Let her shadow you and your abstracts. Make her multivalent."

Zeus's wisdom ruled the world but Hades still had reason to be wary. "This mortal? But she's so ignorant of our history, even for an American. Are you certain?"

Zeus gave a curt nod. "She may not be versed in our history but she will be indispensable to you. Teach her how to work in Hades, Hades. She will not disappoint you."

A complicated expression etched itself onto Hades' stern face. Ultimately, he conceded to his brother's whim and said, "Thank you."

Zeus smiled, reaching over to coerce Hades into another unwilling hug. When they let go, a carnal grin regrouped in Zeus's smile. "So…Since I helped you…I was wondering if I could get a little help with a problem of my own."

"You can't have Rasputin."

"Damn. What about Dr. King?"

"No," Hades barked. Seeing his Zeus' dance, Hades told him, "If you have to have somebody, choose from the Tartarus lot."

Overjoyed, Zeus gave his brother a big fat kiss on the cheek before racing down the house of dead's halls at full speed, singing, "I'm gonna get it on…with Agamemnon! I'm gonna get it on…with Agamemnon!"

*

"Yeah, the internet's got cats and shit, but it's not worth it, knowing you're going to waste two-thirds of your life fighting carpal tunnel and getting really bad at spelling," Tranquila lied to a group of Mennonites. Placated, they were able to retire peacefully inside the House of Dead.

When Cerberus sealed the last of them in, her mood changed entirely. Her ears perked up, her tail of snakes wagged furiously and unhinged her jaw to unleash several ear-shattering barks. It was enough to send Tranquila's heart into cardiac arrest, making it the sixth time she almost died. A voice from behind soothed the Hell Hound.

"Awwww, is my pretty Cerby trying to kill my new employee?"

Clutching her chest, Tranquila lifted her head in time to catch a billow of black robes sweeping past her. Staggering up from her knees, she watched as her boss caressed the beast's cheek and was stunned to see the dog melt at his touch.

After several pets, belly rubs and who's-my-good-girls, Hades turned his head towards Tranquila. He surveyed her, then demanded, "Walk with me."

Tranquila complied, thought lagged far behind Hades. She still tried to walk off the angina.

They went around the corner of the riverbank, venturing down a slender hall where the ceilings were upturned. The walls oozed with energizing magma.

Fifteen or so paces in, Hades spoke first: "I haven't seen you since our little interview. How is everything going for you?"

"Eh, it's going," she replied, as she tried to jumpstart her heart by beating her chest.

"I hope they're keeping you busy."

Punch. "Oh, yeah," she said, relaxing when she heard her heart beat again. With a chuckle she added, "You definitely kept up your end of the deal. I've been everything *but* bored here."

"Good," he said, distracted. "Not many people sell their souls and end up getting a positive experience out of it."

"Wow. How many people have sold their souls to you?"

"Surprisingly, not that many. Usually when people find out I'm real, they chicken out at the last minute," Hades informed. "That's why your situation is all the more unique."

"Yeah that's me," she sighed. "Uniquely stupid."

Hades, who had been staring ahead this whole time, glanced over at Tranquila and recognized her self-disappointment. How many times had he been there? What with recently, when he had to stand in the middle of Olympus and declare, in front of his entire family, that his marriage was less successful than Zeus and Hera's, the epitome of shitty relationships. Probably his biggest regret in life was not seeing Biggie Smalls in concert when he had the chance ("Western hemisphere y'all!")

"Do you know why I made that deal with you, Tranquila?"

"Because I didn't say anything about you being black?" she asked.

"No." With that thought, he had to ask, "Were you shocked, though?"

"I mean a little. But only 'cause I thought you were gonna be blue," she replied with honesty. (*Damn that fucking movie!* Hades cursed internally.) "Then again, the first people came out of Africa. Makes sense that the gods or Zeus or whoever made us would make man based on themselves."

Her answer made him smile. And here he had assumed her to be an ignoramus. Going back to the original topic, he said, "I agreed to that deal because I admired your ambition."

"Oh, I'm not ambitious," she quickly denied. Ambitious was a superlative for the college-bound who worked on the side; for kids who went to vocational school with a ten-year plan to start a business. Ambition did not describe people who took a year off from school because they never liked anything the school counselors suggested.

"But you wanted to work," Hades countered. "You looked at Hades and said to yourself, 'I'd rather sweat and toil in Hell than coast by, doing nothing on Earth'. Not many people are like that, Tranquila." *Mortal or immortal,* he said to himself. Then he asked, "What are your plans?"

"For *life*?"

"For when you get off probation," he heartened, pointing to her electronic anklet.

"Oh," She paused to think. "God…s, I have no idea. I dunno…probably just try to find a full-time job somewhere. Work for the rest of my life…I dunno."

Hades nodded. It was a reasonable plan. "How about here?"

"Y-you're offering me a job?" she stammered, thinking she'd misheard him.

"I'm not going to lie to you, Tranquila, it's gone to hell here. No pun intended. You've seen how huge our turnouts are. With all the suicides in Japan, all the homicides in America and genocides in Africa and the Middle East, I'm up to my neck in dead people. I need help and I need someone who isn't sick to death of death yet," Hades said frankly.

Tranquila mulled over his words. Then she asked, "What would I do?"

"You'd be trained in a little bit of everything: screening out the near-deaths, managing the real deaths, controlling correspondence between the dead and those who've betrayed them, filing punishment proposals, preparing vessels for reincarnation, making referrals. I know it's a lot I'm throwing at you, but in all fairness, there's a lot to be done. I'm not going to lie to you about to it. It's fast-paced, there's a lot coming at you. But it's full-time and there's a lot of room for mobility," Hades informed, speeding through the details like a general manager who had four other interviews to do before he could take lunch. "Does that sound like anything you'd be interested in?"

Tranquila was being offered a highly lucrative job that guaranteed exotic travel, great hours, a chance to meet famous clientele, indispensable experience AND it didn't require a master's degree toppled by six years' worth of experience—*right out of high school*. If she *didn't* take this job, American grad students were going to steal into her room in the middle of the night and beat her with their student loan bank statements.

"Uh, yeah, that sounds like something I'd want to do."

"Excellent! So now, unfortunately—" *Here it comes*, she thought bitterly. *I knew this was too good to be true. If there can't be dream jobs in America, why would the Underworld be any different?* "—I'm afraid I don't have currency to pay you with down here." *Okay, so this is going to be some unpaid internship bullshit.* "So you would be paid in gold. Does that sound okay to you?"

Of course Hades knew that would be acceptable to her, he just wanted to amuse himself by seeing Tranquila's jaw unhinge and the color drain from her tanned skin. He wasn't sure how he kept himself from laughing as he watched her struggle to stay composed. In a dizzy stutter that was the antithesis of calm, she said "Th-that's cool…"

CLAP FOR YOUR DAMN SELF

That night, Tranquila celebrated by not letting Grandma Sobriquet know of her good news. While she bubbled with intense joy at landing such a great opportunity, she had no desire for the good news to be mashed like a rotten pumpkin being slammed into the sidewalk the day after Halloween. At some point she would have to tell her; she was going to need someone to trade in her gold for cash, but not tonight.

Sure, she wished she had friends to relay the good news to. She loathed not keeping in touch with anyone from high school, until she recalled the day her mugshot was posted on the internet by the police department's Facebook page and all the disparaging remarks that followed, made by the people she remembered fondly. Or worse when someone posted the mugshot on an Instagram account titled "cny_Mugshots" and how her drunk-eyed and sobbing police portrait got a staggering 9,000 likes.

Fuck 'em, she thought that night before drifting to sleep. *I can clap for my damn self.*

*

At 4:30 in the morning Mama Sobriquet was awake. No alarm went off; her dreams slipped away while her eyes fluttered awake like dreary moths in the midst of darkness. She didn't stretch. She just rose, spun her legs off the bed and marched out of the bedroom without so much as turning on a light.

Darkness spread evenly throughout the house. Even the living room television was dead. Yet she was able to navigate effortlessly without bumping into any furniture. She couldn't bear to turn on the lights without heating the tea kettle first. Mama Sobriquet was one of the few American adults who wasn't fueled by coffee, which was surprising given the number of hours she worked. When she went into the kitchen, though, the small light above the stove glowed. In her blurry-eyed state of wake, she saw the teapot already blowing steam.

"I was gonna turn it off," she heard a voice from behind say, as she twisted the knob on the stove.

Mama Sobriquet turned to see Tranquila with a mug in her hand. The string of a teabag dangled off the side of the handle.

"You're up early," she remarked. "Did you have another Komodo Dragon nightmare?"

"Nah," Tranquila replied, handing over the mug. "I only get those when it's really hot out. I went to bed early last night so now I'm up."

"Oh," she said, as she poured piping hot water into the cup, readjusting her grip so her fingers wouldn't get burnt by the ceramic. "Well, now you're gonna be bored all day."

"I'll be fine."

Mama Sobriquet gave her a small, weary, early-morning smile. She looked over her shoulder and saw that a near empty gallon of milk sat on the counter. The smile disappeared.

"Tran, don't leave the milk out. I've already bought three gallons this week," she scolded, turning to the cabinets to retrieve admixtures for her tea. Rummaging, she found the bear-shaped honey bottle and was dismayed to see it only had two squirts left in it. "What the hell! We're almost out of honey, too?"

She emptied the bottle into her cup and discarded the honey bear into the trash. With her cup in hand, she went into the living room to log onto Facebook for a half-hour before she took her shower, prepping for the ten-hour shift that awaited. Tranquila followed her. As her mom watched the computer screen turn on, Tranquila asked, "Mom...um, when you get a chance this week, would you mind going to the library for me and picking up this book?"

She slipped a piece of paper to Mama Sobriquet.

"Greek Mythology?" she looked up at Tranquila. "Seriously?"

"Yeah." Seeing the suspicion in her mother's face, she added defensively, "What? Can't a girl want to learn new things?"

Mama Sobriquet scoffed. "Tran, I could teach you about Greek mythology."

"Really?"

"Yeah," she said casually, turning to face the computer screen. "Ninety percent of it is just Zeus putting his Dick in things and everyone dealing with blowback. The other ten percent are just adventures that take way too fucking long."

Typing in her password, Mama Sobriquet asked, "Why the sudden interest in Greek mythology? Or in reading, for that matter?" Mama Sobriquet stared into Tranquila's face, inquiring why this same student that paid her misguided, seriously in-debt older brother into doing all her reading assignments from 10th grade on, suddenly found interest in the most boring of subjects.

"I dunno. I mean, with all the *Jerry Springer* I've been watching lately, I need to start doing something before my mind melts into fake cheese," Tranquila lied. "Yesterday, Grandma was watching two midget hookers fight in a pool of hot fudge and I swear to god…s—" she made sure to pluralize that noun quietly "—deadass, I felt a stroke coming on."

Mama Sobriquet laughed. "Sure, baby. I'll get you that book."

Tranquila smiled. She gave her mom a kiss on the forehead before retreating back into the kitchen. "I'm gonna go hide before Grandma comes over. Have a good day, Mom."

"Alright sweetie," Mama's voice trailed off, no doubt distracted by whatever post or news thread popped up on her timeline. Tranquila made sure she heard the clicky-clacky sounds of the keyboard before opening the fridge to retrieve the peanut butter and banana sandwich she had for lunch. Quietly, she tiptoed to the toaster and grabbed a thermos full of black tea—hidden earlier when she heard her mom coming—and snuck out through the screen door, gently pushing it shut to the rhythm of Mama Sobriquet's typing.

Cloaked beneath the navy veneer of pre-dawn, Tranquila trotted over to the sacred pit and stood atop the dirt now soggy from the milk, honey and water offering she cautiously made ten minutes before her mom woke. She was able to get away without dumping out wine, which was good because Mama Sobriquet would forgive the missing milk and honey but gods help them if she started missing her white wine.

She imagined that she looked like an office worker going down in the elevator whilst sipping black tea. Her lunch dangled at her side. She wished she could have told Mama Sobriquet of her true intentions for being up so early. But with the electronic bracelet hanging off her ankle like a tawdry charm, Tranquila had to accept that the good news would have to wait, much like her nervous system had to accept the eighty-mile-per-hour fall she put her body through every day to commute to the Underworld.

Although it took her weeks to adjust, Tranquila was able to land on her feet with the same grace other people used to go down a single step. With her thermos full and her sandwich only slightly squished, Tranquila looked around to see where she landed today.

She must have done something right because she found herself standing in the only room in the Underworld with any proper lighting. It looked like a cavern, only the dirt floors were solid and smooth. In the middle stood a tower of white uncut opal which touched the ceiling. Another towering source of light in its base, magnifying the minerals and emitting a natural glow that was enough to keep the entire room visible for the next forty million years.

Tranquila would have spent the next sixty years of her life staring into the mesmerizing light had she not felt a presence behind her. When she turned her head in this moment of paranoia, she was startled to find Hermes staring back at her with those terrible yellow eyes.

"FUCK!"

"Nice to see you again, Tranquila," Hermes drawled out, unoffended. When she stopped panting, he handed her some papers and a pen. "Sit with me. We have to go over a few things."

They walked over to a two-person table comprised entirely out of priceless gems.

"Where are we?" Tranquila inquired in awe. "And why is my poor ass sitting on a diamond?"

"This is the break room," Hermes said, as he reviewed his documents. He casually pointed over to a bland-looking microwave which sat unnoticed against the wall. "And as for your seat, all the furniture in the Underworld was made out of precious gems and stones."

"*Seriously?*"

"Well, save Hades' desk chair which is made out of the bones of a mortal who made the egregious mistake of trying to steal his ex-wife from him long ago," Hermes recounted, with the bored drawl of a storyteller giving away a trivial detail. Meanwhile, Tranquila still sat trout-mouthed over the beauty of her surroundings. Hermes laid out a copy of his notes before her and dictated, "Okay, this simply states that you are now an official employee of Hades, unlike two weeks prior, when you were negating any time you spent down here in regards to the oral contract you agreed to with the lord of the Underworld. Now," he read from the document, "'as an official worker of the lower kingdom you are expected to adhere to a specific code of conduct. This includes a confidentiality clause stating you will not discuss what you have seen, heard or were asked to do in the Underworld. You will not inform others that this part of the world exists nor will you admit to anyone on the surface world that Hades and his realm exists, nor will you discuss anything about the persons you have seen dwelling in Hades, either famous, infamous or otherwise known to you. Signing this contract means you understand that you are never to discuss with anyone your job in Hades or that you know Hades to exist. Failure to comply will result in immediate termination and will eradicate any and all memories of your time spent in Hades.'"

Hermes read all of this in one seemingly long breath and when he was done, he looked up from the document and asked redundantly, "Do you understand what I just read to you?"

Tranquila was visibly troubled. "So, I can never tell anybody that I work here?"

"No."

"Not even my mom?"

"Especially your mother," Hermes said. "If Jeanette never told her of the existence of the Underworld, then you certainly can't."

"This fucking blows," Tranquila whined, folding her arms in dissatisfaction. "I finally get a full-time job and I can't even brag about it to my mom?" A suspicion crawled inside her head. "How come Grandma Jeanette got to spill the beans to me, then? What did she do to get that kind of immunity?"

If Hermes could, he would have rolled his eyes. "Listen, maiden, I'm in Human Resources not Human Services. You can figure out that family drama on your own time. Do you want the job or not?"

And pass up getting paid in gold? Tranquila pushed away the disappointment and distrust in her grandmother and agreed to the confidentiality clause. Signing her name, Hermes tucked the document into a folder and flipped over to the next page.

Hermes continued, "'In Hades, you will receive hands-on training for an unlimited amount of time. So long as the employee is willing and enthusiastic to learn, there will be no time frame in which the employee's training should last. However, the employee is expected to have open availability and be willing to tackle new and exciting situations, if they were to arise. This includes, but is not limited to, the event of a nuclear holocaust, devastations due to global warming, the return of the Titans, zombie apocalypse, the eruption of the underground super volcano, technological takeover of Apple products, the second-coming of International Hitler, etcetera, etcetera'."

When Hermes lifted his head to gauge Tranquila's reaction, he rightfully found her flabbergasted.

"What do you mean 'underground super volcano'?" she blurted out.

"Those are just hypothetical scenarios," Hermes reassured, leaving out the actuality that there are twelve of those bad boys, all active, all waiting and all within killing proximity of her family.

"Oh," she said, still on edge. "So, he's just guessing that there *might* be a nuclear holocaust?"

Hermes shrugged obliquely, omitting North Korea's missile tests and America's inherent habit of entering wars they couldn't finish. "Sure."

Tranquila said, "Cool," but on the inside her intestines felt like they were freezer-burnt.

"This wasn't meant to scare you, Tranquila," Hermes insisted, sensing her malaise. "It's just stating if something huge were to happen, that you would be ready to handle it."

She stared at the papers for a while, finding herself unable to read past all those impact words. At least if the world ended, she guessed, it wouldn't be like she'd never see her loved ones again. Reluctantly, she placed her signature and date on the according lines.

"Now, payment."

"Oh, thank gods," she said aloud, thrilled that the conversation was going somewhere positive.

"You will be paid weekly."

"Yeah!"

"And you will be paid in gold and precious gems such as opals, amethyst clusters, uncut emeralds and topaz when permitted. I assume this is alright."

"Hell yeah, that's alright."

"Good. Now, your pay rate is going to start off at two pieces a week. At the end of your training, you'll receive a pay increase of three. There is an annual raise in which you will go up this pay scale," Hermes informed, whipping out a flow chart. Using an index finger, he went through the chart: "Now, there is a cap on of how much you can make, which you can see here. This is when you will be paid your current weight in gold. Is that acceptable?"

Of course it was. As she signed that off, she commented, "Wow. For once in my life I can't wait to tell someone how much I weigh."

"Yes, Hades is aware of the dangerous obsession you mortal women have with your weight. You can blame Pandora and the patriarchy on that one," Hermes remarked, as he took her copy and placed it in his pile. Clicking his pen, he bravely asked the one question not even doctors dared to ask, "Now, how much do you weigh?"

"Three hundred and ninety-eight pounds."

Hermes looked up at her, unamused. "Okay, I don't blame you for trying but I wouldn't get greedy down here, Tranquila. Especially since you're going to see very soon what we do to avarice."

Tranquila dropped her head, then admitted, "One hundred and fifty-five."

"That's better." He jotted down the three digit number then shuffled the page along with the rest. He reached to the bottom of his pile and handed her a packet as thick as a manuscript. He explained, "This is your training packet. As you go along, check off what you have learned or what has been touched upon. By the end you should be knowledgeable in every category."

Flipping through the pages, she scanned down the litany of expectations and caught sight of keywords such as MAINTAINING UPKEEP FOR THE TREE OF FALSE DREAMS; PROPER SANITIZATION FOR THE POOLS OF LETHE; MONEY; HANDLING THE OFFERINGS TO CHARON. Like anyone else given a training packet, she didn't actually read anything.

"Okay," Hermes murmured to himself. He gathered up his documents and hopped off his stool of tanzanite to coast over to some prehistoric-looking contraption. She watched as Hermes picked up a curly-tailed headpiece the size of a box of cereal hanging off the wall like some kind of desecrated animal head. He dialed three numbers and said into the speaker, "Hey… Yeah…Yeah…Cool." He hung up the phone and addressed Tranquila, "Alright, so we are done here. If you have any questions, do not hesitate to ask someone else."

"Where are you going?" Tranquila asked, as he tried to edge out of the break room.

"I'm gonna give these to Hades, then I'm getting the hell out of Hell."

"Should I come?"

"Mmm….No."

"Okay, then what should I do?"

"Well, Hades is having a meeting, so…" he left before finishing the sentence.

"Wait!" Tranquila called, chasing him out of the break room. "What about my training?"

Hermes, who was clearly in a hurry, stopped mid-step and let out a heavy, irritated sigh. Looking over his shoulder, he replied, "I *was* going to just zap over to the boss but I guess I can take you too."

Tranquila pinched her nose at the snippiness in his tone. "Jesus, don't do *me* any favors."

"Actually I am," Hermes said, snarky. "Mortals can't travel at light speed. If you did, your bodies would melt faster than steel beams in a jet-fuel fight."

"Jet fuel can't melt steel beams."

Pause. "What did I say about talking like an asshole?" Hermes demanded.

Tranquila relented, knowing that an argument with a fool made two. Besides, how could she fight a guy with no eyelids? He would literally see anything she had coming. Off they went.

*

Hermes' rudeness turned out, in Tranquila's mind, to be justifiable. In order to save Tranquila's subpar physiology, they had to catch a ride with Charon on his boat, which he only agreed to if they rode with a dozen of the fresh souls. This should not have been a big ordeal. Normally, the newly dead are too busy lamenting, or being horrified by the sights and sounds of the Underworld to be annoying. Unfortunately, they had to catch a ride with Charon while he was ferrying the latest white terrorist to come out of America and six of his pissed-off looking victims.

The spindly little white bastard didn't last long in Charon's boat and neither did Tranquila and Hermes who, thanks to karmic justice, were knocked into the Acheron River—twice—forcing Hermes to calmly float to shore while Tranquila doggy-paddled ashore in order to not get accidentally shredded by vengeful spirits or get their shit rocked by Charon's oar. "GODS FUCKING DAMN IT ALL! THIS IS THE FORTIETH TIME THIS YEAR THIS HAS HAPPENED!"

Doggy-paddling through forty yards of thick ooze, archaic muck and discarded Gorgon skin, left Tranquila enervated and sobbing like an infant by the time they'd managed to land onshore.

"I…think…I…swallowed…bird shit," she wailed through a hyperventilating wheeze the second she could swallow air. She let her head flop dramatically into the black clay of the shore, as she loudly grieved the tragedy that had just betook her.

Hermes, despite being daubed in gunk thanks to her limitations, looked at the maiden with pity. "There, there, maiden," he said, rubbing her backside—observing mortals for a stretch of time told him that comforting humans meant rubbing their backs and patronizing their feelings. "It's only harpy feces. Consuming it will not affect your overall health."

His compassion warranted Tranquila to splatter a regurgitated mixture of last night's meatloaf, this morning's Cinnamon Toast Crunch and harpy shit onto the waterlogged soil.

"Jesus Christ," Hermes murmured, watching her spit away a strand of recoil.

"Jesus Christ," she grunted, throat aflame.

"You puke *a lot*." Hermes thought for a second. "Is that normal for mortals?"

"Not really." Spit. Struggling with an agonizing stomach cramp that hurt even more when she tried to sit up, Tranquila bent her knees up so she could rest her pounding head. "Maybe this is a sign."

"To what? Quit?"

"Maybe," Tranquila said, easing her neck straight, blinking away the stars.

Hermes didn't put up the argument in Hades' defense she would've expected, or patronize her feelings the way mortals taught him. Instead he got up, looked down on her with his unsettling yellow eyes and opened up his palm.

Anyone else would have vilified the creep and rebuked the gesture but Tranquila was an expert in ignoring reason. She took his black hand and he helped the wobbly human homo erectus. If it weren't for his levitation, they would have been the same height.

In a quiet tone meant for encouraging words, he offered this to Tranquila: "Don't talk like an asshole." Pointing to a massive heap of solidified lava behind them, hardened by age and blacker than space, he informed, "That's where the Underworld holds all their meetings. If I were you, I'd go in there and use this as an excuse to sit on your ass for the rest of your shift." He handed her the pile of unrecognizable documents that were now dripping in nightmarish slop. "Give these to the boss. At least he won't accuse me of not doing my job right."

With that, Hermes turned into a ball of fire and propelled himself upward into the dank darkness of the Underworld and out of sight.

CAN'T SPELL CRISIS WITHOUT ISIS

Tranquila stood, gulping down giant breaths. She took a second to spit out the last of the harpy-shit. She then made loud, squishy, wet footfalls towards the basaltic conclave, trying not to think about how long it was going to take to clean her hair, or how this was the second pair of clothes ruined because of work.

She plodded into the building that looked like a giant scoop of black potato salad that some forgotten picnic God plopped one day. She went through an enormous crevice that substituted as an entrance. Once inside, she understood the lack of security: it was gloomier than all the other monuments she'd seen in Hades. The hallways looked like someone merely spooned out a pathway from a mass of fresh tar, with barely enough space for two bodies to walk side by side. She remained as close to the middle of the pathway as possible. As she walked, her waterlogged clothes and shoes grew warm...which is when she noticed heat emanating from the walls. Cusps of steam danced upward from her clothes, like when drops of water hit against a hot iron as the warmth met the damp. It was like she was walking into a dryer. And when she glanced up to the side, she noticed steam coming from the minerals and bubble like air pockets trapped on a painted wall.

At first, it alarmed her and tricked her mind into believing she could hear the dying roar of a primordial creature. At the same time, she found she could no longer hear her own footsteps. Her body ceased shivering beneath the cold, soaked clothes. Was this a coincidence, or was the Underworld that accommodating to the needs of its employees? Either way, it freaked Tranquila out.

C'mon Tran, she told herself, *it's a full-time job. It's a full-time job. It's not minimum wage. Yeah it's in a hellish, black, depressing void of the Underworld*, she glanced down at herself, catching sight of the beeping anklet that effectively cut her career options in half and thought, *but it's still better than working in fast food*.

Mentally, she kept that pith playing on loop. Still, it didn't tame the irrevocable dread that weighed in her gut, sitting thick and harmful like puke she was betting on seeing soon. She hadn't taken three steps when she stopped and hung her head. *What am I doing here?* She couldn't tell if this was another regrettable act or not. She didn't have 'good judgment' or 'women's intuition' or 'common sense'. She was constantly betrayed by gut instinct—the same one that told her to get cocky in front of cops; the same one that said to trust that salty, apathetic grandmother of hers; and the same one who'd said getting a free tattoo from a friend of her brother's girlfriend in his kitchen was a sweet deal. She was a criminal in Hades with an amateur tattoo artist's clumsy rendition of an eyeball eating an ice cream permanently fashioned on her left butt cheek. These decisions left her with zero self-confidence.

Tranquila sighed. She thought of just turning around, tossing her contract into the River Styx, bribing Charon with her lunch to take her back to the surface world and spending the next fifty to sixty years working in fast food, praying for a minimum wage increase and affordable health care. But then she looked up and saw the daunting, endless hallway before her had abruptly changed.

In front of her was now a perpendicular hallway. Ten steps further bore a glass wall revealing a conference room. She immediately recognized Hades inside, sitting upfront. He desperately tried to stay awake for the presentation. Behind him were several rows of minions, either drooling on their desks or goofing around with each other. Meetings, no matter in what dimension, no matter what they are about, no matter if they're led by Minos from Judgment or Lynne from Accounting, are nine out of ten times going to bore the living snot out of you.

Tranquila peered at the abstracts—the personifications of ruin and nullity. Subconsciously, she knew which were which without needing introduction. In the corner, drooling peacefully onto his desk was Death. Beside him, wide awake trying to flick paper footballs into his cousin's gaping mouth, was Sleep. Behind them sat an entity with nasty carbuncles scattered across its grapefruit-looking face, who was no doubt Disease. Beside Disease were Agony and Fear, the Underworld's power couple. They always sat next to each other, surreptitiously making inside joke after inside joke during every meeting. To the left, sat the incarnate of discord, Eris, doodling away after an honest effort to take notes hadn't worked out. And behind Eris was the rival of Youth, Old Age, trying to teach herself how to fishtail braid, having given up entirely on paying attention.

Did these creatures frighten her? Of course they did. They'd be bad at their jobs if they didn't give the mortal heart palpitations. But Tranquila had survived her share of heart attacks and knew how to punch them away and calm herself enough to recognize these were not dark, evil forces hell-bent on the inner turmoil of man; they were her coworkers now. And, much like prison, you can't win over your coworkers by being scared chicken-shit of everyone.

With that, Tranquila used a knuckle to gently rap on the glass door.

"Um, sorry I'm interrupting," she began, stepping inside.

"Oh, good," Hades cried, in that overzealous nice-guy voice managers use to make new employees feel welcome. Waving a theatrical arm, he announced to the rest, "Entities! Abstracts! Minor gods! This is Tranquila, the newest edition to the lower kingdom staff."

This warranted a couple of hellos and grunts from everyone, sans Death, who slept skillfully like a college senior.

Tranquila gave a tucked-in-lip smile before handing the pile of destroyed documents to Hades. She took the only available seat in the back, beside Old Age.

"Rhadamanthus," Hades said to the man responsible for making this meeting boring, "If you could recap for Tranquila."

The ghostly figure searched for Tranquila in the back. In a bland, unmoving voice he remarked, "You are mortal. No doubt you are aware of what is happening to the Yazidis women in the al-Qahtaniya area of Iraq."

Tranquila, like many Americans, wasn't perspicacious on the dynamics of the ethno-religions in the Middle East. Nor could she keep up with the details of which city was under attack, what village was in protest, which terrorist group had done what. To her, the constant controversies over seas were merely fodder the news media frequently—but dispassionately—reported on. All she had was a vague notion that the Middle East was in perpetual trouble.

"Uh—yeah…yeah, that—that shit's awful."

Rhadamanthus, who had a good sense of judgment, could tell she had no clue to what he referred. Nonetheless, a boring presentation is more boring to the presenter than to anyone else. Thus her ignorance didn't matter. He just didn't want to backtrack any further.

"Good. Well a bunch of ISIS members were killed recently. We're trying to exact a proper punishment befitting of the evil they have done," he explained, clicking a small remote he held to change the screen. "Now, a favorite option would be to just shoot these guys in the face, wait for their faces to regrow and continue in this manner for the next thousands of years."

The meeting erupted in a concession of boos.

"We've been shooting rapists in the face for years," avowed Eris. "That penalty's no fun anymore."

Tranquila's interest peaked at the mention of rapists. While the other entities complained, she whispered to Old Age, "Who are we trying to punish?"

"Well, you know what's been happening in al-Qahtaniya, right?" Old Age asked casually.

"Uh…"

Old Age, after a moment of struggling to finagle her fingers into creating a fishtail braid, gave up on her long gray hair to explain, "ISIS members are kidnapping this group of Yazidist believers and raping them with the idea that they'll be converted into Islam. And a couple days ago, a bunch of them were killed, and we're trying to figure out what to do with them."

"Wait. They raped people *to make them Muslim?*" Tranquila whispered, appalled.

"Yep. The worst part is these Yazidis are like Lutheran to Catholics. They're basically a part of the same faith. They are getting beaten, raped and sold into slavery because these extremist fucks don't think they're Muslim enough."

Disgust wasn't the proper adjective anymore. Implicit outrage and sadness took the mortal by force. In her naivety, she berated herself for being so ignorant of the world around her. Diluting her thoughts, she overheard the abstracts shout, "Why don't we just drown them in wasps and beat them with two-by-fours with nails sticking out?" Agony suggested.

"No, we've been using that on Oliver Cromwell for years. What about turning them inside out and making them take a bath in lemon juice and salt for eternity?" Fear interjected.

Soon the room was loud with the babel of bad ideas. Finally, Hades stood up and spoke over the voices, "Guys, Guys, GUYS! All of these ideas suck! We don't need mindless torture or generalized brutality. We need a penalty that surpasses the atrocities that they have put their own women and children through. We don't need cruel and unusual punishments—we need cruel and specific punishments, the likes of which would induce their ghosts to plague the nightmares of man for generations to come. Now, entities, minor gods and personifications—*think*! What do sexist, male, religious fanatics hate more than anything in the world?"

No one spoke for a moment. Timidly, Sleep raised his hand and said, "Women?"

Hades groaned, embroiled by the lack of thinking. "We're not about to give a bunch of barbaric rapists a woman to degrade."

Sleep sheepishly lowered his hand. The others around him, save Death, sniggered. But Tranquila was inspired by Sleep's bad idea. Bravely, she raised her hand, like a student readying themselves for an intellectual smack down.

"Tranquila?" Hades called, taken aback by the sight of her hand.

*

Humans always refer to *that special place in Hell*. They would be shocked to know that when they die there is, in fact, a special place in Hades. But it isn't reserved for the people they would imagine. It's not for those who didn't believe in the 'true God'. It is not for those who stood on either side of the abortion argument. It's not even for those who didn't vote Democrat. It is for the sinners of infamy. It is a capacious place borne on the edge of existence and resigned solely for the defects of the Iron Race; for people who choose to live by hatred, because hatred is an alternative lifestyle no god can forgive. The special place is for those who choose to bedevil, beat, murder and violate others. It is a bastille in which all of life's bastards are clumped together like cockroaches beneath a table waiting in pestilence for the lights to flip off.

This special place is called Tartarus. Normally, even Hades would avoid it, but today he and the rest of the Underworld staff made an exception.

Tartarus perpetuated a darkness that black holes couldn't fathom. Imagine walking in the middle of the night with no aid from streetlights or the moon and with a blindfold on even though you are already blind. Thus, the god of death had to carry with him a torch into Tartarus, ignited by the luminosity of a red giant star. The light allowed Tranquila visibility up to three feet ahead—a favor to her, since none of the other workers were in danger of losing functioning eyes. Chaos didn't even have eyes. He was merely a floating cloud of atoms and club lights. Prolonged exposure to such an environment would devolve her sight, leaving her as blind and eyeless as a cavefish.

Eventually, the immutable ebony conceded beneath the awesome light of Hades' torch. Soon they found the fettered ISIS members strapped to slabs of jagged crags, perched intentionally at knee level so that when their torturers approached, the terrorists could cower at their gigantic presence.

To Hades and the minor gods, whenever the despicable came to Tartarus it was better than Christmas. Especially when degenerates were officially ripped of their righteousness, when their crimes could no longer be sanctified by a god that was never real for starters, when they were dead, captured, half-blind and prepped for eternal torture—it was better than Christmas. It was better than love. It was better than fast food. It was cosmic retribution.

A kind of satisfaction that made Hades hand the torch to Tranquila, who nearly dropped the beacon for it weighed so much, as he stepped towards the harbingers of rape and suffering. The rest of the Underworld staff made their way over to these shameful excuses for Islamists. The gods marveled at their snotty, punk faces. Hades breathed in their fear like a divine fragrance.

"How cute…" cooed Old Age.

"Precious!" said Fear and Agony, their heads bent together as they stared lovingly at a grown man slobbering.

"Oh my Gaia, how a-dor-a-ble!" Hades nearly cried as one of the men started praying fervently to his useless prophet. Looking over his shoulder into a billowing darkness, he instructed, "Tranquila, come look. This guy's actually praying!"

"O Allah be gracious unto Muhammad…"

"Eh…I'll pass," Tranquila replied, busy keeping her eyes from searching for what she could hear was chewing.

"Surely you are the praiseworthy one…"

"Dude, really?" Hades asked, more incredulous than offended. "You're still holding onto that dream?"

"It's not a dream!" the Arabic man cried out. "Allah is real! He's real, he's got super powers a billion times better than what you possess and he's going to lay waste to all of you for having treated his people like this!"

Tranquila held her breath after that outburst. Her fears shifted from the skin-eating snake monster that she was nine hundred percent sure just slithered over her foot, to Hades. Though she never saw him mad before, she could see the glorious reckoning ignite in his eyes.

For an unsettling second, Hades merely chuckled, giggled even. With an unaffected smile, he leaned into the man's face and said with captivating sweetness, "Oh Youman."

Then he chuckled again. This time, in the red iridescent glow of Tranquila's torch, she saw his face become savage. In a low rumble he bequeathed, "If Allah met you, he'd take one look at you and switch religions."

No one spoke after that. Not even the many vacuous chambers of Tartarus dared to echo the message. "Aww," Hades' voice gaped, erratically affectionate. "You guys can't see it but Mr. Yassif definitely crapped himself. How delightful."

Hades turned away from the wretched men. Even in near-total darkness, she could sense his affections had turned. It was like the Earth turning from the sun. In a stern voice he ordered, "Read them their sentences."

She obeyed. Walking alongside the bonded men, carrying the torch in one hand and a clipboard in another, she beseeched: "Each of you have done such fucked-up crimes, nobody in the Underworld Staff could think of a punishment fitting to have done unto you. This is because none of us can truly grasp the horror that your actions have inflicted. So..."

Disease lifted the slabs of each of the men so they would be laying upward. Tranquila, using every ounce of upper body stretch she had, wielded the light of the starfire to the left. They saw Death once again. Only this time, he wasn't leading them away, he was leading an Exodus.

Dozens of bodies followed the sleep-deprived Reaper and as the masses marched closer to the madmen. Tranquila finally finished her sentence, "We thought why not let the women decide."

Standing before the Islamic Extremists were not the seventy-two virgins they were promised—but, the thirty-seven women that they had, collectively, violated. If it didn't smell strongly of feces before, it surely did now.

"This is Samia, Suhalia, Sarah, Ania, Ezraa, Baligah, Howraa, Jihan, Hiba, Athraa, Anfal, Manala, Suroar, Iqbal, Sama, Methaq, Perla, Fatima, Rooba, Amal, Maysa, Nasima, Nisma, Muna, Shadi, Delvin, Hana, Sevian, Narin, Yasmin, Samara, Maryanne, Kordija, Norah, Fatima, and Aleisa." Hades introduced each woman without effort. "And between the three of you, you have managed to systematically extinguish any source of happiness and humanity from their short lives. You took these women and you tore them from their families, their homes and their lives. But that doesn't matter. Because they are dead. And you are dead. And there's nothing, not even I, can change about that.

"And just because I can't reverse Death, doesn't mean the Underworld's not a place of pain."

Like some routine in a vindictive marching band, Hades slid backwards from the front. All the women who stood behind him came forward. Seventy-two eyes held a death ray focus on the strapped men. And the men knew that, helpless, essentially fucked. For the first time since their separate kidnappings and subsequent bondage into slavery, these women were going to be pretty damn close to getting some justice.

Since this was Tranquila's idea, she spoke up again and instructed the women, "Okay! Ladies who were victimized by Dickturd number one, have you thought of what you want for his comeuppance?"

The women fashioned themselves into a tight huddle. Only two seconds later, they broke apart and the woman named Perla spoke on their behalf, "We have."

Agony told each of them their statements would be more effective if they took dramatic pauses. In the spirit of drama,

Perla took six dramatic pauses. "And we have decided..." Two more dramatic pauses later. "To forgive."

Tartarus erupted with the sounds of both the Underworld Staff and the rest of the Yazidis women's boos.

"Screw that Buddhist crap!" Iqbal cried. "I say we give them vaginas and force them to give birth to a billion babies! If he tries to chicken out and not push, have the baby kick the crotch from the inside!"

"You can't have a penis and give birth at the same time!" argued Dickturd number one.

"You can here!" Hades insisted. With a snap of his fingers the man formerly known as Dickturd number one's stomach swelled to the size of a watermelon, while his face contorted with an all-consuming pain. And when his contractions caused him to wail and his insides burst forth like butcher's confetti, the Yazidis cheered out Iqbal's name.

After their cheering died down, Tranquila said to the second set, "Victims of Dickturd number two, what say you?"

The second group quickly whispered before they broke apart. Their speaker, Samia, said, "Mr. God sir, we are simple women. We come from small villages. In past lives, we were farmers' wives and mothers. We will be happy cutting off the man's head and carrying it around with us for the rest of forever."

"Did you guys want to take turns cutting off his head before you carry it around with you?"

She looked to Hades as if he just asked her to dance. "That would be lovely. Yes, thank you."

Hades gave her a warm smile before snapping his fingers and a giant sword appeared out of thin air. He handed it to Samia and her group, saying, "Remember: No matter how many times you cut his throat, he'll still feel everything. So have fun!"

"Thank you, Mr. God!" sang Samia and her group.

"Anytime ladies…" replied Hades in the same sing-song voice, his eyes and cruel smile aimed solely on the doomed, "Anytime…"

Hades once again fell backwards, this time to stand with his staff. They reveled in the cosmic-justice glory. At some point, just as the blood splatter began, he leaned over to Tranquila and said, "Nice suggestion, Tranquila."

"Um, thanks?" she replied and then casually added, "Who said that?"

Hades thought this was a joke that he didn't understand. He almost laughed at it, too. He looked over—a panic snapped him out of his quiet content. Tranquila's eyes, once dark brown, were now a pale, haunting azure.

Hades placed his hand on Tranquila's shoulder. Transforming them into smoke, he swept them out of Tartarus, swiftly guided by the wind of the rapists' tortured screams.

When they rematerialized, Tranquila was stunned to see Hades didn't travel back to the conference room. She wasn't even sure if they were still in the Underworld. They stood in a place that was a thousand times classier than anywhere she visited in Hades.

Towers of black rock carved exquisitely into pillars stood, dominating every corner. The contents of the room shone. The ceiling, which seemed to take up three stadium fields in length, textured with innumerable amounts of uncut emeralds, glittered overhead like a stationary aurora borealis. Tranquila was hypnotized by the barrage of green, nearly giving herself vertigo by keeping her head so straight.

She could feel a stinging in her eyes as she uttered a profound, "Holy…fuck."

Then Hades' voice snapped her out of the trance, "Tranquila."

She dropped her head, finding her boss standing in front of her, beside an all-black desk.

"Tranquila, I must apologize to you," he began, sounding full of regret. "I'm afraid I have indentured you in a position of—"

"Oh my gods! Is that your filling cabinet, made out of crystals?" Tranquila blurted out.

"Uh, yes…it…" he began abashed, as Tranquila sprinted over to caress the desk.

Up close, it was even more majestic. The polished surface was unspoiled by a jewelry maker's hand, the contrasting overtones exciting the eye so that it was hard to focus on any one area of unrefined beauty. Unable to control herself, Tranquila ran a flat hand over the rectangular base and shuddered in ecstasy.

"Ahhh, I've never seen something so classy in my entire life," she said, nearly drooling. "What is this made out of?"

"Obsidian."

"Obsidian," she whispered. "Wow. I've never even heard of it. Is that like rich people's diamonds?"

Hades' lips twitched into a smile. *Oh, right. America is poor now*, he thought. Although finding Tranquila's pecuniary innocence adorable, he was reminded of the purpose of their visit to his office. Shaking himself from his thoughts, he said, "Tranquila, stop petting my filing cabinet. I have to talk to you."

She complied instantly. "Sorry, boss."

He chuckled. "It's alright. If anyone should apologize, it should be me. I'm afraid I was the one who was too ambitious. I've made this deal with you and I didn't even consider the consequences. I forget that mortals are fallible. I have put you in a situation that, one, could have pulverized your eyeballs and, two, could have jeopardized your well-being."

He ceased from his speech to gauge Tranquila's reaction.

"So…" she sounded uncertain, "I could have lost my eyes back there?"

"Well, staying that long in excessive darkness, your body could have gone into hyper-evolution to adapt to the harsh environment."

"Oh."

Hades sighed, "See, this is what I meant. Which is why I am offering a rare, *a very rare*, opportunity to void the contract you've signed. If you wish to step down and remove yourself permanently from the Underworld, then let no one say that I am a cruel god."

His proposal made her eyebrow burrow in what he thought was deliberation.

"Are you kidding me? I don't want to give up this job," Tranquila said at once.

"Tranquila, do not let your hubris—"

"This isn't about pride. I've quit many jobs in my life: fast-food worker, gas-station attendant, newspaper carrier, counterfeit-purse salesmen. I lasted nine hours in a call center before I said 'fuck this' to that. If I didn't like a job, I didn't wait around just to get more miserable," Tranquila said adamantly. "You're worried about me being in danger? Boss, since I've met you I've had four heart attacks, seven near-death experiences, two close calls with insanity; I've thrown up on myself more times than I can count. As of today, I've wrecked four shirts being down here. And you think I wanna quit? I want this job more than ever now."

It took a lot to surprise a deity who was present when Pangea broke up, but Tranquila had just stunned the hell out of Hades. To confirm what she was saying was genuine, Hades brandished before her a clean copy of her work contract. "Are you certain? Are you certain that you want to work down here?

Because it's not all fucking up ISIS and rapists, Tranquila. Some days are nothing but paperwork and soul counting."

She shook her head. "I want this job."

*

At 4:35 in the morning, Mama Sobriquet stood in the downstairs shower, depleting gallons of hot water. She let the steaming water—suitable for cooking lobsters—pour all over her body. Yet, she was still cold. She reached to turn the dial a quarter inch when a startling noise made her hand slip. She unleashed searing torrents of water the same temperature as lava onto her bare skin.

She screamed in pain, then terminated the shower. With the running water off her, she could hear that it was only the sound of dogs barking that frightened her.

"God fucking dammit," she said as she stepped out from the steam, thinking some idiot canine barked at the newspaper carrier again.

Getting dressed, she was agitated that the barking failed to stop. The annoyance continued while she brushed her teeth and dried her hair. By the time she'd stepped out of the bathroom, it had progressed into wolf-like howling. Suddenly, it occurred to her the creature might be hurt. She was stirred by compassion to seek out the helpless thing. She followed the dog's cries in the direction of the kitchen. As she reached the screen door that led to the backyard, the dog's urgent alerts ceased at once.

Mama Sobriquet thought the caprice strange, however, her emotions flew in a different direction at the sound of the front door slamming.

"Darla! Move your damn car," Grandma Sobriquet's bumptious voice demanded on entry. "I'm not going to get a fucking parking ticket just because you park like a dildo."

All at once, Mama Sobriquet's concern for the distressed dog was replaced with rancor and fantasies of delivering a long-awaited eulogy at her mother's funeral. She turned away from the screen door.

Good thing, though. To see her backyard tear asunder into a perfect fault line with her youngest child popping out of the ground like a gravity-and-probation-defying witch, would have pushed her right into catatonia.

DOGS DON'T EAT YOGURT

Her boss wasn't bullshitting when he said most days in the Underworld weren't spent torturing the defects of man. With the exception of ISIS and a few instances of observing Disease give the cosmic what-for to female educators who preyed on male students, Tranquila's shifts comprised very little of the justice and wrath that was sorely lacking up on Earth.

It became very disheartening to go from brainstorming creative ways to torture terrorists with minor deities, to going back to being the hated coworker of Cerberus. Tranquila had no idea dogs could even produce hatred, until she met the triple-headed queen of bitches. She assumed that level of emotional assholery was reserved for cats, wasps and mall geese. Then she'd met the Hell Hound and was proven wrong.

For weeks, she would sit on the edge of the River Acheron, sometimes with her feet submerged in the filthy water, in order to appease Cerberus' temperament. If she dared to move an inch closer, one of Cerberus' untrusting heads would catch her instantly and unleash a deliberate arsenal against her inferior hearing. Cerberus barked with the same intensity as standing directly in front of the sound speakers of a thousand heavy metal concerts. So, Tranquila kept her distance.

All that time, her feet would freeze. Her ass became uncomfortably damp from the wet sand she was forced to sit on. The only exercise she was allotted was when she would rise to greet the shipment of newly dead. Even her enthusiasm for this dissipated, as the questions became routine and their reactions repeated the four D's: Denial, Despair, Disbelief and Dickheadedry. It became so mundane she could identify a person's emotional state of mind before they landed; a banality that was starting to affect her Meet n' Greet Speech.

There used to be patience, understanding and empathy reserved for the new arrivals. In the beginning she even used to introduce herself. Eventually, anonymity became preferable when all the 'weepys' started to use her friendliness as a sign to unload their failures and woes onto her, like whiny dump trucks. Now she had all the comradery of an automatic telemarketer: "Hey, what's up? Welcome to Hades. Yes, you heard it right, folks: Hades. Not Hell with two l's or Hel with one, not Samsara, not Chinvat Bridge, not Bardo, not whatever it is Scientologists believe in. Just plain ol' Hades." At this point, she'd interrupt the stiff, who would unbar their mouth to ask the obvious, "Yes, that means none of the other gods are real. No, this does not mean it's a bad thing. Unlike all the other religions, Greeks don't believe you gotta pay for dying. So, spend your afterlife thinking over your life. Figure out why you were the way you were. Maybe you'll figure out some useful shit.

"Once you walk past that boner goblin-looking dog—" She'd point to Cerberus who up until then lay indifferently on her side. Recognizing she was being insulted, she would unleash a series of growls and glares directed at the back of Tranquila's head, which the paranoid dead always assumed was really for them. "—your soul is bound to Hades. So, get going, people. Unless you wanna sit here with me for the rest of forever."

Thus concluded Tranquila's speech. Sometimes she'd add in a sarcastic little "Enjoy" or "Peace" but after so many boatloads of dead people, she lost her verve.

That day in particular, the normally speedy time spent in
Hades dragged and dragged. Hardly anybody was dying on the
surface world. Sure, the troubles that beset the Middle East kept
business in Hades steady and, sure, the police in America were
doing their part in keeping the mortality rates of young black
men up, but with autumn making people sensible again and
midterm suicides not for another couple of months, traffic in the
Underworld slowed. Even the steadfast staff of old felt the
interminableness of the shifts.

Tranquila and Charon hung together more during these
slower than slow days. Charon, with so few to ferry, would often
dock at Tranquila's riverbank, letting her sit in his boat in order
to avoid sitting in the mucky waters and evade displeasing
Cerberus.

"Gaia, this sucks," Charon said with a lit cigarette
pinched in-between his intermediate phalanges, smoke dangling
out from underneath his jaw, through the gapes in his skull.

"Seriously," Tranquila agreed, laying her arm off the
side of the boat, resting it on the cushy fat from her bicep. "How
can no one be dead yet? It's been six hours, I think." She still
had no clue how to configure time in Hades with time measured
on Earth. It probably involved some kind of metric conversion
that she, as an American, was patriotically obligated to never
learn.

The skeleton, without lungs, somehow took another drag
from his cigarette. "I blame modern science. It's keeping
everybody alive much longer than necessary." Exhaling, he
added, "I miss the good ol' days when you'd drop dead at thirty
from a papercut. Business was so much better back then."

"Really? You'd think there'd be more business with the
world population being so big," she remarked without much
thought.

"You'd think, but the Iron Race surprised the fuck out of everyone," Charon replied. "Everyone talks shit about your age of humans, but those Golden jerks would never have lasted a day with all the innumerable evils and pains that Zeus and Hera have sent your way."

Tranquila was interested enough to lift her head from her numb arm and ask, "Who were the 'Golden jerks'?"

Tranquila's ignorance, once alarming, was now an accepted truth that Charon no longer questioned. Taking another scientifically impossible puff of smoke, he began: "Back in a time when Cronus ruled, there was this early edition of man called the Golden Age. They were spoiled as fuck. They lived without ever having to work and were regarded as equals by the Titans, who created them. They mingled freely with the Titans. They did whatever they wanted, and their bodies were forever beautiful. They never aged.

"Then came the Silver Race of Man. They, too, were privileged turds. The Silver Race lived like children…literally. They never grew old and they never had to work; they never moved out of their mother's homes and they happily mooched off of them. But the Silver Age didn't know how good they had it. They grew arrogant and stopped worshipping. As if all the good fortune that befell them was their entitlement. This was under Zeus's reign. He put up with that shit for all of two seconds—the Earth experienced winter for the first time and all those Silver punks died out.

"Soon, came the Bronze Age and they were cool. I mean, they all had the personality of a rock, but they were tough and they knew how to work for their food. They would have done fine if Hera hadn't found out that Zeus was sneaking around. In a fit of rage, she annihilated the entire population.

"Then came everyone's favorite: the Heroic Age, and everyone *loves* to go on and on about how they're the greatest generation, just because they fought in a big-ass war that the gods started, which could have been prevented in the first place. But…whatever. They're all dead now too.

"And finally, the Iron Race. Your people—the people who everyone swore would go extinct during the first Ice Age. You, who are now so advanced they've put almost every Olympian out of work; you, who survived the plagues and the AIDS; you, who taught the blind how to read; you, who made booze cruises the size of small cities; you—the spare wheel of the universe that everyone assumed was a flat—have nearly made the deities obsolete."

"Obsolete?" That word was reserved for hard drives and penmanship programs. What business did he have to use it for the Gods? "How can gods be obsolete? Hades is the god of death, for crying out loud."

"Oh, Hades' job is forever secured. But name one other absolute, other than death?" Charon challenged, eyeing her mischievously with his empty sockets. She had a hard time answering that. He went on: "Besides taxes, you humans have found a way around almost every other aspect of life. You create your own fire. You make your own food. Hell, I was talking to this one guy the other day who said in his former life he was part of the team who were in the process of printing out organs. Your race, while debased and primitive compared to your predecessors, has really shown the others 'we do not have to worship you; we can worship the figments of our own imagination and still survive.'"

Tranquila was speechless after his mini oration. For a while, there were only the sounds of Charon's inhales and the occasional kicking coming from a dreaming Cerberus who lay against the entrance of Hades. She watched, lost in thought, as Cerberus' body heaved up and down slowly. Charon's words made her think of the time she used to gloat, calling herself a 'second-generation atheist' to her schoolmates. They regaled her with horror stories of the many forced religion classes, the wasted Sundays, the strict rules created in correspondence with their parents' beliefs. Now, she understood what those kids must have felt when she embarrassed their parents' faith. Because now she was embarrassed. Here, she assumed Zeus and his fellow gods and goddesses were the invisible ways of the world. But now, now she understood that they were merely clock makers, standing by as everything became digital.

Tranquila was so conflicted, she didn't know what else to do but eat her feelings. She pulled out a Tupperware container that held a simple lunch of a ham sandwich, a chocolate brownie and a can of Chobani's, with fruit at the bottom of a pomegranate yogurt. Popping open the lid, she ate the ham sandwich first. The barely audible *pop* was enough to stir the Hell Hound instantly from its sleep. One eye from each head flung open as three pairs of nostrils began to sniff about with insatiable interest.

Tranquila didn't realize Cerberus awoke, until she felt blasting hot air, like three hairdryers on max power on the top of her head. Steeled by fear, Tranquila somehow stretched her neck nearly ninety degrees. Standing directly over her, panting twenty-mile-per-hour gales of stinky dog breath, the Hell Hound peered down at her, begging.

In all the weeks Tranquila worked with the dog, this was the closest she had come to her, by at least seventy yards. But Tranquila was in a petty mood.

"Oh, now you wanna be my friend?" she sneered without fear. She crammed half of the sandwich into her mouth, gagging herself in the process, and chewed the contents with great spite. With food flying out of her mouth, she taunted, "Too bad, bitch."

But Cerberus didn't show signs of being perturbed, instead she remained hovering over the mortal, eyes captivated on the little square of plastic that sat on her lap.

Tranquila looked down, then back up. "You want my brownie?" The dog's many heads remained fixed on her lap. "Dogs can't have chocolate. You can't have the brownie."

This didn't seem to get through to the beast. Tranquila was bewildered by Cerberus' behavior until Charon spoke up, "The yogurt."

"What?"

"She wants the yogurt."

Tranquila was about to argue that dogs don't eat yogurt when she felt the fierce wind from Cerberus' mighty tail wagging violently. Looking back up, she could see the want in the dog's many eyes and Tranquila's pettiness buckled underneath her weakness for pitbulls.

Nauseous from vertigo, she maneuvered her body so she could face the creature. Cerberus followed her lead, giving her some distance, folding its mighty hind legs and shaking the ground as it came down to sit.

Tranquila tossed the can of yogurt and watched as the three heads barked and fought for the rights, until finally the lower left head won. The other two accepted defeat. With that, the Hell Hound went back to its spot in front of the entrance, flopping onto its back and returning to its hebetude.

"Wow, Cerberus, you fake," Tranquila taunted good-naturedly. Cerberus didn't seem to care what she thought. To Charon, she joked, "What, is she on a diet or something?"

Cerberus made a low growl, signaling that Tranquila better quit talking shit. "Sorry. Damn, that was just a joke."

"She didn't want the yogurt she just wanted the pomegranate inside the yogurt."

"Since when do dogs like fruit?"

"They don't. But Cerberus isn't like the dogs on Earth. Though she lives off the flesh of the dead, she craves the dead's food." Exasperated by her lack of knowledge, he had to ask, "Didn't Jeanette tell you Cerberus isn't like the dogs back home?"

How does everyone know Jeanette, and Jeanette knows everything, but I don't know anything about Jeanette? she thought, stuck on her resentment for the old woman.

Soon, the shift ended and Charon was kind enough to escort Tranquila back to the little entrance reserved for her and her alone. When she returned to Earth, she met with the familiar barks of the neighborhood dogs alerting their masters that there was an unnaturalness nearby. Suddenly, hearing the Earth dogs yelp in desperation to protect the ones they love, two wires in Tranquila's brain connected. She found a new sympathy for the hellish beast of Hades that she hadn't before.

IT'S HARD BEING ASSOCIATED (OR IN CONTACT) WITH JEANETTE

It took a rigorous amount of mental strategy on Tranquila's part to convince Grandma Sobriquet to leave the house during the season finale of cable television's latest drama about bankers, *Emotional Investments*, "What?! I'm not leaving! Rebecca Blackwelt is two dramatic pauses away from announcing at the hedge fund meeting that she's pregnant with her stepson's ex-boyfriend's baby!"

"...Grandma, do you even hear yourself anymore?"

"...Oh my Gaia, I'm getting emotionally invested in trash...Give me that list!"

But it paid off. Because Grandma Sobriquet took the list and went to the store. The next morning, she was able to enter Hades with a bag full of pomegranates.

When she reached the banks of Acheron, Cerberus was alert: standing, vocalizing her contempt for the mortal. Tranquila remained ankle-deep in the waters, her treats tucked away in a backpack. She addressed the dog, "I know you are smart enough to understand me." The beast continued to snarl at her presence. "I also know that you think I'm here to replace your master."

Those words caused the snakes in the dog's mane to hiss and rise, ready to strike poison into her feeble body. "I'm not here to take you away, Cerberus," she promised. "I'm not here to take you from your master. Your master would never abandon you. Your master loves you." She spoke with sincerity. She remembered the brief moment of love she witnessed between Hades and his beloved pet. Her words were fueled by the memories of all the dogs she had once loved on Earth, how no dog owner who had a dog as long as Hades would ever do anything to hurt them. But whether the dog sensed her honesty, Tranquila couldn't tell. Cerberus' tail didn't lower with ease, nor did the arc of her back slacken in anyway.

Tranquila couldn't back down, though. She couldn't lose the alpha's respect. Thus with one hand upraised to her shoulder, she slowly went into the bag that hung against her hip and pulled out a fruit-bearing deciduous shrub. All of Cerberus' eyes darted to the item in her hand with hunger and curiosity.

Tranquila snapped her fingers to get its attention back. "I don't know what day it is here. But on Earth it's a Tuesday. And since nobody kills themselves, or others until Thursday, I say we take this time and get to know each other." She paused, watching the dog, but Cerberus sat, an expressionless creature. Eventually she had to ask, "Is that okay?"

Despite possessing three heads, they all tended to work with a single mind. When she spoke again, the canine's stiff triangle ears eased into their normal position. The central head dipped itself down, using its nose to point at her feet.

Sharing eye contact, Tranquila raised one foot from the filthy waters and made a baby-step onto the waterlogged land. She waited. Nothing. Slowly, she let her arm fall to her side. Cerberus allowed this as well.

They stared at each other with uncertainty for several seconds before Cerberus grew impatient and started barking for the food. Tranquila immediately chucked the ball of arils at the dog who caught it delicately between its heavy, sharp teeth, then chomped it up violently. She chewed on the remains in a complacent and speciously less homicidal fashion.

Though she was panting through yet another mini heart attack, Tranquila couldn't help but laugh. Cerberus may be the undead monster in charge of guarding Hades, but underneath it all, she was nothing more than a dog who just wanted to eat her delicious human food.

*

For the rest of October, Grandma Sobriquet stirred the curiosity of the produce department in their local grocery store. Every day the weathered woman hobbled along on the pigeon-toes that reduced her movements to slow but steady shuffles in her prescribed slippers. She looked every bit the stereotypical grandmother: round like a plum, ice-blonde hair pinned back into curls, blue-eyed and vulnerable-looking.

At the same time every day, 10:45 in the morning, she'd lean an empty cart against her fragile vessel and use it to get to a large display, where they kept the seasonal favorites. She'd let go of the cart, shuffle slowly to the edge of the oversized box and reach down to start throwing pomegranates into the metal shopping cart. Many of the early-morning shoppers were startled out of their trance with her loud clattering. It wasn't until the cart was half full that she'd stop, pull her body on top of the handles and, again using it like a crutch, go to the front of the store to check out.

Every day, for nearly three weeks, this woman would come. The same early-morning cashiers would look on, amazed as she purchased these copious amounts of fruit. Whichever cashier checked her out—either Gabby, Gina, Deena, or Mehmed—would make the same observation, "Wow. You're just like one of those math problems." Grandma Sobriquet would bite back the urge to berate their condescension, pay the total, and manipulate a bagger into putting the cumbersome shrubs into her car—playing on their ideas that women over a certain age were as weak and needy as babies.

But then, one day, the fresh-faced redhead named Gabby made a terrible mistake.

Grandma Sobriquet finished bending up and down, up and down, to retrieve the pomegranates from her cart. Placing them on the conveyer belt, she mumbled to the cashier that she had twenty-seven of them. Gabby didn't bother to count for accuracy. Who's going to lie about wanting to buy twenty-seven pomegranates? As she started rolling the fruit to the other end of the register for the bagger to collect, she decided to entertain her own curiosity with a question disguised as a quip, "You going to share any of that or is it all for you?"

Up until then, Grandma Sobriquet hadn't paid attention to the workers of the store. She mostly kept her head downward, eyes focused on nothing and no one. She navigated around, like a half-asleep drone in his or her own home. But that insipidness, those uninspired jokes, sent to test the mettle of even the most iron-willed of customers—the cashiers' bland attempts at conversation that tried to force a friendship, which would garner them compliments they could brag to their managers about—was a nudge over the edge for Grandma Sobriquet.

That's when Grandma looked into the face of Gabby. She realized that, though not even an eighth her age, this girl was already on a downward spiral. Soon, she would be telling unoriginal jokes at forty-year-old-dads level. Now it behooved Grandma to put the young girl in her place.

"Don't do that," she admonished, her frozen-lake-colored eyes narrow. She spoke with a voice that didn't belong to regular old women who spent their mornings fussing over the quality of bread. This woman, this short, fat, old thing, who tired from walking fourteen steps and used her cart as a crutch, was frighteningly different. At first, Gabby tried to laugh off her discomfort. "What do you mean?"

But Grandma Sobriquet just glared at her as if she—the cashier—impeached on some ancient grocery store law, for which other grocery stores would flog her on sight for gross misconduct. Under the old matron's heavy eyes, Gabby felt her entire body stiffen against her will.

"Don't make the same tired jokes as everyone else, Gabby," Grandma Sobriquet warned, her voice insidiously low. "Don't waste people's time with your bad material and shitty attempts at small talk, Gabby. You're not doing anything by trying to talk to the customers, Gabby." Grandma Sobriquet spat each time she repeated the girl's name. "You're just serving to piss them off and further ensure every time they come back here, they're just going to avoid your line like the goddamn plague. Don't be that cashier, Gabby. Either be unique or *don't speak*, Gabby."

Gabby just stared at the old woman, lips ajar, vocal cords rendered inept. The bagger too watched all of this transpire with the same wide-eyed speechlessness.

"I...I was just..." the cashier began. When she looked into Grandma Sobriquet's face, she beheld every fragile young woman's worse fear: the judgmental stare of a far superior woman. Instantly, she shut down her own defenses. She spoke, only to tell the dreaded woman her total. When Grandma Sobriquet paid by card, Gabby handed her the receipt, without asking if she wanted it.

The bagger, who was equally afraid of the old thing, put her groceries in her cart at record speed. He got out of the old woman's rueful sight, loudly volunteering to gather carts in the pre-ice hell that is New York fall weather.

Relieved, the cashier watched the cruel creature start out of the store with her large amount of fruit. Gabby's insides froze, as the woman paused to review the receipt. Praying to a god she only acknowledged before the results of exams and pregnancy sticks, she waited in terrified silence for the old woman to turn around and attack her again.

Grandma Sobriquet didn't. After pretending to look over her receipt long enough, Gabby was relieved to watch the old woman stroll through the two automatic doors, taking her cart-full of fruit with her.

*

Nothing was different about her grandmother when she returned with the six bags of pomegranates. The same couldn't be said about Tranquila.

"How many more times do I have to go to the store for you?" Grandma Sobriquet demanded, as she struggled through the front door. "Because you're raking up a bill and I'm sick of looking like a shitty math prob—" She stopped short upon finding her granddaughter.

With her shirt soaking in the sink, Tranquila dowsed herself in dish soap, vigorously trying to sponge away all the mud. She looked like a creature of double form with seaweed and tiny pebbles clinging to her hair. Her neck and arms were sodden with a terrible stink comprising of dog, sludge and the Dead Sea. Tranquila glanced over and saw that she had stunned the old woman.

"Jesus…" Grandma Sobriquet let out. "How did you get so ugly?"

Tranquila glowered at her grandmother before turning her attention back to the cleansing water, saying nothing.

Grandma Sobriquet put the groceries on the table. She lumbered over to her kin and studied her from the side. "What happened?"

There was an impulse on Tranquila's part to cold shoulder her grandmother, but she was disgruntled and needed to complain. "That dog fucking hates me."

Grandma Sobriquet scoffed. "I've dropped sixty-four dollars a day on pomegranates for you to just figure this out? No shit Cerberus hates you. That beast's an inveterate fixture of the Underworld, born and trained to terrorize any soul that steps onto its territory. The fact that you get to walk around as freely as you do is such an insult to its senses. Naturally it's not going to trust you, even if you *are* cleared by Hades to work there."

"Why not?" Tranquila demanded, as she pulled fish bones from her hair, throwing them down the garbage disposal. "I've been there for a month and a half. The stupid mutant sees me every day. Hell, I have lunch with the guy who brings the dead to her every fucking day. Why can't she trust me?"

"That beast has been working that position since before day one all by itself. Now it's being told it needs help? You'd be pissed about it too."

Tranquila moaned, miserable that the issue wasn't going to be solved instantly. "So what does that mean?" she asked, placing her shoes in the sink to be hosed down. "I'm just going to have to live with working next to a bitch who's going to chew my ass out every time she sees me?"

Grandma Sobriquet cast her an oblique glance. "Oh, don't be such a pussy. You dealt with me just fine."

"Yeah but you're just verbally abusive," Tranquila replied as she focused her attention on spraying the eons of harpy dung from her shoes. "I'm used to somebody wanting to hurt my feelings not wanting to actually hurt me."

Her grandmother didn't say anything after that. She tossed the store receipt onto the kitchen table as a subtle way of saying you-better-reimburse-me-don't-think-this-shit's-free, before retiring to the room with her beloved recliner, leaving Tranquila to think.

For a while, the only thing that the young woman could do was scrub the filth from her shoes and mop up the mess she'd tracked through the house. She let her body go into autopilot as she stripped down, got into sweatpants and a cami—the last clean clothes she had left. She gathered a week's worth of soiled garments from her bedroom and did her laundry before her mother could smell the stench of the Underworld.

After turning the washer on, Tranquila—exhausted, frustrated and exasperated—collapsed onto a cushy pile of dirty clothes. She listened to the machine rumble and shake, unable to move or think. She would have fallen asleep too, if her body would allow, but the instant she closed her eyes to remove herself from troubles, her mind rebelled.

I hate Cerberus, she thought, as she nuzzled her face in the soft pile of whites. *I hate that fucking dog.* Those words would have been blasphemous back in August. For the first time in her life, Tranquila had found a dog, worse than *just* a dog—a pitbull—her favorite breed, that she didn't like. While it went against her very nature to say such things, the memories of Cerberus taking her by the scruff and tossing her into the deep end of the Acheron River, like she was an empty beer bottle, validated her opinions. She couldn't help but be bitter, as she recalled how she was forced to swim towards land just as Charon delivered a new batch of souls. She was humiliated, drenched in dreck and sick from breathlessness. The sight of her caused a bunch of dead nerds, who died killing each other after a particularly intense game of *Magic: the Gathering*, to scream at the sight of her, thinking they were being approached by Tlazolteotl, goddess of dirt and sexually transmitted disease.

If she had known she was going to trade being bullied and humiliated by Grandma Sobriquet for being bullied by beasts and humiliated by deceased nerds, Tranquila would have just waited out the hebetude with gratitude. At least she knew how to deal with the beast that was Jeanette. At least she knew if she really wanted to get rid of her grandmother, her mother would come to her aid and dispel the old woman from their home like an exorcism. But it was Tranquila's decision to keep her around. She needed the words of insight and guidance that Jeanette provided, however vague and venom-laden. It was one of the most profound lessons school hadn't meant to teach her: that a person can only survive Hell so long as they have some kind of support system. Whether that support came from the last of the compassionate teachers or even one's bitchy—possibly undead—grandmother, it didn't matter. Any support was better than no support.

The washer thumped wildly through the spin cycle, causing the laundry soap to fall off and crash onto the floor. The plastic bottle rolled next to her foot, without making any mess. Tranquila watched it with tired disinterest. She probably should go upstairs but right now her bedroom might as well have been in China. Instead, she made herself comfy in the pile of whites and closed her eyes.

But her mind rebelled again. Though her body cried out for rest, the brain went right to work. Despite exhaustion, by the end of the day, Tranquila mentally laid out an entire scheme for the next shift. Because, like that plastic bottle, she knew how to roll with the punches.

*

Clever Cerberus could tell, even in the prevailing endlessness of her realm, when the worthless adjutant would come. Each time the beast was sure Tranquila would arrive, Cerberus raised herself from slumber just to watch the meat-bag being escorted in the traitor-bone-bag's boat, and Cerberus would greet it by bombarding the meat-stick with a triumvirate of hostile stares. Usually, Tranquila would avert her eyes from them, but today, with head high and eyes harder than stone, she made eye contact at once with the mutant. She continued to hold it, even as she leapt from the boat and touched land.

The monster and the human didn't break their heated gaze, as Tranquila slipped off her book bag, reached into the front zipper, took out a Tupperware container that was pomegranate-purple and tossed the bag onto a drier part of land a few feet over.

Cerberus blinked at the sight of the possible treat. She pacified the ridges in her back, in order to seem approachable enough to be fed. Tranquila took the hint and put one hand on the top of the tub to remove the lid. She walked closer to the beast. Cerberus allowed it, she wanted the treat. But instead of stopping in front of the dog and feeding her, Tranquila took her place beside the beast, dipped her hand into the arils and ate the tart, chewy contents herself.

At once, Cerberus' moment of ceasefire screeched back into hatred and all three heads made threatening barks and growls at the human, delivering an ear-shattering order for her to get back to the allotted space in the watery sand. Instead, Tranquila ate the fruit and ignored her.

Cerberus snapped her jaws—jaws that could pulverize dump trucks—in Tranquila's ear; the last warning she would receive. Tranquila self-imposed a deaf-blindness to the creature. She ate the fruit, even though she didn't really like it, out of spiteful courage.

Consumed with unholy rage, Cerberus spared no time in grabbing Tranquila by the shirt tags in an attempt to send her back into the disgusting river where she belonged. When the great creature hoisted the tiny person in its teeth, Tranquila took the opportunity to take off her shoe and throw it as hard as she could at the left head's right eye. With precise aim, her sneaker hit the beast in the sensitive jelly. The dog made a squeaky yelp of pain, at once releasing its grip on Tranquila and sending her back to the ground.

She landed with perfect ease, that only a person who commutes every day by free-falling sixty thousand feet below ground could make. She watched the beast howl with pain, still chewing on the sweet seeds like she was a bored spectator at a baseball game.

Once the pain subsided, Cerberus' anger sparked anew upon sight of the mortal. She lunged after the human, four paws hitting the Underworld like four bomb detonations, nearly shaking Tranquila from her stance. When the beast came after her, though, Tranquila remained in her spot even as it hurtled at nightmarish speed. As Cerberus neared, Tranquila bent down, grabbed a fistful of sand and whipped it, boomerang-fashion, directly into every single one of the beast's eyes.

The trimorphic creature was reduced into a simple dog, as it screeched in pain, rolling dramatically onto its snake-laden hide, trying to use its mighty paws to rub its eyes.

Seeing Cerberus reduced to this helpless pup made the better part of Tranquila's person melt. She went to her book bag, pulled out the water bottle she brought and tossed her plastic-ware of seeds onto the sand. She went over to the dog, using its coarse fur to climb onto its belly. Trodding across the giant stomach, she used her strength to move the cur's front paws from off its eyes.

The dog, with failing dignity, made a feeble attempt to bare its teeth and growl at her. Tranquila rebuked, "Oh shut up, dumbass. Let me help you."

With that, the dog went silent. Tranquila leaned her body against its wet nose to distribute water evenly into each of its hurt eyeballs. When the water was gone, she hopped from the dog's belly, onto the ground, allowing the beast to blink away the little fragments of sand.

Cerberus rolled off of her back and lay in the sand. Her giant paws stuck out from underneath her. She stayed there batting her eyes, closing then opening them, then closing them again when the air hurt too much. Several seconds later, her sight renewed. Cerberus was shocked to see, with clear vision, the little human right in front of her central nose, smiling and holding out a pomegranate. This time as an offering, not a bribe.

Sheepishly, Cerberus reached forward and took the fruit from her hand so gently that her sharp lion-like teeth barely grazed the tip of her palm. She blinked at Tranquila once before pushing the shrub into the back of her mouth and using her back teeth to macerate the food. When she was done, she lowered all three heads back onto the ground, turning overtly away from Tranquila's general direction.

Tranquila bravely put out her hand again, this time palm down. She slowly advanced until she was touching the soft, smooth fur located on the middle head's nose bridge, which was so big she had to use her whole hand to pet it. She did this for several pets, all without the pooch making a single protest. Suddenly, all the aversion she once had for the creature melted like dirty snow at the close of spring. Her love of dogs extended—with increased admiration—to the robust mutt.

"Sorry, Cerb," she whispered, her voice soft with baby talk. "Least you got soft furs."

*

In a part of the Underworld, far from Tranquila's triumph, Charon paddled his way down the River Acheron. On the opposite bank of the river, a group of souls waited to be carried over. They saw the skeleton man and tried calling his attention.

"Hey! Hey! Come back here."

"We're over here."

"Hey. Where you going? We're over here."

"For Zeus's sake. Just because I don't got eyes doesn't mean I don't see you. I'll pick you guys up on the next round," Charon fired back, continuing with his strokes, speeding away from the impatient dead. As he went along the canal that brought in the River Lethe, he mumbled to himself a litany of curse words that would have made Grandma Sobriquet jealous.

It took him a great while, but alas, the skeleton proved himself impossibly athletic, for he was able to make it down the River Lethe and across to the little island that held a solitary building of immutable ebony. When he landed on the waterfront and made it up to the formidable structure, he came to find he was not the only one who had thought of doing so.

The building, while grand, was made with unnecessary stairs, leading right to a large set of doors where Charon found several other members of the Underworld staff.

"Agony? Fear? What are you doing here?"

"Same as you, Charon," said Fear. "We're worried about Hades."

"That's where you're wrong, Fear," said Charon. "I never worry. Occasionally, I'll get stressed, or more often be vexed, but never suggest for a second that I appear anxious."

"Then why are you here?" asked Agony, annoyed.

Charon pulled a letter out of the creases in his hip joints. "I just got a notice that stated my insurance hasn't been paid for this year. I'm going up there to curse Hades out."

"You have boater's insurance?" Fear asked, perplexed by the prospect. "What protection could you possibly need?

You're a skeleton who ferries dead people from one side to the next."

"Hey, I'm not here to talk about logic. I'm here to talk about facts. And fact is I can't be driving around without insurance," he implored. "Besides, that's my personal boat and just because I'm dead doesn't mean I can't be entitled to have nice things."

Fear and Agony looked at each other, shared a smirk, then completely lost it, bursting forth with laughter. Charon stood, wishing he had eyes so he could glare at them. Over their guffaws he challenged, "If you guys are so concerned, why don't you just go inside and reason with Hades?"

Just like that, their brazen ways ended. "We're not going in to tell the god of dead nothing," cried Agony.

Charon scoffed. "You guys are pansies, you know that? We're talking about the most relaxed god this side of Olympus. It's not like you're going in to talk to Hera or something."

"Yeah but Hades has been…different lately," Agony replied, casting a worrisome look towards the lair. "He's usually so much more resigned. But lately…I dunno."

"What do you expect? The guy just got dumped."

"Oh, I get that. It's just…" she couldn't say the rest. Instead she looked to her lover for reassurance.

Charon studied the two of them, trying to figure out what nonverbal messages they were sending each other. He couldn't read them. Finally he asked, "It's just what?"

Anxiousness traveled from Agony's face to Fear's. But Fear, by name, was duty-bound to spread terror. Hence he was forced to share with Charon something that fraught the abstract with apprehension.

"Charon, he…he hasn't left his office in five hundred and seventy-six weeks."

Like a grenade when the pin is withdrawn, it took a few moments for the explosion to register within the skeleton. When it did, though, what he lacked in facial muscles, or other expressive body parts, he more than supplemented with his superior fury.

"WHAAAAATTT?" he cried, as his arms rankled in the air, making him look like a cheesy Halloween decoration. Self-awareness served to piss him off even further, making his jaw bone almost unhinge to scream at them louder, "YOU GUYS LEFT HIM ALONE FOR A FUCKING DECADE?"

Charon was the apogee of ancestral doom. His wrath cowed the power-couple. Fear and Agony quaked in each other's arms, like the idiots they were.

"We thought he was in a meeting and we didn't want to interrupt," sputtered Agony, tears running down her many boils, warts and festering wounds.

"Who's in a fucking board meeting for five hundred weeks?"

"We thought he was with the Fates," wailed Fear. "You know how the Fates love to waste everyone's time."

Charon didn't have time for asinine logic. Priorities had changed. For the first time in the history of boat ownership, a boat owner didn't care about his boat anymore. Charon pelted through the entrance, his feet clicking furiously, as if a tap dancer was surging down the hall. He bum-rushed the double set of doors to Hades' office. What he found made his metaphorical gut throw up inside itself. There lay the stricken god, chin to the desk, surrounded in his own wasteland of rotten, maggot-infested ambrosia. Hades held a dead-eyed-goose stare on a swirl of opaque that played images at command. Charon thought that Hades' thoughts clouded his hearing, seeing as he made no reaction to Charon's dramatic entrance.

The ferryman let out a dejected sigh. When Fear and Agony finally joined him, they did the same.

"You were right to be concerned," Charon said mournfully to the couple.

"Oh, poor Hades," Agony murmured. "He's...he's..." She couldn't finish. Fear did it for her, "He's gone emo."

As if approaching an injured bird, the three of them made their way to Hades who was so transfixed on the all-seeing sphere, he didn't notice their presence. He continued to goad whomever, "C'mon, *C'mon...Eat the fucking poison.*"

The trio looked into the globe and recognized who he was trying to kill. None of them were surprised.

Charon took the initiative and spoke to Hades: "Sir? Sir, it is Charon." He talked to Hades in the same tone adults use to talk to their Alzheimer-afflicted relatives. "Sir?"

There was no response. Each of them looked to the other with worry.

"How far along do you think he is?" asked Agony, anxiously.

"I dunno. But he looks like he hasn't bathed in years," commented Fear.

"Fear, why would a god need to bathe? None of us have to bathe," corrected Charon.

"Oh. So it's weird for us to groom but it's not weird for a psychopomp to need boater's insurance?" Fear snipped back at him.

"Be fucking careful how you talk about my boat, Fear," spat Charon, uttering his name like it was strong, biting liquor. "Just because I can't eat, doesn't mean I won't chew up and spit out your pansy ass."

"That doesn't even make sense."

They started to squabble when Hades' voice snapped them out of their pettiness. "This is taking too long," he said at once, still speaking to the floating globe, his once sluggish, sad voice now energized by intolerance.

Charon, Fear and Agony were slow to react to Hades' sudden recovery. They watched him lift his head from his desk and pull open a drawer, usually reserved for pens. But instead of a writing utensil, he picked up a piece of thread and a pair of scissors. With each hand occupied, he spoke to the orb threateningly, "This is for making me look bad."

At once the trio leapt into action. "No! Hades, you can't," Agony wailed, hurt by his ruler's obvious pain.

"Sir, no. Stop," Fear screamed, trying desperately to knock the thread of life from his hands.

"Why can't I?" Hades roared defiantly, as he wrestled against his employees' furtive hands.

"'Cause you're better than this, Boss," Charon cried, trying to slap the scissors from his employer's hand.

"No, I'm not!" he bellowed back, maneuvering the string in between the gaping shears while Agony pushed her entire weight onto his arms. "That movie made me look like a dumbass who doesn't do his job! Why wouldn't I know if that someone wasn't dead for 18 years?! That's literally the entirety of my fucking job description! To know when people fucking die! I worked too hard to be turned into some bad car salesman joke!"

"Hades please!" Charon cried, shaking his hands in Hades' face as a signal for rationality. "Yes! *Hercules* was poorly made. Yes, it was unoriginal and badly researched and it portrays you as a quasi-Satan who liked to sell used cars on the side—for some reason. But you can't let that bother you anymore!"

"That's not what bothers me the most!" Hades insisted, shaking off his employees with bravado muscles. Huddled near him, frightened by his unreason, they each saw, quietly, that while his eyes regained lucidity, his normally sonorous tone was getting lower and more dangerous by each delivery. "*Hercules* makes *way* too many outdated movie references to movies that were already corny and unfunny to begin with! Someone has to die for this! And since I gave a bunch of the story board department mega-Syphilis—I'm going after the real Judas in all this."

The staff could only help but to watch as Hades turned away and veered his daunting attention back to the perceptive globe. He whispered, "The guy who turned me into trope. A guy who tarnished my countless years of hard work and turned me into a *swarthy*, *lazy*, *ugly*, kinda-rapey *devil*. James Woods ruined my name. So—I'm going to bury him."

The God of Death was quick. He raised his hand to snip the string that was the mortal's life but the whole point of hiring demons was for their ability to haul proverbial ass. Thus, they clashed and they fought together in a weird jumble of bones, flesh and scales.

"Boss! Don't do this!" Charon screamed. "You do this and you're just like Hera!"

Hades, frustrated at despair he didn't comprehend and enraged at having been compared to his sister, lashed out at them. He abused them. He called them nasty names. He damned Fear and Agony's happiness. He viciously slandered Charon's boat as a whore. None of that fazed them. Their grips didn't lessen. Their struggles didn't weaken. They held together.

With this, Hades compiled all his strength to send the three entities to his jewel-encrusted floor. When Charon, Fear and Agony looked up at the god, they saw in his face nothing but debased spite and misguided grief. With his face haggard by malice, they were powerless. Hades held up the flimsy thread that determined James Woods' life. With his other hand he drew forth the pair of scissors.

The God reached with his cutter, to sever the line between being a servant to life and being a murderer, and Fear and Agony all but gave up on him, relented to his unreason, told themselves maybe it was time for this god to join his killer brothers and sisters, and held their breaths as they waited for him to enter that devastator-of-life role.

Hades would have too, had Charon been of a less brazen and blunt character. For Charon cried out something so crass, it made Hades stop mid-action, "Persephone's a bitch, boss! Don't kill because of her!"

Those bold words stunned not only the Underworld's greatest lovers, but his employer as well. They watched as Hades turned his head to stare at Charon, with eyes so deranged with rage, both Fear and Agony thought for certain he was going to destroy the skeleton. Charon held down the delirious gaze, returning it a quiet, eyeless empathy, palpable enough to sting at the great God. Though his face gravely struck with offense, and while his giant hand trembled with stubborn effort, Hades let his limbs go limp against his person. The shears fell to the floor.

All three of his workers expressed their relief.

Dropping his gaze, Hades stashed the string of life back into his desk drawer. Turning his head to the floating imagery, he gave it a slanted appraisal of pure loathing, to which he said, "You got lucky, James Woods. You got lucky."

Hades then snapped his fingers and the glowing rounder dissipated on the spot.

Embarrassed as he was, he looked to his employees with an earnestness, indicating that he wanted to thank them all. He was interrupted by an unfathomable roar that convulsed his office to the core.

None of the workers knew what creature could possibly make that sound. But Hades did. That's when he thought, for the first time in six Earth months, "Ah shit! I haven't gone to work in 10 years!"

A KING, A MONK AND A PILE OF BARF

By the time it took for the God of the Dead and his faithful employees to clean up his office, tidy himself up, authorize exceedingly-late forms and zoom down to Cerberus' station to apologize to Tranquila for his negligence, Tranquila made Hades' Hell Hound her Hell bitch. She wouldn't have even noticed their presence had Charon been a speechless type. From behind, she heard the familiar skeleton cry, "Holy fuck." She turned around to see the faceless face of disbelief. Alongside Charon, two scaly, wart-covered faces of similar disbelief, gazed upon her. Hades bore a single impression of intrigue.

Strolling up to his newest worker, with his smooth hand extended for her to take, Hades announced, "Congratulations. You've just been promoted."

*

Thus, Tranquila moved on to the other waterways of Hades.

"Okay, this is the River Lethe," Hades announced, as Charon eased them through the perennial, drab waters. The olive color, smell and dynamic all reminiscent of dirty old bong water. "Also known as the River of Forgetfulness. Over there is my office."

The left beheld a sharply designed fortress that normally only existed in the fantasies of the Goth subculture or in the manifestos of death metal bands' concept albums. Hades introduced it with an indication of indifference that would have made both of the aforementioned cry jealous tears of blood.

"Wow," Tranquila commented. "You sure dig black."

"Eh," Hades remarked. "It's kinda hard to have a color scheme when everything is cloaked under abject blackness. Now it goes without saying, but try not to touch the water. One drop and half your memories are gone."

"What happens if you fall in?" Tranquila asked, looking over the edge of the boat with unease.

"You do that and you'll forget how to shit," Charon chimed in abrasively.

Tranquila took the warning and scooted towards the middle of the boat.

"Why do you even have this river? I get the River of Pain, and the River of Fire is pretty badass. But why do you want people to forget who they are?" she asked, remembering Charon's insistence that the Underworld was a place of reflection.

Just as she asked, Charon held up his oar and carefully pulled it inward to allow the boat to coast. They were carried along by steady currents, like an inflatable tube taking a sunburnt grandma down the Lazy River. Through an evanescent light provincial to bayous and corpse-laden marshes, Tranquila saw they were being brought to a cul-de-sac of water. She was stunned to see how the body of water led directly to a land mass consisting entirely of dead people, standing in near-perfect lines, talking animatedly amongst themselves, as if they were patiently waiting to get inside a concert venue.

Charon's guidance brought them to the riverbank with such precision and grace that the boat slid right onto the sand.

Tranquila was able to get out with two feet of separation from the memory-erasure waters. She was so impressed (and grateful to not be another victim of inevitable Alzheimer's jokes) that she was about to hand Charon a couple of crimpled ones. Before she could, the god of underground wealth pulled a diamond the size of a dodgeball from his capacious garments and offered it to the skeleton.

"Aw, thank you, Hades," Charon said, his harsh, guttural voice softening.

Tranquila wondered if Hades was being charitable, aware that perhaps Charon had money troubles. As she pondered what money troubles a skeleton, with his own sweet-ass boat had, her thoughts were interrupted by Charon gripping the diamond, winding-up pitcher-style. He heaved the pressurized rock into the blackness of the Underworld sky, lobbing it high but far. Tranquila watched in amazement, thinking this was just an exercise for the surprisingly fit skeleton until many seconds later when in the distance an unseen unfortunate, no doubt someone impacted by the heavy jewel, screamed out in pain.

"THAT'S WHAT YOU GET, JANE AUSTEN! YOU SLIMEY PILE OF BARF!"

"Dude!" Tranquila cried out, horrified by Charon's abusiveness. "What the hell was that for?"

"She knows what she did," he snarled, shaking his bony wrist in the author's direction. In another striking change of mood, Charon tossed his skull backwards into a hearty cackle before driving his stick into the land, hoisting the boat back on the water, stirring himself away, still guffawing at triumphantly getting even with Jane 'Pile of Barf' Austen.

Tranquila watched the whole incident with her eyebrows disappearing into her hairline she was so shocked and confused. She turned to Hades for an explanation but saw he had already walked up a small incline. She jogged to catch up with him.

"The River Lethe is more valuable to me and more badass than all the other rivers combined. You know why people used to get baptized in lakes and rivers? It's because of the River Lethe," Hades said, as they reached a small plateau where two lines of souls opposed each other, separated by an above-ground pool; mere feet from where they stood, this was the Pool of Lethe. Bordered by red clay bricks in order to stand out noticeably, even in the low lighting, stood a Greco-shaped pool, the kind seen all across state-funded America with uninspired black and white tiles. The water, though, wasn't exactly crystal-blue. The water bore a striking resemblance to a pool of algae-green that emerges when chlorine is forgotten.

"In the Underworld—" Hades never called his kingdom Hades in order to prevent people from assuming he was one of those jerks who spoke in the third person, "—it gets so overcrowded, that in February, March, August and September, we erase a couple of thousand souls so they can be reincarnated and sent back on Earth, to make room for new souls. We push them into the Pool of Lethe, the harpies dry them off so none of the excess travels back on Earth, and thus they are reborn."

Silently, Tranquila watched a handful of souls being taken through the process. It was comical to watch the souls of those who probably found this existence nightmarish enough get to the edge of the pool. Apprehension streaked their faces to the point where the harpies had to intervene, gripping them with their talons and pushing them in. It happened every time, no matter the person: from the kindergartener to the priest to the appropriately dressed teen wearing a 'pro-death' sweatshirt—each wanting nothing to do with their new destinies, preferring to stick to a miserable, predictable death than inure life again.

"Cool," Tranquila said, her eyes hypnotized by the process. "So does everyone just go clean or are they reincarnated based on what they were like before?"

"Unfortunately for a lot of rank-based religions, it's just random," Hades replied, as they watched a harpy throw a newborn afflicted by SIDS into the deep end. "That newborn has an equal chance of being a puppy as it does a male prostitute."

Tranquila watched until the newborn was scooped from the cleansing waters and carried away, gurgling and cooing happily in the arms of a bird-faced mutant as if it were its mother, before she asked, "Who was I reincarnated from? Because I feel like with all the bad decisions I make I used to be a dude."

"I have no idea." Hades did, but there wouldn't be much fun in telling Tranquila she died in a past life getting her noble head cut off by a bunch of bread-obsessed peasants. "But that's the beauty of the Pool of Lethe. All your prejudices, your crimes, your social merits—none of them are contingent to your next life. Everyone dies equal. You die a warlord, you serve your time, you reflect, you come to the Pool of Lethe and all the ancient sins are gone."

"What about those assholes in Tartarus? They never leave right?"

"Hell, no," Hades said, no pun intended. "Tartarus was made specifically as a landfill for the defects of humanity. If they were ever to be reincarnated, the evil is so embedded into their souls, whatever they would be—man, woman, polar bear, laptop charger—they would be such a menace to the community around them, it'd be pointless trying to redeem them. Why bother with the soul of Kim Jong-il if he's just going to be reincarnated into a child predator or one of those asshole wasps?"

"So what should I do?" Tranquila asked, referring to her job. "Should I start pushing people into the pool?"

"No. There's too much risk of you getting backsplash. Besides, the harpies are more than qualified to do that. They run by instinct, not by thinking," Hades replied, as he began walking in the direction of where the harpies were taking the emptied vessels.

They didn't have to journey far. Ducking from the harpies' low-hanging talons, they followed the bird-ladies' migration into a nearby passageway, which like anything in the Underworld was no doubt formed by lava slowly draining over millions of years to leave behind a tube the size of ten blue whales. At the end of the passageway, Tranquila saw where the harpies dropped off the 'reset' souls. Dozens stood around, pure as chaos, dumber than bricks, each bearing a look of utter serenity on their faces. They were the lucky ones, better, in Hades' opinion, than himself. Better than any immortal. They were able to die and be reborn. They could be new. They could transcend. And courageously, humans did it over and over again without any help from superior gifts or superior knowledge. They, simply, lived.

"I'm going to show you how to send the dead through the process of reincarnation and then I want you to clear out all these people," Hades said, unaware that Tranquila was distracted by a face she recognized.

"NO FUCKING WAY!"

He heard her normally effeminate voice turn abrasive with disbelief. When he turned around, she stood face-to-face with the most famous face in American history.

Pie-eyed, dried of wisdom and holding hands absentmindedly with a white man, was the evacuated vessel of Martin Luther King Jr. Tranquila found it exceedingly difficult to maintain dignity in the presence of such a man.

"Holy fu…This is Martin Luther King!" she cried out, star-struck. Turning to Hades, she pointed at the former man wildly and asserted, "I can't believe this. I went to his school. *I went to his school.*"

"Which one? Boston University, Crozer Theological Seminary or Morehouse College?" Hades inquired.

"College? Ew, no. I went to Martin Luther King Elementary," Tranquila explained, clearly elated at meeting the man named after the only school she ever liked attending. "Dude. This is insane. I'm face-to-face with the guy who's— what the hell? Why is Martin Luther King Jr. holding some greasy homeless homie's hand?"

Tranquila's ineptitude in European history revealed itself once again. As she attempted to pry the homeless-looking man's hand from the revenant man's, which were latched together with surprising strength, Hades came to intervene. Ceasing her efforts, Hades had to explain, "That's not a homeless man. That's Grigori Rasputin." He was met with Tranquila's blank stare. "Russian mad monk, Rasputin? Healer for Nicholas II's hemophiliac-afflicted son Alexei?" This warranted only more incomprehensive stares. "Ugh…'*Ra ra Rasputin/ Lover of the Russian Queen/ He was a cat that really was gone.*'" Silence. "OH C'MON! It was on *Just Dance* for the Wii console!"

She was nowhere closer to knowing who this creepy blue-eyed Russian was. She didn't care. All she wanted to know was, "Well, why is the creep holding Dr. King's hand? Are they gay together, or something?"

Hades sputtered, offended by the idea. Martin Luther King could do way better than the guy who lied to everyone and said he deflowered the Romanov Sisters. "Grown men can hold hands and not be gay. What's wrong with you? Don't they teach you anything in America?"

Tranquila pointed to Martin Luther King Jr. "We learn about him, the Holocaust, a little bit of biology and *maybe* some math. Maybe." (Not really)

Hades shook his head. "Poor Americans." Sigh. "Anyway, let's teach you some discernible skills before my head goes numb."

*

"Grandma, I was really having my doubts but I can honestly say after today—I'm really glad you tricked me into selling my soul to Hades," Tranquila said joyously, pacing back and forth in the living room, while Grandma Sobriquet disassociated herself from the conversation by staring mindlessly at her programs.

"Uh-huh," she said listlessly.

"Today I took your advice. I finally showed that bitch Cerberus who was boss."

"Wow..."

"And...and...get this. I got to pet her. Pet. It was like the greatest moment in dog person history when I touched Cerberus' fur, which, I don't know if you know this, is softer than freaking bunny hair."

"Oh wow."

"And today—today I learned reincarnation isn't just some hippie crap Hindus always go on about. It's real. I even got to watch this old Russian dude get reincarnated into a baby tiger—but then it sucked because the baby tiger got poached— but then it was okay because the baby tiger got reincarnated into a baby *human*—"

"Oh geez, that's great, Tran," Grandma Sobriquet said, in a voice devoid of enthusiasm or interest. "Now, how 'bout we stop boring grammy and let her watch *Gross Gangsters Marry Sad Models*?"

Instead of letting Grandma Sobriquet get to her, Tranquila decided she was allowed to boast.

"And," Tranquila began deviously, as she dug into her pockets. "I got paid today."

Tossing the contents right into Grandma Sobriquet's worn-denim-like face, Tranquila showed off the ten gold bullions—glittering beneath the living room light—that she received from the lump sum of paychecks. Instantly, Grandma Sobriquet's interest peaked.

"Holy Zeus!" Grandma Sobriquet cried, straightening up in the recliner chair. "Hades actually paid you?"

"Yep," she replied, full of smug and damn proud of it. "And since you did get me a job, and you dropped mad money on all that fruit, I guess I'll give you a cut. But only if you go to the Cash 4 Gold for me. And the rest is going to Mom so don't you dare try stealing from her."

As usual, Grandma Sobriquet had tuned out the sound of Tranquila's voice. Normally, this was due to the fact that Tranquila, to her, sounded like a hen trying to squeeze out an egg from its cloaca. In that moment, though, she drowned her out for an entirely different reason. Inspecting the gold as closely as she could, without touching it, a shadow fell across her grandmother's face that changed her incredulity into something different.

"Wow," Grandma Sobriquet said. "I can't believe Hades pays you so well. I didn't think he needed much help. What with Persephone…"

"Oh, they got divorced," her granddaughter interrupted.

Grandma Sobriquet's jaw jarred open, exposing false teeth and halitosis. So her suspicions were confirmed, though it didn't alleviate the shock nonetheless. "You're kidding," she gasped.

Tranquila was shocked by her grandmother's shock. Since when did this woman have emotions? "Yeah. I mean, that's what I've been told. Plus I haven't seen any other gods in the Underworld besides him and Eris."

The decrepit woman was visibly thunderstruck. She didn't speak for a while. When she did she let out an uncharacteristic sign of benevolence: "Poor Hades."

Tranquila couldn't believe what she heard. *Did this bitch just have a stroke?* "Poor Hades? Grandma since when do you care about other people's problems?" she said reproachfully. "When Mom called you up and said her husband had a drug problem and she needed your help, you laughed at her and said fuck 'em."

"That was different," Grandma Sobriquet insisted. "Your parents weren't soulmates. Hades and Persephone—those two have been together for so long. It's like finding out Saturn dumped its rings." She shook her head, repeating over and over, "Poor Hades."

Tranquila stared at her grandmother, her eyes narrowed by incertitude. Then at last she asked in a soft, timid voice, "Grandma…are…are you human?"

The question hung in the air like a dense fog that shouldn't be lifted. Slowly, her grandmother tilted her head to meet her granddaughter's wary gaze. They held eye contact for a short minute, each waiting for the other to blink.

"That depends," she said eventually. "Are you a virgin?"

The bluff was enough for Tranquila to fold. Without looking behind her, Tranquila backed out of the room and remained on the second floor of the house until her mother arrived.

Grandma Sobriquet had, at first, smiled with smug triumph, but then dark thoughts reared into her pessimistic mind: *If a marriage like that can fall apart, what will happen to the world when Zeus and Hera's finally ends?*

OPTIONS ARE A GIRL'S BEST FRIEND

Looming on the hollowed grounds of Olympus, Hera of the golden throne looked down from her mighty perch to oversee another one of her son's drunken revelries. An elegant hand propped up her lovely, yet listless face. She was the bored queen of the skies with nothing to do but watch as others engaged in the euphoria which she was long tired of.

Queen Hera was the envy of all, with her flawless, mustang-colored skin which glowed favorably in every light. Even in darkness, her beauty became a beacon for others to be lured in like moths. But while her beauty could not be overshadowed by others, her cruelty, like an icy, unloving wind, is what steered others away. Her lips, though plump and the color of blackberries, wore a constant sneer that ebbed only under relentless boredom. Her eyes, which were the same color as fresh soil, had a cold fury in them, reserved usually for two things: her husband and anything he loved. Including numerous offspring, an endless litany of lovers, his favorite city-states, his favorite warriors and his favorite animal—tough luck, bumblebees. Maybe next evolution.

As the bacchanalia continued, her eyes drifted lazily over to the many mountains of Ida, where she saw Zeus standing on the topmost crest of the universe, leering at what transpired. She loathed him infinitely. Even now, with his back against the sun, making him and his virile beauty illuminant, she felt nothing but hatred. She knew he had resettled there recently, in an attempt at secrecy, following a decade-long disappearance. She knew she could never squelch his wanderlust. She, the queen of nearly everything, could not control her husband's wanderings, his philandering or his idiocy.

Rage as black and ever-growing as space was sculpting her, as the orgy before her continued.

"Ain't no bacchanalia like a Bacchus bacchanalia because a Bacchus bacchanalia don't stop! OH! Ain't no bacchanalia like a Bacchus bacchanalia because a Bacchus bacchanalia don't stop! OH!" The perpetually drunk Dionysus sang in rapture. His parties tended to last two to five days, although since his accidental invention of Pomegranate Zinfandel, the last century was a shaky blur.

Hera would have let them continue, if it were not the time for knavery. Standing up, she decreed, "This orgy is over!"

All, save one, of the participants were relieved at this respite.

"What?" Dionysus cried, dismayed. "You can't stop the party. Didn't you hear the song?"

"Actually, Di, I'm wiped out," Adriane confessed sheepishly, as she searched for her long-forgotten clothes.

"What?"

"Yeah, Di, great party but, you know, I've been in that orgy for so long. I just want to go home to my wife," yawned Hypnos. He, and many other deities, filed out.

"N-no! No-o!" Dionysus slurred vehemently, watching his many guests head back to their respective homes.

"Sorry, Dionysus," apologized one man passing him by, who stretched his sore muscles. "I should probably go check on the countries. Go see how Africa's doing—"

"No! Not *you*, Atlas."

"Sorry man, but the party's gotta end sometime, right?" Atlas said with a shrug, before giving Hera a deep reverent bow as he left.

As Olympus became a place for Olympians again, Dionysus looked up to see that he was caught under the wrathful gaze of Hera.

"Well, I hope you're happy," said Dionysus with a pout. "You just ruined a perfectly good buzz."

Hera rolled her eyes. "Leave, Dionysus. And don't puke on anything on your way out."

Dionysus grumbled underneath his breath, bitter that he would have to go back to day-drinking on Earth, like some kind of savage.

Normally, such insolence, however minor, would have incurred the wrath of Hera comparable to the release of a hydrogen bomb—but Dionysus wasn't deserving. Not today. Hera cast a discreet eye towards Zeus, to find that he was looking down from the stars to engage in his favorite entertainment—watching mortals go about their simple lives. Hera's deep frown was forced into an unnatural smile.

She pulled from the clasps that held up her perfect breasts a small vial, which contained a powerful aphrodisiac made specifically for men: a mixture of musk, the smell of sex and a hint of bacon fat. She tipped it onto her fingers and dabbed it gently behind her ears and on her wrist.

With a quick refastening of her clothes to ensure her assets were better showcased, Hera enshrouded herself in a thick mist. She floated to mount Ida's summit where Zeus was stationed.

He smelled her before she was physically present.

"Oh," he chuckled rapaciously. "I see someone is trying to distract me from my mortals."

Hera gave him a bedroom smile. "Nothing ever gets past you, ye mighty Zeus."

Zeus bared all his teeth in a lascivious display. He turned away from watching humans commuting to work and returned the overeager stare. "What say you, my Queen?" he asked in a low rumble. "You want to make our embrace on the mountain peaks or can we finally join in your humble boudoir?"

Hera twisted her nose playfully, making herself look coy yet hungry. She sauntered over to Zeus and gently sat on his golden-draped lap. Zeus embraced her. He tried to reach his lips to meet hers, when she halted him with a slim finger.

"Oh, Zeus. So quick to start," she breathed. "Can't we go slowly for once?"

Zeus never objected to going slow. It meant everything would last longer. With a broad smile, he said dreamily, "Of course we can. However you please."

Hera smiled, gently clasping soft hands onto his coarsely bearded face. She bent her forehead to his, nuzzling his forehead. Zeus tilted his chin to kiss her again when she interrupted this action to ask, "So, who of the gods this time, my wanderlust one, was hatching plans with you?"

She spoke so coyly that Zeus mistook it as playfulness. They had an anniversary that stemmed millions of years, yet he barely knew his wife. With a gentle chuckle, he tapped her nose and replied, "Ah, ha ha! You and your eternal suspicions. I can never escape you."

Hera's lips squeezed together, making them look even bigger. At first glance, it was just a smile, however the longer it lasted the easier it was to see she was not trying to smile but was trying to suppress chomping his eyes out with her own teeth.

Zeus, mighty god of thunderbolt, who in a clangorous battle that nearly destroyed Earth, defeated the Titans and gutted his siblings from his cruel father's stomach. Chilled, he felt as if the sun itself had run cold beneath Hera's stare. He stood up, letting Hera slip from his lap, and backed away from her. He was already reaching for the bolt strung at his belt, ready to fight her if necessary.

"Hera, I swear to you, I was not being unfaithful," Zeus protested. Hera glowered at his pathetic lies. He started over. "I was not! I went to comfort my brother. He is still in mourning over his failed marriage. I swear to you. That's all."

"You pity your brother?" she roared, her voice made out of thunder. "You pity that immortal but not the one who stands before you—the ruined, bored queen of nothing?"

"Queen of nothing?" Zeus repeated blankly. "Do you not see where you stand? You stand above the very stars. You could forge entire galaxies if you desire. You rule with infinite wonders."

"I rule nothing," she spat. "I am merely the ruined whore who people know as Zeus's wife! I am the wife of a king who goes around and does what he pleases. *Who* he pleases. Always *your* pleasure when *my* back is turned and yet I am expected to sit on my throne and not pay any notice. How is that being the ruler of infinite wonders, I ask of you, Zeus? How is that glorious?"

Those hate-filled words carried through the ever-expanding endlessness of space and yet Hera's rage was still able to reverberate several times, buffeting Zeus and his stunned silence. They stood at arm's length apart, both rankled with resentment and loathing.

Finally Zeus spoke, "Tell me, Hera. What can you do about all this? About all this animosity you collect and all the grudges you bear? Nothing. The only thing you do is estrange yourself from me a little more. All the worse for you."

Thus again, Zeus turned his back on his wife and left Mount Olympus in a flash of white lightning.

"No," Hera hissed. "All the worse for *you*."

In her infinite power, she transformed herself into steam and floated in a thick white cloud away from Paradise.

*

Mama Sobriquet found so much money on the ground lately that she was developing a kink in her neck from bending her head in search of more. It was unreal; just as the clocks fell backwards and Mama Sobriquet's mornings were destined to become colder, blacker and suckier, she walked out to find a wad of twenties somebody lost in their yard. Normally, she would have missed such luck, with her eyes not yet fully open at that hour, but the neighborhood dogs were going berserk. The howling forced her into being more alert, thus she easily spotted the little lump sticking out of the grass.

From then on, fortune seemed to be lying in wait at every turn for the single mother. One day, she found a fifty in the laundry she didn't know she lost; another day a note was stuck in-between the cracks of the sidewalk when she was coming home from her evening walk; she found out she had been selected to win a two hundred dollar gift card to a local grocery store from a Facebook post she happened to 'like' last week.

Since life wasn't always a crystal staircase for Darla Sobriquet—with the decades spent married to an abusive addict; having to raise an entire family on a single income; being bullied for being chubby and oily as a teen; being bullied by Jeanette as an adolescent (and again as an adult) just for *being*—she didn't dare question the source of her newfound luck. And since she was in such a good mood lately, she decided to surprise her daughter.

As Tranquila took her mid-afternoon, post-work nap, her mother creeped into her bedroom: a stuffy space that took up half the attic.

"Tran?" she called, as she came closer to her daughter's sleeping figure. "Tran?" Just as she spoke, the overpowering smell of pigeons bit her nose and made Mama Sobriquet say loudly, "Oh God! Did a bird die in the walls again?"

Immediately, Tranquila's eyes pulled awake, fully aware that the foul smell wasn't coming from inside the walls but from a long shift of cleaning up harpy shit.

"Oh, wow!" Tranquila exclaimed, making a face after two very audible sniffs. She got out of bed, grabbed a nearby bottle of body spray and made a rainbow of spritzes, letting the fragrance rain down on top of her tainted clothes. The attic room now smelled vaguely of a bird cage that had just been cleaned with coconut water and luau flowers. With a refreshed breath, she lied, "It was probably a pigeon. Pigeons are bums who don't know when to migrate."

"Makes no sense," Mama Sobriquet remarked. "It's twenty degrees out. Why would a dead bird smell that bad?"

Tranquila shrugged, "Physics, man."

Her mom was in too good to care about a half-assed lie. With a smile, she pulled out a thick book that she concealed behind her back. "I went to Barnes & Noble after work and got you something."

She handed over a copy of Edith Hamilton's *Mythology: Timeless Tales of Gods and Heroes.*

"Oh thanks, Mom," said Tranquila.

"I figured I'd just buy you the book, since when's the next time either of us are going to go to the library," she explained, adding: "I also brought you something from work."

She pulled out a wrapped half-moon from her coat pocket: a local treat made from a round slab of sugary bread topped with a half-pound of vanilla and a half-pound of chocolate frosting, reminiscent of lunar phasing. It was a personal favorite. Seeing it, Tranquila instantly chucked the book aside in order to get her hands on the bakery treat.

"Yo-o!" she cheered, elated by the surprise pastry which was already unwrapped and halfway between her lips when she said, "Thanks, Mom."

Mama Sobriquet watched her daughter with a satisfied smile.

"Ugm...Thank you so much, Mom," Tranquila said again, in-between bites and lip smacks. "You haven't brought food home from work in forever."

"Yeah, well, you know me...I can't stay mad forever."

Tranquila knew this to be a half-truth. Her mother, like many women who believed they lived by the creed 'forgive and forget', in reality, lived by a more appropriate axiom: 'let it go until the next row, then bring up the past and lambast their ass'.

Regardless, Tranquila, who devoured half of the diabetic bomb already, knew this treat was more than a sweet gesture. She stopped eating the overindulgence long enough to notice a glint of worry in her mother's eyes. That's when Mama Sobriquet saw her opportunity, "You're going to be off probation soon," she said.

Another half-truth. The duration of her house arrest was contingent on the discretion of her probation officer, a man who was as much a friend as Zeus was a feminist.

"Have you thought about what you want to do?"

Tranquila knew what she wanted to do. She wanted to get her laptop unblocked. She wanted to be a part of social media again. She wanted to watch YouTube videos of giraffe fights, Loch Ness Monster conspiracy video-essays and K-Pop music videos again. She wanted to get her smartphone back, so she could test out the service in Hades and maybe even convince her boss to turn the Underworld into a WIFI Hot-Spot. She wanted to continue working in the Underworld, save up her gold and rubies and fly her mom first-class to Italy. She wanted to work more, to give all she could to the woman who had done all she could for her daughter over the last eighteen years. She wanted all of this and more. But being bound by a contract under penalty of permanent amnesia yielded her from speaking these thoughts. So, while Mama Sobriquet waited for a response, all she could offer was a vague, yet honest: "I have a plan, Mom."

"Oh, really? What's the plan, Tran?"

Pause. "It's a surprise."

"Tran—" her mother began, on the verge of a lecture.

"Mom, trust me, I have a plan." When her mother gave a knowing look, Tranquila reiterated, "A law-abiding plan. I'm going to get a job, Mom. I'm going to work my ass off, save up, hopefully get a car and help out around the house more."

"What about school?"

"Ew, school?"

"Yes, Tranquila, *school*! You can't honestly think you're going to get a good job with a high school education and a criminal record. You need to go to college."

"Why?" Tranquila demanded. "Why should I go to school when I have no idea what I wanna be—waste my time, rack up all this debt? I don't wanna owe fifty grand like Lonnie and still be working at a grocery store."

"You don't have to go to a university, Tran," her mother said in a pleading tone, understanding her daughter's stubbornness in the face of harsh economic reality. "There are community colleges, vocational schools. You don't have to major in business management or sociology. All I'm saying is you have to figure something out, sweetheart. You don't have to limit yourself."

"I'm not limiting myself, Mom. I have a plan," Tranquila asserted, annoyed and frustrated by her restrictive situation. "Okay? I—have—a—plan."

Those four words clung to the dense attic air like cobwebs. Yet, they did nothing to assuage the doubt and worry in her parent's face. It took her mom several seconds to speak again. When she did, her voice conveyed something worse than the argument. Her words wavered with a lack of confidence, "Okay, baby. All I'm saying is, options are a girl's best friend."

After that, she left. Tranquila could hear a sigh, followed by the hastened footsteps of someone who'd rather be closer to the roaring sound of trash transmitting through a radio speaker than have another argument.

Tranquila was pissed. Not because she didn't understand. Why wouldn't her mother be concerned? Her résumé consisted of a basic level of education, two years' worth of employment between multiple jobs that didn't last more than six months, and now a blemish that translated to most companies as 'unreliable' and 'will most likely be fired, so why bother hiring her'. In an economy that didn't guarantee jobs to people with master's degrees, how was Mama Sobriquet supposed to believe that her daughter would succeed? With the highest prison population in the world, America was staunchly against criminals. Against low-level criminals that is—it loved serial killers and high-level corruption. Now, Mama's youngest would be branded one forever, however minor the offense. In Mama's eyes, she had every right to worry. How many mothers saw their brown and black babies imprisoned for non-violent crimes, only to bear witness thereafter to their own lives crumbling before them? Treated as if they were plastic being left to rot forever in a landfill, instead of easily being scooped up and recycled.

Tranquila could validate what her mother felt. It didn't stop her from feeling pissed off. Why couldn't she just believe her when she said she had a plan? At least she *had* a plan. Her older brother Lonnie's 'plan' was to get a state job with a bachelor's in business management while working mid-shifts as an apple stocker. Six years later and fifty thousand dollars in debt, he was sharing an apartment with his girlfriend and her brother, not even enjoying his expensive degree. He wanted to major in Obscure Literature and Theory but didn't want to be 'in debt for a degree that wouldn't get me anywhere'. At least if he studied Dostoevsky's rough drafts of the Gambler or analyze Salman Rushdie's Grocery List for four years, he'd be a lot more okay with being down sixty grand.

Furiously, she ripped the rest of the half-moon with her teeth, aggressively chewing the treat, as if it were the head of one of her enemies. When she was done, the thought of going downstairs and dealing with either of the women in her family was too repulsive. Instead, she flopped back onto her bed and glared at the walls for ten minutes. When that became old, she grudgingly picked up the book her mother gave her and immersed herself in escapist literature.

PARAGONS AND PARAWRONGS

If anybody resented Demeter more than Hades, it was Hera. But Hera's reasons for this resentment were different from her brother's. Hades despised Demeter for the control she held over Persephone, for the way she would narcissistically play with her only child, for constantly pitting the goddess against him during their marriage in a cruel contest of who she loved more. In every instance, it proved to be her mother. But none of that bothered the goddess of marriage and women. What bothered Hera was that Demeter was far too much of a frolicking hippie to be considered a real goddess.

Even now, as Hera found the goddess of wheat after searching endlessly for the flighty deity, what was she doing? Frolicking like a fucking hippie in the same fields of wheat Van Gogh painted while he stared out the window from a mental institution in Saint-Rémy. With a sheaf of wheat in one hand, and a bong in the other, Demeter thoroughly enjoyed yet another day as a goddess until Hera flashed before her in a cloud of red smoke, ruthlessly killing a square-mile of crop and her perfect day of skipping.

Demeter laid eyes on the cruel beauty before her. The Nepenthe she ingested made her braver than if she were sober. "Well hello, Hera," the goddess mustered, clearly inconvenienced. "What a pleasant surprise."

Hera nodded curtly. "Demeter. I'm sorry to interrupt your...skipping, but I need to speak to you. Where is your domain? This is urgent."

Demeter waved both arms, as if in a desire to embrace. Instead, she held out her melanin blessed arms and said, "This is my domain, Hera. Whatever it is you wish to discuss, you can discuss here, in the security of nature."

Internally, Hera growled. Fucking hippie. The goddess of agriculture plopped onto the soil, letting the dust and several bugs bedaub her cosmic garments. Hera didn't sit on the earth. After epochs sitting on top of gold, your ass starts to become discriminatory. Instead, she crouched down, letting the hem of her robes mingle with the dust.

Before Hera could start, she heard the sounds of trapped bubbles rapidly popping and water circulating. The patience she would have pretended to have for Demeter burned away as quickly as scorched grain. Demeter took yet another bong hit.

Feeling her liver boil with rage, every second the goddess took to take the hit, Hera said scathingly, "You know you're the goddess of wheat, not the goddess of weed."

Demeter gulped up the smoke. Teary-eyed and hoarse from an onset of coughing, she replied through a choke: "Lighten up, Hera. The only time pot ever hurt anyone was in Cambodia."

In the many, many years they had known each other, there was never any evidence of Hera having a sense of humor. Hera laid waste to her plan of patience, and in a moment of incense, took the drug paraphernalia from Demeter's hand and sent it clear across the cypress.

Demeter watched the object hurl through the air with dry-eyed grief. When the black dot in the distance fell into an unknown location, she dropped her head as if it were a fallen comrade.

"Her name was April," said Demeter, bereft. To Hera, voice shaking, she asked, "Did you even care to know if she had a name?"

Hera's face convulsed, disgusted and dismayed by such attachment to an earthly possession. "No, Demeter. Because I don't have time to get attached to plastic fashioned out of some armpit of a city in Mexico. And I don't have time for your Dead-Headed ways or genocide jokes either."

Demeter turned her nose at her. "She was made in Thailand, thank you kindly."

Hera seethed, but knew if she revealed any more rashness this trip would be a complete waste. As much as she found Demeter a nugatory deity, for the time being, Hera needed her. Hera altered her tone and spoke with great forbearance, "Deme, I'm sorry. I didn't mean to accuse you of enjoying the Grateful Dead music. I realize now that was low. The point I'm trying to make is that you are so much more than those cult victims. I have known you for many years. I have never seen you so inactive, so…lethargic. All this time—laying in the sun, skipping, hiking, immersing yourself in nature, all this tranquility and peace—wasted. I'm asking you, Demeter, honestly, how can you be happy living like this?"

The goddess's entire countenance of peace and contentment crumbled into abject despair.

"I'm not," she wailed, dry-sobbing. "I'm not happy living like this. I'm miserable, Hera. Absolutely miserable. My entire livelihood has been destroyed. The mortals need me no longer. They don't need to pray anymore to get good harvests. They have factory farms. They have soil pH tester kits. They have Dollar Menus."

At this, the voluptuous beauty—the once-adulated goddess, worshipped and loved more than Zeus himself—threw her hands into the air, cursed the cruelty of time and wept. Hera held her with love-starved arms. Even her touch, the goddess of wheat noted as the Queen's hand brushed against her back, robbed her of equilibrium. She wanted to bear away from her like a shadow but she couldn't escape this hug, this unwanted, antithesis of a hug and instead Demeter listened respectfully, as her visitor related her untoward plans.

When Hera finished making her appeal, Demeter took several minutes of silence to sort out what she just heard.

"What say you, Deme?" Hera prompted.

Demeter cast apprehensive eyes to a stock of wheat that was spared from Hera's fiery entrance by luck of location alone.

"How can this work?" she asked finally, still keeping an eye on the golden crop that was once conceived to be the great gift to mankind, the emblem of her enterprise.

"We would need the help of your daughter, for one."

Demeter's head flicked backwards. "She'd never work with us. She—" She didn't need to finish the sentence. Still, she rerouted it out of fear. "How do you know she'll go for this?"

Hera rolled her eyes. "Because I'm a paragon not a para-wrong, Deme."

*

It was 4:50 the following morning back on Earth. Grandma Sobriquet came through the front door, already bitching.

"The front door's wide open," she hollered. "It's mid-November and it's ten degrees out but the front door's still open."

No one responded to her outrage, though she hadn't expected anyone to respond; she didn't complain for an audience, she just liked to complain. Satisfied, Grandma Sobriquet hobbled on pigeon-toes towards the coveted armchair fitted with her own ass imprint, perfectly aligned with the television. The fabric throne, however, was usurped by her granddaughter. Grandma Sobriquet would have verbally abused her, if she hadn't recognized the tightness in her stare and the way her arms folded across her chest.

"What's your problem?"

Tranquila shot the old woman a hot glare, stood from the chair, and towering the shrunken creature by half a foot, looked her in the eye demanding, "You sent me down to the Underworld—miles and miles away from anybody else—*knowing* I would be working with a rapist."

The sharp tongue lay paralyzed in Grandma Sobriquet's dry mouth.

Tranquila picked up the book that her mother gave her yesterday. She didn't even have to flip through the pages; she had ruined four pages folding them in half for this occasion. The page opened to a fresh chapter, one that read—in big black letters—four terrifying words: **THE RAPE OF PERSEPHONE.**

But her grandmother was not phased. Instead, she took the book from Tranquila's hands, lowered it in order to see, then read for a second. Silently, she flipped through the pages, glossing over the words. She skipped to the back of the book where the book jacket revealed a brief description of the author.

"University of Munich?" she read with a scoff. "That farmer from Tomis knew his shit better."

Tranquila, enraged by this indifference, stepped closer until she was inches from the woman's saggy body. "Do you even have a soul anymore?" she snarled.

Grandma Sobriquet pinched her nose into a smug grin that she knew would piss off her granddaughter. "Souls take up too much space. Less room for food."

Tranquila's insides felt like they were freezer-burnt. She always disliked the mother of her mother but never before had such loathing filtered in. Now, in the dark of the early November morning, Tranquila could honestly say she hated this vile person.

"You have a garbage bag for a soul," she stated as fact. Tranquila turned away, determined to disown her and march back into her bedroom but Grandma Sobriquet's voice caught her mid-step with words imposed in cold fury: "Well you're a big bag of turtle dicks if you believe a book over what you have seen."

Tranquila whipped around to unleash her own barrage of insults but her grandmother wasn't finished, "No god is more compassionate and more just than Hades." Though she was passionate, her words were weighted with authority, not affection. "He didn't kidnap her. He didn't trick her. He didn't r—force himself upon her in any way."

She spoke with conviction. Something unexplainable— something persistent yet crazy—made Tranquila believe her, just as she had when Grandma Sobriquet said she could open the pathway to the Underworld from an anthill in their backyard. Still, she didn't understand. "But the book—"

"Tran. Do you know who Persephone is?"

She hesitated, thinking back to the author's introduction of the gods. "She's a goddess. Of fertility."

Grandma Sobriquet nodded once. "She's a goddess. She's also the only daughter of Spring and one of many daughters of Zeus. Such a woman of noble birth would never let herself be taken advantage of like that."

The trickle of rapport between them dissolved as Tranquila's face contorted, appalled. "That's the most sexist thing I've ever heard," she fired back. "Women don't allow themselves to be raped."

"Tran, I know *mortal* women don't let themselves get violated," Grandma Sobriquet said, edgy with impatience. "But when you're a goddess and you have the cosmic power to turn a man's Dick into an inside-out cactus just by looking at it, then you tend to fend off unwanted advances pretty easily."

Tranquila was humbled by the light of this new information. "Oh," she said. "Well...I'm...Then why does everyone say that's what happened? I looked it up. Everyone from Homer to greekmythology.com says Hades snatched Persephone and made her his queen."

Grandma Sobriquet growled, clearly wanting to berate such ignorance. Remaining surprisingly disciplined long enough to stress, "Tran. These. Are. Fables. These aren't meant to be taken literally. The 'Rape of Persephone' is supposed to be a metaphor for how shitty the arrival of winter is. That and—if you really wanna get metaphorical—it's the reason we put flowers on people's tombstones."

"Yeah, but everyone—"

"Everyone hates death, Tran," Grandma Sobriquet cut her off, needing to get her point across. "Everyone has and always will hate death. Ergo, they're going to hate Hades. Ever notice how your employer is the bad guy in every story he's ever mentioned in? It's because, despite all the rapes, all the murders, all the wars and plagues and evil that the other gods have caused, nothing will scare a mortal man more than the prospect of the lord of the dead. And since Hades takes his job seriously and doesn't budge when it comes to mortality, he will forever be seen as the villain. Zeus, changes his mind on a whim, who can be swayed into having favorites, who slacks and lets things slide, will always be seen as the good god.

"It's the reason why, when the mortals found out the god of dead had a wife, they were convinced the terrible god had to do something terrible to get her. But when his brother turns into a bird to fuck women, people just laugh it off as folklore."

Her speech proselytized Tranquila. She stood before her grandmother, humbled and apologetic. "Oh, wow," she uttered. "Grandma, I—"

Thankfully, her grandmother hated apologies. "Go to work. If there's anything Hades hates, it's a no-call-no-show."

Tranquila nodded agreeably and headed to the kitchen. Before she passed the threshold, she turned back and asked, "How long have you known him, Grandma?"

Grandma Sobriquet, who had already taken comfort in her designated chair, scrunched her face at Tranquila. "Don't be slick, Tran. I'll tell you when I'll tell you; not a minute before or after. Now go to work."

As she started to leave, Grandma Sobriquet called her again: "Oh, Tran? One more thing. You ever call me a dildo again and I'll bash in your nose and use your face for an ashtray."

Tranquila cocked an eyebrow. "You don't smoke."

A devious smile slid its way across the ridges of the old woman's face. "How would you know?"

*

Tranquila would have been forty minutes late to work on Earth, but when she tried calculating how late that would be in Hades, all she could determine was that it probably involved some kind of metric conversion they hadn't bothered to teach back home. Thus, when she dug the pit and sacrificed the gas-station wine, she prayed to Zeus, Hera *and* Apollo, hoping at least one was the god of small favors.

"Please don't let me be late." She took a brave step into the Underworld and hoped to whomever that there wasn't a plain of pain for the late.

Working in the Underworld for close to three months might have taught Tranquila discernible skills, made her more worldly and even broadened her vocabulary. In contrast, it had totally destroyed her faith in her math and science capabilities. Which was the reason why no matter how she stood or what time she stood on the consecrated hill, she could never figure out how to direct her landing. However, it didn't shock her at all today to find that she had landed directly in the chair before Hades.

"You're late."

Tranquila cringed. "Yeah, I know. I'm sorry. I…" *Was busy calling you a rapist? Na, he probably wouldn't find that funny right now. I'll tell him later.*

Hades didn't notice her trailing sentence. "You realize you are sixty-four hours tardy, right?"

"What? No I'm not. I'm forty minutes late."

"Well, in this realm you are sixty-four hours tardy" Hades repeated. "Tranquila, you must be conscientious of our differences in time zones. I know Earth is slow but when I offered you this job on the premise that you were on house arrest, I assumed I would never have to lecture you on timeliness and responsibility."

Tranquila bowed her head in the same way a dog does when they are shamed for eating out of the trash again. "Sorry, Hades."

"That's alright. Normally its standard practice for an employee this late to be given a step one, but I realize you cannot help the rate of rotation of your planet, so I'm just going to give you a coaching memo."

She was taken aback by how managerially he spoke in that moment. "Step one?"

"Like the strike ones you get in that boring game you Americans seem to enjoy. Lacrosse, I guess?" (Tranquila opened her mouth to correct him but Hades cared so little he cut her off) "Whatever it's called, you get three steps until your position is terminated. But you're not getting a strike, so don't worry."

She wasn't going to worry, even if she did get a step one. Still she made a point to look like she was relieved. Inwardly, she was more touched than anything. Eons ago, there was a time and place in her life when a superior would throw green beans in her face if she forgot to season them, but here the dreaded god of dead barely raised his voice at her. He merely acknowledged and explained to his employee how she had messed up, without degrading or humiliating her in the process. It was so simple and humane, it was almost revolutionary.

"Thanks, Hades."

The god gave her a small smile to assure her of his lack of anger. He rose from his desk with a pair of hedge clippers in his hand and said, "Alright. Let's go do your coaching memo."

*

Hades took them to the entrance of the Underworld where the souls must first pass by Cerberus. From there, in a small patch of sun-deprived soil, grew a shadowy elm with two sets of trunks and a neglected frenzy of branches and leaves.

"A couple of years back, the roots from the Tree of Truth became inosculated with the Tree of False Dreams. It's becoming an eyesore. Your coaching memo is going to involve pruning the leaves of truth from the leaves of verisimilitude," Hades explained as he handed her the pair of clippers.

Thanks to the Underworld, she had become better at assessing sentences out of context. She mentally paraphrased the last word as, 'shit that seems true'. What boggled her was how she was supposed to figure true from false with her fallible judgment.

"What if I can't tell which is which?"

"I thought you were from New York City?" Hades said. "Don't you all have built-in bullshit detectors?"

"Hades, I'm from *Central* New York. CNY not NYC."

Pause. "Ah, crap. Well what do you guys have going for you?"

"Refugees and chicken riggies." When the look of dismay didn't leave Hades' face, she added, "For a while we were the first city to have a bath salts epidemic."

Hades sighed. "Just do your best."

He turned to leave when Tranquila called after him with another question, "What happens if I cut off some leaves that turn out to be true?"

"Nothing," replied Hades, starting to walk away. "I just don't like how much of an eyesore that tree has become. Plus, it is super annoying when all dead people start hanging around the Tree and think they know everything."

When he was gone, Tranquila approached the Gemini tree. As she worked her way closer, she started to hear things. The longer she listened, the more pronounced the sounds became. She knew that she was hearing voices yet again.

"Oh great," she grumbled. "This tree is trying to defend itself with psychological bullshit. Well I'm not losing to a fucking tree. Not this time."

She gripped the handles of the clippers, pulled apart their giant teeth and stepped towards the tree, ready to show it who was in charge. That's when she heard the voices again, realizing they weren't the same insidious babbles she'd heard when the Gates dispelled her.

"In 2019, Nike will launch a new kind of sandal with wheels in an attempt to appeal to the busy beach bum on the go. It will fail."

Tranquila stepped back involuntarily. The voices stopped. Stepping forward, she heard the same message again. She did this twice more before she understood that she could only hear the leaves speak if she stood on their soil. With *both* feet on the soil, she saw that not only could the leaves speak, they shook as they did so. Searching carefully, she found the speaking Nike leaf just to her left. She used the clippers on it and it dropped it to the ground, silent and dead.

Its loss it seemed, though, signaled for more to speak, and within seconds Tranquila was taking life's only real-world true-false test:

"Planet Earth will enter a worldwide era of peace by 3013 AD, after which they will focus all their military exploits against Earth's evil twin, Kepler-186 f."

"That's too stupid not to be true," she determined, snipping away at a branch.

"In France, a person can legally marry a corpse."

Tranquila shuddered. "That's too gross not to be true."

"One day, restaurants will be able to serve Pepsi and Coke products in harmony."

"Yeah, right," she scoffed, leaving the leaf alone.

"Businessman and reality TV star Donald Trump will be kicked to death by donkeys after attempting to engage the animal in bestiality."

This one made Tranquila cry out, as if in pain, as she waffled on whether or not to cut the leaf off. Ultimately she was forced to snip the specious leaf. "Ohh! No wonder they call you a false dream."

Tranquila continued on with her adventures in horticulture until, after many fallacies and interesting facts, Hades came back to see how she was doing.

"I think I'm done," she replied, stepping away from the tree to get a better look at it.

Hades scanned it over and pointed to the far right. "Get that last one and you're done."

She complied and stepped onto the soil again. She could see how she'd missed this one; it had such a quiet little whimper that Tranquila had to look around in order to determine where it was coming from. When she found it, she saw it wasn't even a leaf yet, just a pale green bud full of promise and want. Tranquila ducked underneath a cluster of branches just to reach it. When she came closer, she could finally hear the bud's whispers, "*Tranquila Obiit of Utica, New York, will one day be her own boss and be considered a success amongst her peers.*"

Instantly Tranquila felt her face flush and her nose sting, warning her she was about to cry. She withheld the tears, out of fear of further humiliation. She settled herself just long enough to emerge from the tree and stand beside her boss without looking affected.

To his enquiring expression, she said, "It was just a false dream."

THE TRAGEDY THAT BEGETS JEALOUSY

Sunbathing in a remote emerald field, unsullied as of yet by the Iron Race, lay Persephone. She was reunited with the blades of grass, wild flowers and a loving sun, feeling spoiled that she could enjoy this all the long years, instead of only 6 months of the year. With her hands behind her head, allowing the sun to kiss her bare arms, her toes tucked into the dirt. Her dress hem fell, so that a comfortable breeze caressed her thighs. Persephone was truly happy.

Persephone's happiness was cut short by the terrible sound of the earth being thrown apart. The fields trembled and roared, as if struck by an inverted avalanche, sending Persephone from her back onto her feet. Panic induced her to act instead of freeze. She was already breezing past several large cracks when she felt her body being yanked to a halt.

"Whoa, whoa! Slow down, Persephone." A female voice came from behind, sounding amused, as Persephone began to skid backwards involuntarily. Accepting that she was being reeled in like a fish, she let her body go limp and succumbed to being pulled backwards. When the movement stopped, she didn't need to look behind her. There was only one goddess she knew of that treated her equals with such dishonor. When Persephone tossed her head back to confirm her suspicions, she saw, adding even more insult to injury, that her kind but malleable mother had followed her.

Demeter ran up to comfort and smother her dead-eyed daughter with skunk-smelling kisses. "Oh! Smooch. My baby. Smooch, smooch." She turned to Hera, cradling Persephone's head in-between her elbow and armpit like a basketball. She explained, "My sweet, sweet Kore. She's got that Tee-Pee disease."

"Deme," Hera said, though her eyes lingered on Persephone, who was struggling to be released from her mother's concerned headlock. "It's *PT*SD."

"Yeah," Persephone confirmed, as she yanked herself free from her mother's grip. Standing up, trying to maintain dignity, she added, "And I don't have it, Mom."

"Oh, baby, that's just the Stockholder Syndrome talking," Demeter cooed.

Persephone opened her mouth to correct her but found it moot. Instead, she saw the cat-grin lying dormant on Hera's beautiful lips and frowned. Speaking to Demeter, but with eyes laid squarely on Hera she asked, "What are you two doing here, together?"

Hearing the suspicion provoked the cat-grin. "Oh, Persephone," Hera crooned, "it's been so long…"

"Not for me," Persephone hissed.

"Oh, Kore, don't talk like that," Demeter gently scolded.

"Yes, Kore, don't talk like that," Hera mimicked, half-mocking, half-warning.

No one spoke for a moment. Persephone seethed with unconcealed loathing at Demeter's condescending fawn and at Hera, whom she simply hated. The intensity was enough to make an oak succumb into a weeping willow.

Hera turned to Demeter. In a voice that was more commanding than asking, "Deme, will you give Kore and me a moment in private?"

As if the goddess of wheat had the autonomy to deny such a request. Bowing her eye, while casting a fearful glance to her daughter, Demeter transformed herself into a pile of leaves and allowed the summer wind to carry her away.

Alone, Persephone, the darkest of all goddesses who possessed skin the color of peat, grew black with rage. Lunging at Hera like a viper, she stopped mere inches from the Queen's face. She took one last, long look before pulling back and hocking a juicy stream of spit into the woman's left eye.

Sure, it was unrefined, life-threateningly reckless and beneath Persephone's status as a former queen herself; it was the fattest, wettest, most perfectly precise loogy ever spat. Persephone was proud to have begot that wad of spit directly into that bitch's face.

Hera, with a level of sangfroid that was borderline schizoid, raised an elegant hand to her insulted eye. She wiped the liquid free and flicked the excess onto the ground, all while looking at Persephone. She waited. As the substance hit the ground, it sizzled on impact, shooting sparks onto the dry grass, until soon small flames grew. Within seconds, all the vegetation in the area was on fire, with the exception of a small circle within which the two goddesses stood.

Still, Hera waited. The look of horror paled Persephone's recusant face. Hera saw those two beautiful, black lips part into a horrified oval and let out an unsettling scream at her beloved field, engulfed in wildfire. Only then did Hera bellow above the inferno, "What's the matter, Persephone? Not used to fire anymore?"

Persephone watched as the greenness crisped up and burned. She began to sob when Hera grabbed the hem of her dress to create galling winds with one swoop. In those winds, the flames were reified into skyscrapers of dizzying heights, entrapping them both inside a manufactured hell.

Hera dropped the hem of her dress and raised a hand to touch Persephone's wet cheeks. The feline smile returned. Using a thumb to caress her jawline, she spoke evenly, "Listen well. Your untamed rage means nothing to me. But you mustn't hold a woman, not even one with a face as hated as mine, as the cause of your rage. All your woes didn't begin with women—it was begot from men. From your father to your husband, to all your male relatives who think they reside over you—it is they who beset you. They beset you, they beset me and they beset all women they deem too strong, too forceful. But now I come to you pledging an armistice. Help me, Persephone. Help me and help your mother to prove yourself the goddess Hades never presumed you to be."

Tears flowed from Persephone's Black-eyed-Susan eyes throughout Hera's speech. With a dry, almost sick voice, she inquired, "What are you asking of me, O Queen?"

Hera stared at her until the tears transformed into steam, disappearing into the carbonized atmosphere. Hera let go of Persephone in order to use her hands to make one loud demanding clap. In an instant, the fire was gone, though the land remained barren and bleak.

"I want to take Hades."

"Take him," Persephone scoffed without thought.

"No, not him. *It*. I want to take his house of death."

"Why?" Persephone inquired, rudely. "Have you *been* to Hades? That place sucks. It's always crowded, you get Vitamin D deficiency from lack of sun, the harpies shit *everywhere*, and the Vale of Mourning losers literally—never—stop—complaining— ugh! Why would you *want* to live in Hades?"

"I don't want to live there. I want to *rule* there," Hera
implored. "And with me, Persephone, you can rule there too.
We'll take back what should have been our spoils from the Titan
War."

"Well, *you* can have it," Persephone replied. "I've ruled
Hell and it's not as fun as it sounds."

"No, Persephone, you didn't rule Hades. Hades ruled
Hades," Hera corrected. "Hades had all the power. Hades had all
the final says. Hades took all the glory and commanded all the
respect while you did half the work with none of the ceremonial
sacrifices."

"Hey! I did rule Hades. I was just as feared as my
husband—FUCK! Ex-husband. Ex."

"Hm. That's why his name was never uttered and the
poets were quick to call you Dreaded Persephone."

Persephone was bitten by a bitterness that Hera found
succulent—a joy not just reserved for the deathless. Mortal
women were just as guilty in making the easy call to their fellow
sex, to despise and analyze the depths of wrongs done by men.

"I'm not going to lie to you, Persephone, Olympus
sucks. It sucks worse than Hades. At least in the Underworld you
have work to do, tasks to complete, mortals to kick around.
There's purpose in Hades. And I'd rather spend the rest of
forever toiling in Hell than spend another pointless afternoon in
Paradise. So, Persephone—proud, dreadful, rightful ruler of
Hades—what say you?"

Hera's demagogy was riveting. Even to someone who
was adamantly hell-bent on getting out of Hell, as she once was.
But Persephone wasn't as controlling as one would believe an
ex-queen to be. She shook her head.

"I'm sorry, Hera. But I have no desire to spend the rest
of forever in Hades. Even if you get rid of him, it would still be a
palace full of painful memories to me," Persephone said. "I'm

sorry." She turned her back on Hera and began kneeling to tend the smote earth, hoping to repair the damage her recklessness had done. Hera watched the despaired goddess whimper as she held a burnt flower in her hand.

"Did I mention…he has a mortal down there?" Hera added. She smiled at the stillness in Persephone's body and continued: "Rumor has it, he's prepping her to be his new queen."

Persephone was very quiet for a short time.

"A…mortal?"

Hera's sharp eyes gleamed at the effect this had on Persephone's tender voice; sweet milk that spoiled upon uttering a hated noun. A mortal? A mortal was going to usurp her old title? A mortal?! The very notion was beyond insult. The best way to compare how she felt in that moment would be if a professor with three doctorates and a Mensa fellowship retired from his post and the university he worked at decided to fill the position with the first Johnny-Heroin fiend with a GED they could find.

Jealousy and rage trivialized the way Persephone felt in that second. Such passions enveloped the goddess. It was easier, now, to turn towards Hera—the deathless bitch queen who Persephone chanced everything just to spit at—and look her in the very eye she sullied and recant all previous objections.

"Fuck that," Persephone hissed, her voice sick with vengeance. "What's your plan?"

ENNUI'S NOT FOR ME

There was only one entity that could outdo Hera's pettiness and arbitration: The American justice system. But Tranquila didn't understand that. All she knew was that her probation officer was a dick, and after today, that wouldn't matter. Because whether Mr. Dicklager liked it or not, she had done her time, paid the price and she would be given her freedom back.

Weeks before today arrived, she came home from work, tossed aside the shirt and pants destroyed by the inevitable messes of working with monsters, abstracts, corpses and Chaos. She went to her closet and threw on three articles of clothing that were separate and superior to the rest. One was a modest, earth-toned skirt with Aztec patterns at the hem that draped at her calves; the other a white, fitted, scoop-neck shirt with quarter-length sleeves which tucked into the skirt without revealing unflattering bulges nor producing wrinkles; and finally a black, smart-looking blazer that every magazine deemed a must-have for a professional image.

She looked like a waitress at an indie café that served gluten-free Mexican entrees and blasted death metal on the speakers. But she didn't care. This was going to be The Last Outfit. She wore this outfit to every interview she ever went to. It was her good luck outfit. If she ever were trialed and sentenced to death, and she had the option to pick what she was going to wear to the chair or needle or guillotine, wherever, she would pick these exact clothes. Paradoxically, she felt this outfit was the last chance she had for freedom. Because today was going to go one of two ways for Tranquila: either she was going to get off house arrest today and be free once again or she was going to flee the human realm all together and live full time in the Underworld. She was five-thousand percent sure that if it came down to it, it would be because she ended up killing her probation officer.

Finally, this day had come. After a night of dreamless sleep, she woke, showered, washed her hair, spent twenty minutes drying it and putting on her makeup. All whilst listening to a playlist she had made especially for this occasion, entitled *Freedom/ Runaway Forever Music*, which contained a collection of the most violent, energizing music from the world of rap, heavy metal and steampunk-magical-realism-electronica.

After ignoring her mother's screams to 'turn down that screaming shit' a couple of times, she finally heard the call, "Ten minutes, Tranquila!"

She inspected herself for the last time before running downstairs with a pair of plain, black flats in her hand. At last, with her mother waiting at the door to take her; they left for the county office building.

*

Ten o'clock, on the dot, Tranquila entered through the office doors. She was met by a state worker, who had occupied a desk without refute for the last couple decades. His name was Richard. G. Dicklager. Tranquila would forever remember their first day together—an indistinguishable rage burned in her memory, after he introduced himself by saying: "You know, it's a small world. I think I was your father's parole officer at one time." He went on to ask with false concern questions about her mother and how she 'dealt with this generational refractory'. A middle-aged white man whose power went back generations. His clients ranged from young to old, were mostly black, and while the offenses may have differed in the eyes of the law, not in his opinion. They were all in 'for drugs' even if the records detailed otherwise. He had no interest in helping them, even though his job title demanded otherwise.

"So, Miss Obiit, it's almost time for that little charm tracker to get cut off," Mr. Dicklager said, after a quick skim through her file. He flashed her a big Kool-Aid Man smile, the file still in his big, furtive hands. "You must be excited."

Of course she was, but she knew better than to be honest with criminal justice people. In her best Caucasian English, she said, "Yes. Yes I am."

"Good," he crooned. He lay the documents flat and laced his fingers together. "But the date's still tentative. That is, it's still up in the air. The Board and I have to make sure you won't fall back into recidivistic ways."

What recidivism? her thoughts shouted. *This was my first offense!* But she knew damn well in *his* eyes it wasn't—he saw a punk junkie who managed to cheat the bimonthly drug screenings. Someone who the State wanted to play keep-away with her rights but lacked any evidence to do so, yet.

Tranquila had to hold back the glares and the curse words that demanded to break free. In a professional tone she said, "Cool....Cool. I can't wait to prove to you guys that I've learned my lesson. I hope once this is all done I will never see you again." Tranquila said with a laugh, thinking to herself *until you die, Dick Dicklager. Then your saggy ass is mine!*

Mr. Dicklager chuckled once at her little joke. "I hope so too, Miss Obiit, I hope so too. Now, what are your plans for when you are off probation? Because that's what today is about,

Miss Obiit. Setting goals. Making objectives. Getting you back on the right track."

Tranquila opened her mouth, ready to tell him she wanted a job in management. She even prepared to list all the qualities she knew she possessed, that would make her valuable to an employer. But Mr. Dicklager already ignored her. His attention swerved to his computer screen.

"Now, given your criminal record and your level of education, I would suggest you start putting out applications to as many fast-food places as you can. Of course," he looked over her head and spoke to her hairline, "there might be some drawbacks in regards to your...fashion statement." She tried speaking again but was cut off. "Maybe try some of those new *hipster* cafes. I see most of them do not object to unusual hairstyles. Or, if you are not interested in the food industry, maybe servicing. I see here a lot of hotels are looking for cleaning maids."

She could feel her cheeks burning while he spoke. She was already thinking of how she would approach this to her boss: 'Heeeyyy, Hades! How's it going, Ay-Dees?' 'Oh, you know it's going, it's going...' 'Cool! So, I was just wondering...What's your stance on pushing a guy's time of death forward a little?'

Her murderous thoughts were interrupted by a fake gasp of joy that's made when people have some smug news to divulge. "Oh, look!" Mr. Dicklager cried with mock enthusiasm, before giving her a barely concealed smile of triumph. "There's a hotel in Methtown that needs a cleaning lady!"

*

Tranquila left with an armful of printed applications and a white, sun-deprived band just above her ankle. Her mother, patient and wise, didn't start a conversation until they reached the safety of her silver Honda. Once the doors were closed, she reached over and gave her daughter a huge shoulder hug.

"I'm so happy for you, Tranquila," she said into her hair, before administering a dry kiss to the forehead. Once she was in drive, she went on to talk about how they would celebrate with chicken fried steak and French fries tonight, after she came back from a manager's meeting—a well-known favorite of Tranquila's.

Tranquila wanted to be happy and jump into conversation with her mother, but she was too preoccupied with fury to recognize she possessed more freedom and power in that moment than that civil servant ever could.

Mama Sobriquet kept glancing sideways at her passenger, watching and waiting. She saw a rage lying in wait in the young woman's face, like magma melting rocks to move up further into the Earth's crust, ready to volcanically fuck-up any living creature that got in its way. It made her smile. Her daughter was so readable. Tranquila didn't possess the clichéd female knack for 'knowing how to fake it'. Tranquila couldn't push away emotions, pretend things were okay when they weren't, even if she wanted to.

Mama Sobriquet started chuckling. "Oh, baby," she said, using one hand to squeeze the fat on Tranquila's thigh. "It's a beautiful day. The temperature is above the negatives again. You just got your freedom back." She gave her thigh a firm pat. "Don't waste your time dumpster-diving for recyclables."

Tranquila frowned. Not because she was annoyed at her mother, nor in confusion about her mother's odd diction. She just knew, no matter what her mom said, no matter how many times she proclaimed her pride, she couldn't be happy until she was back in the Underworld earning some gold and proving to herself that she wasn't a crazy, lazy, dumb fuckup the way that people saw her.

*

After swinging by Burger King for two celebratory MilkshakeBurgers™ with cheese, Mama Sobriquet dropped Tranquila back home before returning to work.

As the squealing sounds of a car with brake problems faded away, Grandma Sobriquet said to Tranquila, "Look at you. Free as a Canadian. You must be excited."

"Yeah....I'm going to Hades. Peace!"

"You're going to work?" Grandma Sobriquet's voice called after her in surprise.

"What else am I going to do?" Tranquila shrugged. "It's fucking twenty degrees out. Might as well go to the Underworld and work next to the River of Fire for a couple hours."

She shook her head. "You got that workaholic gene. Your mother got that bad when she was your age. Always had to make that money."

The broad generalization offended Tranquila. "No, Mom was always at work because she didn't want to be around you."

"Well, good," Grandma Sobriquet replied. "If that's what motivated her from being lazy, then I'm glad."

Tranquila balked, somehow shocked. "You don't even care!"

"Hey, I wasn't supposed to be her friend."

"Yeah, but you were so hard on her that she ended up having shitty self-esteem and stayed with Dad for fifteen years."

"Yeah but eventually she smartened up, got her bachelor's and now you guys got a nice house in the nice part of West Side," she argued, so smug that she was speaking to the TV instead of her granddaughter. "It all ended up working out. Look,

I'll admit I made mistakes. I always punished her, even if she didn't deserve it. But you can't argue with results. Face it, Tran. Sometimes a parent's gotta bully their kid to greatness."

Tranquila shook her head. She could have argued all day on her mother's behalf, but ultimately she knew it would be pointless. "I'm going to work."

She left. Quickly, the house became desolate, leaving Jeanette to the familiar loneliness that sagged against her face, zapping away the haughtiness. All she could do was drown herself in the garbage-infested waters of publicized DNA testing until her granddaughter and daughter returned from work.

*

Grandma Sobriquet couldn't enjoy her morning shows. She had a fit of fidgeting that made it impossible to zone out. Shifting weight, crossing legs, even adjusting the seat brought her no comfort. She couldn't fathom the reason. It could have been the bed sores on her ass, that she chose to ignore. For a brief, frightening moment, she worried she had suddenly become cultured and was unable to watch such trash any longer. Thankfully, TV sensed her doubt and the commercial ended. The midday woman-talk/cooking-show came on. Her faith in garbage was restored. Still, Grandma Sobriquet was perplexed. What could the body be aware of that the mind wasn't?

"Ladies!" the host, a woman with the voice of a hyperactive howler monkey, sing-song-shouted at her audience. "It's eleven a.m. and you know what that means!" In unison, all the women in the studio sing-song-chanted: "*W(H)INE TIME!*"

While lady-host-chef went on to glamorize day-drinking and irresponsibly promote pseudo-psychotherapy babble, a flash went off in Grandma Sobriquet's head. Cooking with Maggie May doesn't come on until eleven. Tranquila is never gone when

Cooking with Maggie May is on. She usually comes back just before Long Topical Dialogues ends. Grandma looked at the clock then did the math. Tranquila had been gone for a solid eight minutes.

At first, she discounted the thoughts that told her to worry and ended up watching some of the show without fidgeting. But then a few more moments passed before she dropped her head, looked down at her plump, worn self and let out a heavy sigh. "This *fucking* kid…" she said to herself. She gripped the arms of her chair hard and used three scoots to push herself up and onto her pigeon-toed feet.

She went down a litany of curse words as she made her way to the kitchen "Turd burglar, bum tag pizzle". Even while she opened the cabinets to retrieve the honey and cups "Sister-brother-motherfucker, Type 2 ass fucker". The ferocity of the obscenities increased dramatically as she shuffled unevenly through the snow and ice-laden backyard "Ass scurvy, whale cunt, shit sucker, Clytemnestra." She shoveled through the frozen tundra with gnarled hands. She only stopped after she performed the consecrated song and gave libations to the ceremonial mound. Then as the earth gulped open to allow her in, she tossed the contents to the ground in anger and took one step into the plunge, grunting one last expletive into the whipping winds, "This *fucking* kid."

Unlike her kin, she hurtled into the secret compartment of the Earth with the same indifference of a person riding in an elevator. Dropping into the Underworld like a meteor, she emerged from the smoking collision with athletic ease, as if she were stepping off of a porch step. She did not land on the outer banks of River Acheron, where the dead were brought, nor on the pillar where Tranquila first entered, but on an isthmus rendered in the middle of the Styx.

She waited patiently amidst rolling flame waves and wailing currents, unperturbed. Not even the smoky, penetrating voice that rang out from above made her flinch.

"Well, well, well." There, Hades, the blackened King of Dead, wearing garments threaded by the souls that displeased him most. As he walked, the wretched shifted in pain and created mouths that hollowed for help but no sound came out of them. He met her on the tiny divider betwixt flame and pain. He greeted her with a smile. "Jeanette. Back from retirement."

Flashing two sets of old, yellowed teeth, Grandma Sobriquet looked pleased for once. "You wish."

Her response made him bear his teeth wider. "Indeed I do, *Jeanette*," he laughed as he said her name. "To what do I owe the pleasure? Undoubtedly, you miss this helm."

Grandma Sobriquet glanced over to watch a screaming, condemned man drown in a vat of wasps. She sighed wistfully, "Not going to lie. Watching people deplete their dignity and brain cells for fifteen seconds of daytime TV fame doesn't exactly satisfy. Still, I'm afraid you're going to have to continue on without me, Hades."

Hades clucked his tongue. "Too bad. You're missing out. We just invented a Piranha-Castrating-Machine that I know you would have been proud of."

Grandma Sobriquet's face softened. "How's my granddaughter doing, Hades?"

"Good."

"Just good?"

"Amazing," he admitted, his smoky voice tender with sincerity. "Really, she's got your work ethic. At first, I was wary of taking on a kid who wanted to work here but, man, did I luck out. If I wasn't so against cloning, I'd make three of her."

The sad smile that she gave him was completely gone by the end of his statement.

"I can tell you value her," she said, her voice no longer hard with its usual snippiness. Loaded with gravity she added, "It must be hard down here, with Persephone gone." Hades went quiet. She went on with more caution: "All this helm to control, harpies to supervise, and skeletal-boaters' insurance to pay…and no one to help you."

The gaiety in his face vanished, replaced by budding consternation; the connection they had shared disappearing, just like the man in the wasps.

"Hades," the old creature said, shaking her head. "Do you *want* to punish yourself for the divorce even further by replacing Persephone with a mortal? That's asking for an ass-kicking."

Hades scoffed. "Jeez, all those years of watching trash has really melted your brain," he laughed, gauging her response. But her eyes, squinty from bags and wrinkles, narrowed further into suspicious slits. "Jeanette."

"Do not try to placate me with that stupid name," she hissed, her voice screeching like a bat going through cardiac arrest.

Hades, Lord of the Dead, flinched at the little old woman. "Jesus, Jea—" he stopped himself. Catching his breath, he reasoned, "I am almost a trillion years old. I'm nearly as old as time itself. Tranquila, she's…she's what? Eighteen? That'd be like flirting with a fetus."

"Just because *you* know that, doesn't mean shit to me," Grandma Sobriquet retorted. She sighed, realizing how bitchy she sounded, and relented, "Look, Hades. I didn't come down here to lecture you and to give you the old 'stay away from my grandbaby' gig. I get it, Hades. I know you. I know how lonely it gets down here. It's hard. And, Tranquila…she's…she's a hard worker; she's generous and sometimes she's cool to be around. Why wouldn't you want her down here? But—we both know how jealous the goddesses get. They smite and they rue over the pettiest shit..." She shuffled half a step forward and took her wrinkled, withered hands into his shiny black ones. "That's why—I'm asking you, as an old coworker, *as a friend,* please...don't let her get killed."

Hades hadn't looked her in the eye throughout the duration of her plea, but when she took his hands, he raised his head to watch her white, delicate fingers rub his calluses. How long had it been since a woman held his hands? Or anyone...

Shaking himself from his selfish thoughts, he touched the back of her hand, looked into her eyes and with a weak smile, "What made you worry?"

She glared at him. "Piss off, I wasn't worried. I just happened to notice that the house was a lot more enjoyable and that's when I realized that she had been gone for longer than usual."

Hades' smile grew. "Aww. I didn't figure you a doter." When she glared at him, he added quickly, "Ease, Grandmother, ease. The Winter Rush came a little early this year and the Underworld is teeming with stiffs. I needed help and Tranquila wanted the overtime. I assure you, she is not being held here against her will."

The answer was plausible but it didn't comfort the old woman and her countenance reflected as much. *"Promise me,"* she said in a tone that didn't suit her at all; a tone one octave lower than normal. She was serious, but more than that, she was beseeching him, pleading even. It shocked Hades to hear and see her so anguished. He remembered her as someone who always threatened. But, now, she was begging. *"Promise me, Hades."*

She held out her hand. Without hesitating, he took it. "I promise."

In that instant, the flames of the River Styx began to curdle and hiss. Within moments, a giant wave of bones, blood and pain beat against the cave walls with a fantastic wail; the souls that clothed him cried out in a deafening crescendo. The River Styx heard the god's words and sanctified their troth.

Grandma Sobriquet was so grateful she reached for Hades' face and kissed him gently on the lips.

DEADASS STOP JAMES WOODING AROUND

When Hera kicked out Dionysus, Olympus briefly enjoyed being the heavenly home of temperance, grace and quiet splendor. Then Zeus came back.

Upon seeing his domain, the great god wept at its lameness. For a little while, he feared the lameness was so strong that it was like a stain that sat too long, becoming impervious to handmaid tricks. When he searched for his friend, whose magical booze could change a library into a rave, he found Dionysus chained against his will in an unspeakable prison.

Zeus had to fight hard to regain his friend's freedom. At first, it seemed tragedy had struck twice against the Olympians. But Zeus, formidable god of all, finally did it. He struck down against the prison and broke the oenophile out of rehab. Thus, his kingdom was safe from sucking, and soon—following the scariest fourteen minutes of Zeus's eternal life—crapulous was back in Olympus.

While Zeus flipped between orgies like Grandma Sobriquet switched between channels during commercials, Hermes came into Olympus with a different desire. Scouting through the pell-mell of limbs, butts, vaginas and satyrs, somehow he was able to locate his king, and approached him without prudency.

"Hey Zeus, have you seen the Queen?" enquired Hermes, looking completely out of place. He stood with a manila folder under his arm, amidst such utter decadence and incest as would have made Caligula blush.

"Hey baby, we related?" Zeus asked, shamelessly.

If Hermes could, he would have rolled his eyes at him. Unfortunately, he just had to deal with his own dad, the so-called superior Olympian, copulating with three of his aunts.

Hermes held out the manila folder and asked again, "Do you know where the Queen is? I wanted to give her the quarterly update on the treatment of wives and widows back on Earth."

Zeus's interests decidedly changed. He pushed himself out of the pile of nymphs and nephews to stand beside his retinue and read whatever information Hermes tried to hand off to his wife.

"I wanted to share the news with Hera that Earth is now a hundred years closer to banishing child marriages and dowry killings," Hermes replied.

Zeus smiled as he read the documents. When he looked up he said to Hermes, chuckling, "Why would they want to ban child brides? That sounds adorable."

"Well, Zeus, it's not as if two children are trying to get married. Usually it's a very young girl getting sold off to a much older man."

Zeus let out a hearty laugh. "And?"

Normally Hermes had the stomach for Zeus's more revolting traits, but the god's personality, mixed with his musk of choice—did he detect bacon grease?—made Hermes nauseous. He suddenly wanted to leave Olympus as soon as possible. Holding back the urge to puke, he took back his papers and hastily asked, "Is Hera here?"

"Hera?" Zeus said blankly. "She's not here?"

Seeing Hermes' pupils shrink into pinpoints, Zeus gave him a boisterous guffaw. "You honestly think I'd have this going on if she were around?"

"Then where is she?"

Zeus shrugged. "I haven't the faintest idea."

"Well how long has she been gone?"

"Gaia, I couldn't tell you," Zeus said, using both hands to scratch his penetralia, which apparently helped him solve problems more easily. He was able to answer with more confidence, "At least a couple years."

Hermes' piebald face paled. "Hera's been gone…away…for at least a couple of years?"

"Yeah."

"Even though you are here—openly fornicating—in the home that you both share?"

"Yeah."

"And…you're not in the least bit suspicious as to why?"

Zeus shook his head with unjustified earnest. "Why should I be? I've done nothing."

Hermes would have balked, but horrified surprise took him first. *How much wine does one have to drink to forget all the times your wife flew into a wild, virus-like rage and made it rain the blood of your bastards? Or to make you forget how you brought the subjugation of women to men in the presence of the goddess of married women?* Hermes felt sick standing next to a god so ignorant. He kept the thoughts to himself and told Zeus, "I'm just saying, Zeus, quiet is violent. Especially in your queen's case."

Zeus scoffed, laughing off the idea. "Hera knows better." Laughing a little harder, he said, "Re…remember the last time she tried to rebel against me? He, he, he. Trust me, my Hera knows better than to defy me."

Zeus referred to a time when Hera was caught rounding up the other gods and goddesses, preparing to overthrow him. She came close too, until Zeus lucked out and beat her like a blacksmith beats bronze into a blade. When he tired of that, he dangled her from the stars by her thumbs. Hermes had to suppress a cringe when he remembered she was only reprieved because Zeus lost a night's sleep from the sounds of her weeping.

"You don't think she's up to some untoward plan, then?" Hermes said, trying to cancel out his dark thoughts.

His suspicion transferred to Zeus. The god started to lose his mild temperament. "You doubt me, Hermes?" Zeus asked, an overcast shadow staining his brilliant good-looks.

"Zeus, never," Hermes said, quickly shaking his head, then insisting as Zeus started towards him threateningly, "I doubt Hera! Her jealous moods beset me. She can never seem to get a grip on herself whenever…"

"Whenever what?" barked Zeus, his eyes flashing with an irrevocable furor at Hermes' hesitation. Grabbing the god of commerce by the scruff, he glared at him with a violent stare and pressed, "Whenever I decide to take a lover? Are you inferring I am the cause for Hera's inclemency?"

"No! O Zeus, Lord of all and any, why would I—" Hermes began but Zeus interrupted his puffery.

"That's fucking right I'm the 'lord of all and any'," Zeus scowled, flinging Hermes to the ground with the flick of his wrist, as if he were an article of clothing. Towering above the overturned god, he howled, so all in attendance could hear, "I didn't get eaten by my own father, launch a crusade against the Titans, and forge Olympus out of the blast of a meganova just to be *cowed* into fucking the same bitch for all of eternity! You got that, Hermes?"

"Yes! Yes! Yes!" avowed the god who feared nothing—not death, sickness or wounds—but he surely feared Zeus. "I would never imply you should, O Zeus. I am only accusing Hera...Hera of being too harsh and unforgiving. I accuse Hera of being imperfect. Never you."

The impassioned flattery and uxorial slander was enough to convince Zeus. Mirth mercurially returned like sun poking from in-between a little scattered rain. Yanking Hermes back up by the shoulder and embracing him forcefully, he told the god: "Hermes, worry not. I am her husband. I would know before anybody if Hera were up to something."

Hermes gave Zeus a tight-lipped smile and left the god. Zeus returned to his carnality.

*

The speed of light didn't compare to the awesome kinetic fury that is the messenger god, who— once he knew Zeus was back to being distracted by vice—bolted out of Olympus and hurtled through the vacuity of space at the neck-breaking speed of four point five million miles per second. He plummeted through two dimensions, shattering through the Earth's three protective layers with insane ease and whooping the cement-like surface of the Indian Ocean like it was the reddest red-headed step-child, the impact of which created a super-cyclone that swept up six fishing boats and instantly liquefied the men and their cargo.

Hermes shuttled through the Earth's crust, then its mantle, passed the core, and finally found himself in the secret compartment of the Underworld. He jetted to Hades' office and burst through the door covered in rock, seaweed and geodes. Upon his arrival, he shouted, "Hera's up to something!"

Hades, who quietly tried to complete fourteen thousand hours of paperwork for the Federation for the Unionization of Kreatures, Monsters and Entities, looked up at Hermes with wide-eyed horror, then instantly began to panic. Flying from his desk, he bombarded the god with questions, "What! How do you know this? When did you learn this? Did Zeus tell you of this? Why won't you tell me how you learned of this?"

"I know this because Zeus thinks everything is alright," Hermes blurted out.

Immediately, horror befell Hades' face. He stood there speechless—mostly because he was struggling to choose what language and what phrase expressed his loathing, sullenness, and vexation best. Out of all the concise little bon mots, and out of all the many languages he acquired over the endless span of time, he settled for English, "Fuck!"

Hades began pacing around the room, shouting the mot juste every few steps: "Fuck! Fuck! FUCK!" Whipping around to face Hermes, he asked, "How did all of this come about?"

"I went to Olympus to find Hera and discuss with her the news that Zimbabwe had finally abolished child marriages. When I found Zeus, up to his neck in literal pussy—"

Hades groaned. "It's like he doesn't even try to conceal his infidelities anymore."

"Right?! Like…c'mon, Zeus. How many Atlantises do we have to go through before you realize Hera don't fuck around lightly with your cheating?" Hermes blurted out, getting overly chatty with panic. "So, anyway, I ask him 'where's Hera' and he tells me he hasn't seen her. So I asks him…I ask, 'when was the last time you've seen her' and you know what he says? You know what he says?"

"Piss off with the psittacisms, Hermes! *What does he says?*"

"He says he hasn't seen her in years. YEARS, Hades!"

Hades let out a sharp-pitched gasp. "NO."

"Yes. And when I kept asking him 'don't you think that's suspicious'? And he has the nerve to say 'Hera knows better than that'. Like…you're fucking kidding me, Zeus! This woman lives to fuck with you. It's like he doesn't even remember the Fall of Troy."

Zeus' voluntary ignorance provoked a madness in Hermes. He was breathless, his eyes looked like gold that had reached the melting point. But for Hades—he became the daunting epitome of ennui. Many gods, in the face of their absoluteness, become either besotted with vainglorious delusions like Zeus, or driven to bouts of restless melancholy. Hades felt one of those episodes coming on.

He stalked back to his desk, collapsed in his throne and buttressed his head with his hands. For several seconds, he kept this position rigidly, no doubt daunted by the responsibility at hand.

"For fuck's sake!" he shouted abruptly, startling Hermes. Hades let go of his head and slammed his fists against his desk. "This is going to be Pompeii all over again."

"So you agree? Hera is scheming and she must be stopped?" Hermes asked, jovial that his concerns were being validated.

"No shit she's scheming," Hades snarled, his moods bouncing from depression to distress to pissed off. Upset further by the roller coaster of emotions, he added, "The Hera I know probably has some untoward plan that she's readying to shoot up her husband's ass."

"Then whatever she has plotted, we have to stop," Hermes cried anxiously.

"Yes, but how?" Hades spat, getting more frustrated as the dialogue continued. "I'm too swamped to go out there and find Zeus's wayward goddess. I have unions on my ass. The

Underworld is backed up with stiffs. I've got a dog addicted to pomegranates. It's too busy to leave work right now. I can't just leave."

Like any dialogue, there was an eventual discovery of truth. Hermes knew what they could do, but he feared that veridical would make the god homicidal.

"Hades, I know of a way…"

Hades recognized the reluctance in his colleague's voice and tried apprising the deity in order to guess what his thought process was. But Hermes' expression was unreadable.

"What say you, Hermes?" Hades asked quietly.

"Hades, you must summon Persephone and see what she knows."

Predictably, Hades disagreed. "No."

"Hades, please—"

"I'd rather endure the backlash of a thousand Pompeiis than spend one second talking to that goddess," Hades said. "As the mortals would say: fuck 'em!"

"Oh please, Hades. Are you really going to let bias against your ex be your hamartia?"

"Why the hell not? I'd rather have a hamartia than be some pompous paragon," Hades rebuked, folding his arms stubbornly across his chest. "Besides, when Persephone and I had problems, we didn't need the super team to get involved. We stopped communicating, started resenting each other in silence and gradually let our love life melt away like snow off a cliff. *That's* what good couples do. This is my brother's marriage; this should be my brother's problem."

"But…but their shitty marriage will destroy us all."

"Fuck 'em," Hades reiterated, turning himself away from Hermes.

Hermes let out a small sigh. He dealt with the petty, irascible ways of gods for a long time and though he hated resorting to such tawdry tactics, Hermes wasn't above using a little puffery to rock them back into sensibility. Thus, Hermes changed his tune and tried again. "Hades: fair god, caretaker to the old and sick, bouncer for life's weak and stupid, please reconsider. Do what behooves you, as you have always done. Do not let your feelings affect you, as they would your siblings. Do what is right, Hades. Be the god you are and not the god your petty feelings want you to be.

"Either stop being butt-hurt and talk to your ex-wife, or let all the tragedies that are sure to come fall squarely onto your lap."

With all the respect that one can offer after calling someone butt-hurt, Hermes kissed Hades' hand, gave a low bow and left his office, to allow the deity to think over what he had just said.

For Hades, there was nothing to think about. Lifting his head, he threw his voice out and summoned Hermes back into the room. When the swift-footed god returned, he gave him the command: "Summon Persephone."

"Yes, Hades," Hermes replied, through a barely concealed smile.

The god rolled his eyes at the blink-less deity's triumph and proclaimed, just as he left for his mission, "Let no one say I was ever a butt-hurt god!"

*

When Hermes was gone, Hades went to find Tranquila. Like the good worker he knew her to be, she was exactly where she was assigned—just beyond the river bend, forty hours into 'resettlement'. This process was relatively simple; merely an inverse of birth, where instead of pushing simpletons out of a hole, they were being pushed back into one. To Tranquila, it was less like being a mom and more like being a nightclub bouncer.

When Hades came in, she wasn't even looking at the dead as they passed by her anymore; under pressure of time constraints and an endless line, she reached to the side, grabbed them by their clothing, and using her new muscles, heaved them out like a professional bouncer hurling the bums from the bar.

"Hey, Tranquila. How's it going?"

She shoved a fully grown man into the Resettlement Pit. "Eh, it's going."

"Look at you," Hades remarked, after he watched her do this a couple of times. "Showing those stiffs whose boss. You could have been an excellent cop."

Tranquila kept her eyes on him while she mindlessly shoved an elderly man into the pit. Usually when he complimented her, she'd just brush it off and say 'no prob', but today she beamed. "Deadass? Thanks, Hades."

"*Deadass*?" he said to himself in alarm. "Did one of the harpies get loose and slay another donkey?"

"No," Tranquila said, "Deadass is one of those New York curse words, often just a predecessor for more curse words. For example, 'deadass, I love that bitch', or 'deadass, it's fucking minus six degrees out', or the more widely used 'deadass, yo fuck fractions'."

"Oh, thank Gaia" Hades replied, as relief washed over him. With a smile and sigh, he added, "New York has such a fascinating culture of vulgarity."

"Fuck ye," she said, proud.

"Hey, I don't know if you heard," Hades broached, nonchalant, "but a bunch of random fishing boats just exploded, killing a crap-ton of fishermen off the coast of Myanmar a couple of minutes ago."

"Boats that randomly explode? How does that happen?" Tranquila enquired, more baffled than concerned.

"Um..." he had to think fast. He blamed science for the last couple of things he couldn't explain, so he'd have to scapegoat something else now. "Communism." Tranquila bought it. She, like many Americans, assumed communism meant murder and Russian-specific anarchy. "Anyway," he moved on swiftly. "I need you to help Charon out while I'm in a meeting."

*

Charon was minding his own business, rowing gently down the River of Pain, when over an invisible intercom, he heard the page, "Charon, please call extension two one one."

He bent down inside his wooden boat, made in 900 BC, to pull out an ancient-looking phone from 1992. He propped the phone where an ear should be and dialed the numbers.

"Yeah?"

"Charon. It's Hermes."

"I know who it fucking is, Hermes," Charon snapped. "I've worked with you for sixteen million years. What do you want?"

"We have a three one three."

"Hermes, we use words down here not numbers. We're not freaking cops."

"Persephone's here, Charon."

The phone nearly jumped out of Charon's hand, and he had to scramble just to keep a grip on it. Pressing the receiver back to his invisible ear, his harsh, unpleasant voice was breathless with confused elation. "What! She's back. Is…is that a good thing?"

"Since when is the crazy ex-wife coming back ever a good thing?" said Hermes.

"She wasn't *that* crazy," he replied, his sharp, reaper-effect index finger twirling around the curly rubber cord.

"Well, regardless, Hades is meeting with her and he needs you to babysit the mortal until she's gone."

On the other side of the river, he spotted them. Tranquila was barely recognizable—a bright green speck—but she stood out with Hades as her protective backdrop.

"Just keep her away from the River Lethe for a couple of hours."

Charon was able to veer himself in their direction but was slow to paddle, wanting to stay on the line with Hermes.

"Persephone wouldn't harm a mortal," he said firmly, then in a whisper stated, "Particularly one that's practically a zygote compared to how old *she* is."

He heard Hermes scoff on the other line. "You sure about that, Charon? That woman turned a nymph into a mint just for saying she liked Hades' sandals."

"Yeah, but he wasn't even wearing sandals," Charon argued, remembering the incident clearly. When he heard the snickering, he added vehemently, "Only homewreckers and gay people compliment another man's shoes, Hermes. It's simple science."

Hermes was downright laughing at this point and Charon had to stop rowing out of fear his guffaws would be overheard. As he coasted to the bank, coming closer to his boss and coworker, Charon could see Hades' expression more clearly. All he saw was a forced, lopsided smile smearing the god's handsome face.

The laughter finally stopped on the other end of the phone and Charon could hear him bleat, "Whatever, Charon, you believe what you wanna believe. All I know is no goddess, malevolent or benign, is going be cordial to the maiden who replaced her."

*

Hades didn't budge from his spot on the littoral crest, watching the rickety old boat get smaller and smaller into the distance. He heard Hermes' voice call for him over the PA system, *"Lord of the Underworld to your office, please."*

No part of him wanted to take his feet from the sticky, detrital soil to walk on hard, sharp, unforgiving stone. Though, his feet had generated a thick layer of calluses over the bottom of his soles and toes in order to survive the floors of the Underworld, they still tingled and welcomed the soft, wet particles of clay.

"Lord of the Underworld to your office, please."

Alas, those moments in the sand were infrequent and fleeting. Begrudgingly, Hades turned himself into smoke to be carried south of the River Styx by an invisible wind, and over to his castle where he was more servant than god.

He materialized in his office where Hermes and Persephone waited for him. Hades tried looking at her but saw her green eyes were firmly planted on anything that wasn't him. Hermes stood beside her, his black and white face now pale with two kinds of gray.

"Thank you, Hermes," Hades said, giving him a chance to leave, which he took without refute, speeding out of the office, away from them and their inevitable drama.

Persephone still refused his gaze, her head now tilted to the side. Hades had to deny himself staring at her neck, her sharp jawline, her perfect nose. "Did Hermes tell you why I asked you here?"

She still didn't look at him but at least said, "No."

"Have you been to Olympus lately?"

This garnered another repressed 'no'.

"Zeus is running wild up there," he informed. "Flagrant sex, bestiality, unending booze and ambrosia. From what I hear, it's worse than a roman emperor's birthday up there." No reaction. No change. No lol—as Tranquila would say—for the witty joke. Though disheartened, he continued, "There's no way in Catholic Hell that Hera would let all of this hedonism slide if she were not occupied with her own misdeeds."

Persephone finally turned her head to look at him. And when her intense green eyes appraised him, they weren't reminiscent of spring breezes and lush grasslands—they were a reminder that she was an unrelenting sun and he was dirty, leftover snow that should've melted by now.

"Are you asking me if I know the whereabouts of Hera?" she spoke with a cold fury only the scorned and disgruntled could create.

"Do you?"

"No!"

"Are you sure?" Hades enquired, trying to soften his voice so she could see this wasn't an interrogation. "Just think back, Persephone. You speak to more gods than I do. Have any of them mentioned anything?"

"I don't like talking to you, why would I waste time making up lies for you?" she spat, looking at him as if he were pigeon shit on the windshield of a pristinely cleaned car.

While the anatomical construct of the immortal was still up for debate, Hades was sure—more than anything—that he did indeed possess a heart because he was certain it had just seized, froze and broke. If he could, he would've flung himself into the sun.

"This was foolish," he whispered.

"You're Gaia-damned right this was foolish," she snarled at him.

"I don't know why I thought you would be in contact with Hera," Hades replied, his voice on a steady incline back to refined dignity. "I just thought, perchance, you'd have some insight on the mind of a vindictive queen."

Somehow, Persephone's elegant face turned ugly with undignified rage. Instead of coming out and screaming, she took a dramatic step closer to him as if preparing herself to assault, she hissed, "Oooohhhh…So it's gonna be like that, *ain't it, Hades?*"

This time it was Hades' turn to glare, saying nothing. He couldn't speak. He was too busy loading up his arsenal of verbal attacks. For a moment, neither of them moved, spoke or even breathed. Priorities had changed. Hera was no longer an eminent danger. One thing mattered and one thing was certain: it was time to argue. And like mortal couples, they weren't in it to resolve anything. They were in it to win.

"So, I'm spiteful and crazy, am I?" Persephone started, her full lips already curled into a sneer.

"If the chiton fits, Persephone."

"Crazy is what crazy becomes and you can only do so much when your family's got more drama in it than the House of Thebes!"

"Oh, here we go. Blame it all on me that your parents are siblings."

"No. This is more than just the ravenous incest. You never, ever, defended me when Zeus hit on me."

"Oh, boo hoo, 'Zeus hit on me'. Zeus hits on everyone. He hit on me forty-two seconds before we were divorced."

"So fucking typical of you. You'll defend your fucked-up brother to the end of dawn but in all our years of marriage you couldn't find one decent thing to say about my mother."

"That's not true. I've always complimented Demeter on the bricks of fucking weed she smokes a day."

"You hate my mother. Admit it. Admit it. You *hate* her."

"OF COURSE I HATE HER," Hades bellowed, his voice so uncharacteristically loud and unsettled that it startled Persephone; she forgot what she had wanted to say next. With his metaphorical heart aflame, he raged, "And you should too. She's the hot fucking mess that destroyed our marriage. She's the one who refused to accept us, who refused to see you as the goddess that you are. *She's* the one who had a mental fucking breakdown on the day we eloped and *she* was the one who would have let the Earth die if you hadn't placated her and promised to spend half the year under her thumb again. But you...*you* let her drive us apart!"

"I didn't let her drive us apart," Persephone retorted, sounding more like a wail than an assertion. "She would have let the Earth die if I hadn't gone back to her."

"But she let winter commence regardless, didn't she?" he reminded her.

Silence.

"You expect me to rewrite poetry, to defend your honor, to...to read your mind, but how long...how often did I beg you not to leave? How many springs did you spend with me? I'm asking you. In our sixteen million years of marriage, how many springs did you stay home?"

She didn't answer because there wasn't an answer.

"You never thought what those half-years alone would do to me? I used to fall apart every day you were gone," Hades beseeched, moving her to meet his gaze. And when her softened green eyes embarrassed him, he said jokingly, "Do you know what it's like to be the clichéd lord of the dead...who constantly cries? Gaia, it was pathetic."

She didn't laugh but she did give him a small, tight-lipped smile. It was the first smile she'd given him in ages. "You know, when we were in the Magistrate," she began. "I thought the only thing I wanted from you was an apology. But now I know it is I who need to apologize." With that, she sandwiched her hands on top of his and looked him right in the eyes and said, "I'm sorry, Hades. I am so, so sorry."

At first, Hades froze from the shock at having actually won an argument. A male winning an argument against a female? What else were sitcoms wrong about? Then he burned from the thrill of holding her hand again. Suddenly, he was smiling at her. She returned the smile. He thought his lips would break from how hard he was smiling.

"Bet you thought you'd never see the day when your husband—ex-husband—could be right," he said in jest.

Persephone gave him a wild grin. For a tender second, neither of them spoke. They simply held hands and looked into each other's eyes, as if something was rekindling. Then, a wild, sudden realization saddled her thoughts. Before Hades knew it, she had waved her arms in a wide circle, causing huge, gray storm clouds to envelop them. She tackled Hades to the ground. Shrouded in an ethereal cloak and with Persephone on top of him, Hades became fervently excited.

"Alright!" he cried, full of zeal, as he tugged at her chiton.

"Hades, we don't have a lot of time," Persephone began.

"Don't worry, it's been so long, it probably won't take very long."

"No, Hades! That's not what I mean," she whispered urgently, giving his furtive hand a good slap to assert she meant business.

Palpable disappointment ran through the god. "Oh…so, you didn't wanna get some James Woods?"

"No!" she scolded. "And stop calling your dick that! It's creepy."

"You used to think it was funny," Hades said, almost offended.

"Hades, please listen," she pleaded in a near-whisper. "Hera has a plan, this I know. I lied to you earlier. I'm sorry."

Once again, priorities shifted. He sat up. His body was stiff, though the lust he felt was gone. "Did she try to persuade you?"

Persephone nodded.

"Were you persuaded?"

Another nod, this time full of shame.

"But...but you hate her," he stammered, perplexed by the admission. "How could you work with her?"

Persephone bowed her head and Hades knew it was because she started to cry. It was something their marriage hadn't changed—her weakness—being seen as weak.

"You replaced me," she whimpered, as jealousy destroyed her sensibility.

"What? I didn't replace you!" Hades exclaimed. Persephone didn't believe it.

"Yes, you did," she shouted, turning on him, revealing the hot ugly face of hurt and betrayal. "You replaced me with a mortal. With a mortal, Hades. How could you think some little pile of puke could do what I did? I worked my fingers to the...the...whatever our fingers are made of—bone, galaxies, solidified chewing gum...whatever. Regardless, I worked my ass off with the powers that I had. All of that just be usurped by some Earth whore—"

"Whore? You think I would copulate with Jeanette's granddaughter? You're out of your goddamn galactic skull," he cried.

The mention of Jeanette killed Persephone's diatribe instantly, leaving her incredulous and perplexed. "What?"

"That mortal that you think I'm sleeping with—which I'm not—is Jeanette's granddaughter," Hades stated flatly. "She sold her soul to me a little after you left so she could get a job down here."

"She sold her soul to you—to get a job?" Persephone echoed, thinking it a joke. After a brief moment of reflection, she commented, "Wow, that's ambitious."

Hades smiled but said nothing. He merely took her hand again and stroked her knuckles. She watched quietly for a couple seconds before they found themselves looking into each other's eyes once again. For a fleeting Earth second, they might have kissed.

Their tender moment was tarnished by the mood-killing noise of what sounded like a sumo wrestler getting punched in the stomach. "OOOOOOGGGHHHHH!"

Waving her arms again, as if she were drawing back a pair of large curtains, Persephone dispelled their cloudy enclosure and exclaimed: "What the hell was that?"

THE TILTING OF GRANDMA SOBRIQUET

The pained moan rang out again, louder and more gnarled: "OOOOOOOOOOGGGGGHHHH!"

Charon's distinctive voice yelled from outside the office, "Boss! Boss! Come quick."

Hades ran out of his office doors, followed by Persephone. Just outside his castle of black crystal, they found Charon, kneeling in the black soil, trying to hold up Tranquila's head. Hades bolted over to them and demanded, "What happened to her?"

"I don't know," Charon insisted. "We made it to the River Acheron when she started dry heaving and, you know, she pukes a lot so, I didn't think anything of it. But then she started making that unholy racket. Hades, I think she's dying."

Lying pale and gray, clutching her stomach like it was going to rip apart if she didn't, Tranquila's mouth hung open like a gaping wound and out sprang that horrible groan, "OOOOOOOOGGGHHH!"

"What do we do?" Charon cried.

Persephone chimed in on this one. "Feed her."

"What?" Charon nearly cried; the concept was lost on the skeleton.

"The poor girl's got low blood sugar and she's hungry. Just give her a bit of fruit or something and she'll be fine after an hour."

"How the hell is food supposed to make her feel better? She's clearly dying. Food doesn't keep people from dying." Charon argued.

Persephone rolled her eyes. Instead of arguing she took a couple of paces towards Tranquila, bent to her side, touched her cheek and bade her, "Maiden? Maiden? Can you hear me?"

Slowly, two brown and black-colored eyelids fluttered open to behold a beauty a thousand times greater than the photoshopped wonders daubed on the covers of magazines back home. Whoever she was—Aphrodite, Miss Universe, Africa's Cinderella—Tranquila had never been more intimidated, insecure and somehow amorous. Nonetheless, she found strength in her presence.

"I forgot to pack a lunch today."

Persephone nodded, understanding. She looked at Charon and Hades, her eyes full of silent 'I told you bitches'.

"You haven't eaten since getting here?" Hades enquired.

Tranquila shook her head, meekly.

"Tranquila! You've been down here for five days. Why didn't you say anything?"

A hunger pang stabbed Tranquila, just as he asked. With an anguished groan she said, "I'm bad at taking care of myself."

"Oh, you poor creature." Persephone cooed, sympathetically. "No person should have to go six hours without eating."

Hades sighed, "At least you didn't starve to death. Starvation is the most agonizing death that can befall a human."

"Yeah," she grunted, trying to roll around to distract herself from the fact that her stomach was eating itself. "That would've sucked."

Standing up, Hades rifled through his robes searching for food. Persephone beat him to it. She held out a ripe, pre-cut pomegranate, giving him a sly look in the process. Hades smiled knowingly before he bent down to Tranquila to offer it to her. But when she saw it, she flinched, as if it were roadkill. "Ew...fruit? Don't you have any real food? Like chicken tenders? Or tacos?"

*

She felt something seize control her body, so suddenly, that she confused it for arthritis. But it didn't surge like it normally would in the bones or in the joints. It was like a nag that couldn't be ignored—more powerful than intuition, more urgent than common sense. Grandma Sobriquet didn't know what to make of it at first, it was so foreign to her. She almost assumed it was a mild stroke. But something pestered at her, something concentrated and unyielding, and in a blinding moment of truth she recognized the meaning: a primal grandmother instinct was letting her know that somebody was trying to hurt and/ or feed her grandchild. Needless to say, she was pissed the fuck off.

It was in this verve that all of Grandma Sobriquet's health problems: the bad knees that caused walking to be slow and painful; the bunions on her feet that gave her a penguin gait; the osteoporosis that threatened to pulverize her hip bone into dust every time she accidentally banged it against the corner of something, fell away from her like a thin, tattered blanket. With this youthfulness, she rushed into the kitchen to find the offerings. Accessing a secret wine rack teeming with expensive wine, Grandma Sobriquet used her chest to hold seven bottles at once. She race outside without bothering with the milk or honey.

She stomped on top of the opening, rose her head to the heavens and made those dead-language chants, smashing a bottle of wine into the ground after each appointed caesura.

Directly above, the heavens closed themselves to her, and as she shattered a new bottle—thick glass shards cutting her ankles and feet, staining her lower half dark red—clouds came and overruled the sun. What was once a clear but brisk November day, turned dour and warm like the moments before a thunderstorm.

She was down to five bottles by the time the wind tore through the neighborhood and stole what it could: recycling bins, mailboxes, a couple of screen doors. While New York experienced its first real life Midwestern tornado, all the glass around her lay subjugated.

Ankle-deep in a puddle of her own blood by the time she was down to two bottles of wine, Grandma Sobriquet didn't wince or pause from the prayers. She kept right along, motivated by an unexplained zeal. Her face, already the same texture of aged denim, became further ravaged. She looked, in that moment—in the backyard, wasting good wine, reciting an occultist's prayer— like the masochist priest of some tenebrist image held in the hearts of only Catholicism's most hell-obsessed minds.

At last, she held the last bottle of wine over her head. Before slamming it down to her feet and letting it slash her legs, just like the rest, she punctuated the prayer by saying something in English, "HADES!"

Thunder rang out like a gunshot in compliant reply. Just like that, Grandma Sobriquet shot into the Underworld like an inward lightning.

*

It took them a solid minute to explain to her: "No, Tranquila, the Underworld does not have *Hot Pockets*," before she relented and chose the fruit over starvation. She plucked a few seeds from the halved shrub and popped them into her mouth when an impetuous force stormed its way over to them, slapping the fruit from her hand.

Standing above her, as if shielding the young woman with her quiescent, old person's body, was Grandma Sobriquet.

"DON'T YOU DARE TRY TO FEED MY GRANDBABY!" she screamed at Persephone.

"Jeanette!" Hades yelled, dumbfounded.

"Grandbaby!?" Tranquila blurted out, also dumbfounded. "Since when am I your *grandbaby*?"

"Shut up, grandbaby," Grandma Sobriquet snapped. She reared her mutinous rage on Hades. Through her teeth, she hissed, "We—had—a—deal! I said you let harm come to her Hades, and then I come down here and see you're trying to kill her—with fruit!"

"You know I'm not a dog, right?" Tranquila remarked, but was promptly ignored.

"Jeanette, please. If you would just hear me out," Hades began patiently but was promptly ignored.

"Nobody—AND I MEAN NOBODY—tricks my grandbaby into doing something dangerous and short-sighted if I have anything to do with it."

"*You* tricked me into doing something dangerous and short-sighted," Tranquila interjected, hunger no longer hindering her from sitting upright.

"I did it because I thought I could help you," Grandma Sobriquet fired back. She turned her head to berate Hades more, but Tranquila wouldn't have it.

"You did it because you were bored," she harangued, standing now and fully confronting her.

"Tranquila," Hades began, as if he was about to tell Tranquila not to raise her voice at her grandmother.

"No!" Tranquila cut him off. Rearing back at Grandma Sobriquet, she screamed, "You can't come down here, bully my boss and try to make people believe that you suddenly care about me."

"I do care about you," she fired back, lacking any evidential warmth.

"Why should I believe you?" Tranquila demanded. "All my life you've been nothing but a salty bitch to me and my family. You laugh at everyone's bad luck. You call me stupid and ugly. Christ, every year for my birthday you used to send me a card that said 'here's to another year of getting uglier.'" Charon let out a tiny chuckle. It was quickly cut short by Persephone's slap to the head, "And now this whole time, since I've worked in the Underworld, you haven't talked to me once about who you are or what you are. So, no, I don't fucking believe that you care about me because you don't respect me and you don't trust me."

Grandma Sobriquet lost all the hellfire that possessed her earlier. In front of Tranquila, hearing what she'd heard, she was dowsed. She looked up towards Hades for help, but in her line of vision she found Persephone's and Hades' hands intertwined. Grandma Sobriquet blinked in disbelief at the tender gesture. Her incredulity behooved Persephone to give an amused smile, one that said 'Yeah, I'm back, baby'. Though she was happy for Hades, Grandma Sobriquet was angry with herself. If Grandma Sobriquet wasn't so busy being angry when she'd arrived, she would have noticed how the Underworld smelled like spring. A trail of flower petals even lay at their feet, leading right up to where Tranquila stood.

Regret humbled the old woman. With a sigh she confessed, "A long time ago, I was an Erinyes."

Tranquila was too angry to use context clues, so without thinking she snapped, "Just because you're transgendered doesn't mean you get to be a bi—"

"No. No. Don't embarrass me, Tranquila," she said, spitting. Already her patience for the young woman was waning. Working hard to control her temper, she started again. "I was a Fury." When Tranquila's incomprehensible look still didn't ebb, she explained: "You know how there were supposedly three Fates that manifested divine destiny? Well, there were three Furies manifesting the divine beat-down. I was the divine beat-down. I brought cosmic justice to those who deserved it."

Tranquila snorted. "You're full of crap if you think I'm gonna stand here and believe that you could get along and work with two other people—"

"I didn't say there were three of us," Grandma Sobriquet said, getting irritated with the constant interruptions. "Your classical poets thought that. You could tell them one god rules the skies but tell them one woman does the workload of three and suddenly that's 'impossible'."

Tranquila didn't realize it, but she shook her head at the admission. None of it made sense.

"It's true, Tranquila," Hades' voice rang out from the side. "She used to work here."

"Work?" Tranquila repeated, the very term ludicrous. Pointing, she said, "This woman doesn't work. I've seen her sit in the same spot for so long I had to turn her around just so she wouldn't get ass sores."

"Hey," Grandma Sobriquet cried out, clearly offended. "I earned those ass sores. I worked my metaphorical ass off every day, all day, for sixteen million years."

"So…what? Are you retired?" Tranquila guessed, struggling to make sense of all this. "Is that what you're saying?"

Shrug. "Yeah, pretty much."

"B-but how can an abstract retire?" Tranquila blurted out. "Weren't you specifically destined to be a Fury? How can you just retire from serving your destiny?"

"You can when you get replaced by another servant of fate."

"You got laid off?"

"I prefer to say I opted out to make way for fresher blood."

Tranquila was boggled. It was like she was sitting in college-level calculus when all she knew was grade-school addition. Turning to Hades, she silently begged him for some plainer explanation. Charon took up the challenge, instead. In the harsh, blunt rhetoric befitting of a skeleton, he told her, "Her job became obsolete."

"Fuck off, Charon! You're two decades away from being replaced by a self-steering cruise liner," Grandma Sobriquet barked back at him.

"You wanna go, old ass human?" Charon fired back, fists up, already in a fighting stance. "Because my bony ass can whoop the shit out of yours."

The ensuing fight was lost on Tranquila. Everything felt backwards and slanted, like time and gravity had contrived to stop right then and there, just to mess with her.

"That…that doesn't make sense," Tranquila spoke up at last, as Persephone pried a wiry skeleton from on top of a body of a soon-to-be skeleton. "'Jeanette' is a French person's name. You've got blonde hair and blue eyes. You're not Greek."

Hades grabbed Grandma Sobriquet in one hand and Charon in the other, flinging them forty feet apart. While Charon reattached his femur to his knee joint, Grandma Sobriquet fretted over the eye that would surely go black soon. Grandma Sobriquet then explained, "I know you're going to find this hard to believe, Tran, but this disgusting old person's body isn't mine.

This saggy, gross and disease-riddled body belonged to some Frenchwoman whose ass I identity-thefted many, many decades ago."

"Then…" Tranquila began warily, looking at the old woman with a new kind of revulsion. "What did you used to look like?"

The answer never came. She was interrupted by a monstrous eruption, like the detonation of a sub-terrestrial bomb; echoing like smaller cannons going off. Soon, the Underworld was daft with the screams of scared dead people.

"What the fuck was that?" yelled out Charon, but his voice was drowned out by the sounds of another, dangerously closer, BLA CHA CHA explosion. This time, the aftermath produced a nasty-smelling wave of blinding, bilious smoke—the kind that suffocated and subjugated them into darkness.

"IT'S THE SUPER VOLCANO!" Tranquila screamed, latching herself onto Grandma Sobriquet's body like a baby monkey on the back of its mother during a rain storm.

But nothing lasted in Hades without its namesake's say. With one grand gesture, Hades drove the smoke out like pagans from a St. Patrick's homestead. In that atmospheric cleansing, the cause of the ruckus was revealed. Grandma Sobriquet said to her former boss, "Either Zeus needs his Dick sucked or you got yourself an invasion."

AN UNTOWARD PLAN

Carried on the back of Cerberus, using the poor dog's ears as reigns and driving the beast to trample over the rubble of a wall forged from volcanic ash nearly two billion years prior, sat two of the most insanely beautiful women Tranquila had ever been terrified of.

"How's it going, Hades?" projected one of the goddesses, as she commanded the dog to walk closer to the ground. Forcing her to heel, the goddess jumped from the animal's back and sauntered over, casually saying, "How's my favorite brother/brother-in-law?"

"Under what great delusion of Cronus did I ever become your favorite?" demanded Hades, whose even temper and sympathy never stretched to Hera.

The goddess gave him a wicked smile, the kind that one hopes a dangerous woman will never give. "You've always been my favorite, Hades," she said. "It's why I'm about to make your day a thousand percent less stressful."

She reached down and pulled from her hip what appeared to be a white, extremely long and thin tree branch. In one swift motion, she jacked her arm up and whipped the branch like a softball player. It sped through the air for miles and miles, until it became apparent with a shattering clash, that she had struck the top of the lower kingdom.

To Hades' horror, the dead must have sensed freedom, for like a ghoulish gust of wind, thousands upon thousands of unfettered souls—and a couple of disgruntled harpies—shot through the opening of the Underworld, journeying through the secret compartments of Earth in search of their once-allotted homes.

"No! Nooo!" Hades shrieked, unable to stop them. He watched helplessly as the lucky dead made the ultimate escape. Within seconds, the house of dead looked like a vacated parking lot for mole people. To Hera—in a black rage Tranquila was fortunate to have never seen before—he bellowed, "YOU BITTER BITCH OF UNREASON! DO YOU KNOW WHAT YOU HAVE DONE?"

"I've cleared your over-populated kingdom, sent the dead back to their loved ones and given ghost hunters a steady increase of jobs," Hera replied serenely. "Seems like I did a lot of people a lot of favors."

"You've done no such thing!" Hades screeched. "You have undone me. It will take me centuries to undo the tragedy you have just beset man."

"Oh Hades, that's where you're wrong. This isn't your problem, anymore," Hera replied, speaking with a gilded sweetness. She reached to her hip and drew another white branch from her side, pointing it straight at Hades' chest. "I'm relieving you of your status as God of the Underworld."

The white branch in Hera's hand snapped and crackled with tremendous raw energy, which was when Tranquila recognized it for what it really was—a lightning bolt.

Despite a brilliancy that illuminated his upper half, Hades was dark with pure, foul loathing. His voice was the apogee of cold fury when he asked Hera, "How did you get that?"

"This?" Hera said, with mock embarrassment, as if someone were complimenting her on an old purse. Turning her head to her companion she said, "Why, Demeter got this for me. Didn't you, Deme?"

The second goddess didn't speak. She went completely rigid and white-faced. It was clear that a great trauma had undone her recently.

"Mom?" called Persephone, anxious at the distress in her mother's visage. "Mom?"

"Oh, she'll be fine, Kore," Hera interjected, off-hand. "She just took one for the team."

"What did you do?!" Persephone nearly screamed, terrified at the possibilities.

For whatever reason, the implication infuriated Hera. All the forced politeness and beauty-pageant smiles that she slapped across her face disappeared instantly, replaced by malicious sneers and spiteful glares.

"*I—didn't—do—a—thing—to—her!*" Hera roared, waving the bolt of electricity at the goddess, as if it were a cosmic gun.

"Then who did?" Persephone spat, unable to conceal her hatred for the woman.

"Who else could brutalize a goddess like that? Who else could degrade and humiliate a great woman with impetuous ease? Who else would do that to their fellow gods? Who else but my husband! Who else but Zeus!"

Persephone's flawless skin was ruined by pale fear. She turned her head and called for her mother, but it was clear the goddess was beyond speech.

"She'll be fine," Hera sneered. "She'll get over what he did. I know I did. Besides, she made the sacrifice. She did her part and it'll be worth it in the end. Unlike you, Persephone.

How easy it was for you to betray me. I guess that hoes before bros saying is all but a lie."

"You're so backed up with bullshit it's getting clogged in-between your ears, Hera," Charon cried out, courageously. "There's no fucking way Hades will give up his kingdom. So you're just going to have to figure out another way to get back at Zeus—"

"Zeus? Who said this was about Zeus? I didn't say this was about Zeus."

"Bull-fucking-shit, Hera. It's always about Zeus," Hades cursed at her. "Every plan, every scheme, every failed miserable plot you've ever had always came back to getting revenge on my brother."

Hera wasn't affected by his insults. In fact, hearing them brought back the wicked smile that man feared most on a woman's lips.

"No, Hades. That is where you're wrong," she said, in a dangerous whisper.

Hera turned her head. Those beautiful amber eyes searched and found exactly what they were looking for. Grandma Sobriquet.

A split second later, Hera came forth hurling lightning bolts thick and fast from her hand, directed right into the old woman's face. Immediate and blinding, contact in a searing white flash, they could see Jeanette's body being thrown from the ground. Out of her shoes in fact, like something out of a cartoon. Then came a white explosion that impacted the ground and shook the kingdom to its core. Fat, gray, acrid smoke followed. Tranquila screamed into the thick of it, crying out the only name she trusted: "Grandma! Grandma!"

After a painful succession of moments, the smoke dissipated and visibility returned. On the ground, not far from them, lay a twisted carnage of shoes. Not far from those were its human counterpart: a perished husk, cauterized to the bone. Not even her dentures survived.

Tranquila's bones collapsed at the sight. She crawled on her hands and knees to curl up next to the remains in the dirt, giving way to a horrible, howl-like weeping.

"Grandma, Grandma..."

Hades, Persephone and Charon watched Tranquila's squalid mourning of Jeanette's ashes with stinging sadness. Hera, who didn't bother with a second glance, seized this distraction. A second bolt was produced and she held it with deliriously precise aim at one of Persephone's many hearts. Her threat, which crackled and singed within the Goddess' hand with insane fury, marred any bravery Persephone, or Hades and Charon, had. The bitter Queen robbed another kingdom of its equilibrium.

"Your choice, brother." Hera commanded, her voice hard and cold. "Give me the Underworld or I will send this bolt straight into Persephone's heart and she will be nothing more than a pox on this realm."

For the first time since Hera had arrived, Hades looked petrified. It made his insides burn to see Persephone stand before eminent destruction. He could hear her breathing start to quicken and he saw her gaze dart from the lightning bolt to Hera's eyes. Hades noticed how difficult it became for her eyes to resist tearing.

"Hera, don't do this," Persephone begged, fencing between fright and fury. "What happened to the Hera that cared about women and families?" she yelled, fencing between rage and sadness. "In a past life you would never have laid a hand on an innocent like this. Twice you try to shape Woman's life with tragedy. What has become of you, Hera? What impiety has made you so heartless and starved your sight for love?"

"You know nothing of what lies in my heart," lambasted the Queen, and though she still addressed Persephone, her eyes lay squarely on Hades. "But you will. You will..."

Tears stung Hades' eyes. His good friend was murdered. His wife—ex-wife—was going to be killed right in front of him. Behind him, Tranquila's sobs shredded his insides until his grief became ineffable. Hades, king of Death, could never bear suffering. He couldn't bear tragedies, especially the preventable. He was much too kind to allow this pain to continue, even at such a price, even if it meant bending to his sister's terror. Hera's sadism knew no bounds. If he said no, she would unleash cruelties upon any and all rhythms of life—until the world was nothing but trauma and casualties.

Hades opened his mouth to speak when another voice interrupted him.

"Give it up, Hades," squeaked a tiny voice from behind.

Hades looked over his shoulder and saw Tranquila getting up from her knees. Her face was ugly from intense crying but she did her best to wipe them away, as she walked towards the God.

"There's no point anymore." She continued, wiping snot on the back of her free hand as the other carried the pomegranate half that Grandma Sobriquet tried swatting away from her. Tranquila made her way over to Hades' side. She tilted her head back to look her boss in the eyes and gave him a brave little smile. "We might as well come clean."

With that, Tranquila reached down and laced her fingers inside of Hades'.

Hera smirked, smug. "I knew it." To Persephone she said, "Told you human females are slutty."

Persephone said nothing. Her entire face constricted tighter and tighter, as if physically holding in vicious ornery.

"We were going to get married today." Tranquila spoke up again. "That's why my grandma was here. That's why Persephone is here. She heard and was trying to stop us. I was going to be the new Queen of the Underworld. But, I don't want Persephone to die over me. I don't want to cause her anymore pain. I mean, I already banged her husband so there's no point in adding insult to injury.

"Anyway," Tranquila extended her arm, brandishing the cut pomegranate to Hera, who looked at it with sanctimonious delight. "This is for you Hera. This is what we were going to use to seal the deal."

"Thank you, earth whore." Hera replied, ripe with arrogance as she took the fruit from Tranquila.

"May your enemies reach your gaze and shit themselves with fear." Tranquila proclaimed, using her hands to engage in a hearty round of applause for the newly appointed head of the Underworld.

Tranquila clapped as hard as she could, until the vacuous air of the Underworld was teeming with the sounds of her applause. Until the sounds of her clapping reached Cerberus' ears and the Beast Canine raised its head from its humiliating animal abuse and searched for the source of such noise. Its six eyes found what they searched—then found something even better.

Cerberus spotted the pomegranate. Instantly, the three-headed dog was reduced by the shameless desire for a treat. The sounds of Tranquila's clapping only solidified its want, which charged its tripled-heart the way crowds excite team players to run harder.

Tranquila kept clapping until Hades was clapping and then Charon. She clapped until Hera, high from victory, was too distracted to see Cerberus get back on its paws and bend its head down, signifying the urge to run.

She kept clapping, even as Cerberus made a single, giant, soundless leap into the air, forward, towards the coveted fruit. It wasn't until she could see her own reflection within the beast's razor-sharp teeth that she stopped with her applause and crouched down and covered her head.

By the time Hera saw what she was doing and realized the dangers that surely followed—the heat of Cerberus' tire-burning breath was already on her neck.

A second later, Hera was slurped up in a single motion by Cerberus' giant tongue and it was too late for the goddess. Hera and the fruit that she held onto were inside the three-headed beast's belly.

Tranquila lifted her head from underneath her arms and saw a Hera shaped bulge stick out of Cerberus' stomach. She raised herself up again and a giant smile burst from her face. She turned to Hades, Persephone and Charon, who stood back, still awe-struck.

She shot both arms in the air and screamed, victoriously. She even ran in a circle a few times, pumping her arms, exhilarated, thrilled, happy-to-be-alive. Tranquila was proud of herself.

Thunder-struck, none of the entities said or did anything for a few seconds, still trying to process the situation. But then Hades crossed over from incredulous to pure joy and ran over to Tranquila, shouting, "THAT—WAS—AMAZING!"

Persephone and Charon stood back stunned, as they watched the consecrated leader of the dead run around in circles with a teenager, shouting with brilliant joy, chanting, "U-S-A! U-S-A! U-S-A!" After a while, he felt too silly and he stopped running, only to grab Tranquila by the shoulders. "Tranquila that was the most ingenious thing I've ever seen! Tranquila: more brilliant than Athena, more cunning than Hercules! How did you come up with such a plan?"

"Oh, I learned a long time ago from going to public schools that if you want to beat up a big bitch then you're going to need help from an even bigger bitch." Tranquila answered, earnestly. Waving a grateful arm to Cerberus, who was licking its privates, she said, "And Cerberus is the biggest bitch I know." Cerberus stopped licking herself to growl at Tranquila contemptuously. "See?"

Hades' face dropped, as if disappointed by Tranquila's explanation. He dropped his hands from her shoulders.

"So, did I do good?" Tranquila inquired, sensing the shift in Hades' demeanor.

Hades smiled. "Of course."

Tranquila beamed, truly proud.

As the pair stood smiling, Persephone, still insecure and unsure of how to feel about being saved by a mortal, broke their moment by crying out in agitation, "Pomegranates! Why is it always pomegranates?"

Hades looked over to his former spouse and rushed to embrace her. Holding her tenderly, he whispered, "Thank Gaia, you're okay."

Persephone smiled, despite herself, into his shoulder. She missed his hugs. When they separated, she looked at Tranquila and said, "Thank you. Sincerely."

Tranquila smiled. "Hey it was your fruit that saved the day. If it were up to me, I would have just tossed it in the River Styx when you weren't looking."

Persephone chuckled, faintly. But then a second past and her insecurities took hold of her again. She blurted out, "Okay I know you probably were lying just to distract Hera but—you didn't really sleep with Hades, did you?"

"No!" Hades cried.

"Ew! Gods no!" Tranquila cried, simultaneously.

"What do you mean 'ew no'?" Hades demanded, offended.

"Hades, you're three billion years older than me. That's gross." Tranquila insisted.

"Okay, yeah, but *physically*, I'm still good-looking, right?"

Fortunately, Tranquila didn't have to answer. They were distracted by the muffled screams and threats coming from Cerberus' overactive stomach.

"Release me! Release me!" They could hear the goddess bellow out in vain.

Tranquila sucked her teeth at the goddess' cries. "Yeah fucking right. Enjoy those stomach acids, bitch!"

"She won't be digested anytime soon." Hades replied. "Cerberus has sixteen stomachs. It takes centuries for her to metabolize anything."

"Oh man!" Tranquila whined. "So I gotta listen to this crazy bitch scream and beg for mercy any time I go to work now?"

"Well," Hades began, his voice strange and soft, as if he were in the throes of a plan he didn't understand fully himself yet. "I wouldn't say that. You're probably not going to work besides Cerberus much longer."

Tranquila paused. She surveyed Hades' face for new understanding but was stymied. "Are you firing me?" She inquired. "Is this for calling you old and gross?!"

"No!" Hades said, laughing. "No! Tranquila, I'm trying to promote you."

Tranquila sighed with relief. "Oh good. Because you know you're not old and gross Hades. Sure you are hella old but you're not gross. I mean, you are always covered in dirt but you got really nice skin."

"Tran, stop."

"Okay."

Letting go of his ex-wife, Hades strode towards Tranquila. He said next, in all seriousness, "Tranquila Obiit, how would you like to take over this realm, for me?"

"Like, as a temp? So you can go on vacation or something?"

"No." Hades said, gently. "As a new ruler. As a goddess."

Tranquila heard the words but it was as if her brain purposely blocked it from the processing center of her mind. It was thoroughly inconceivable to her.

"But…but…How?" Tranquila stammered, her lips separated wide from perplexity. "I can't be a god! I'm from New York! We're morally tone-deaf!"

"What, and the rest of us are perfect?" Hades replied, laughing. "Look at us: Zeus' a rapist, Hera's violent and cruel, I'm a pathetic workaholic and Persephone's got jealousy problems."

"It's true Tran." Persephone confirmed. "We are but strange, flawed gods with amazing gifts and even better bodies."

Tranquila continued to stammer out in protest, feeling underserving.

"I-I-I can't rule Hades. Hades should rule Hades!" She argued. "Besides, I don't know how to do anything. I'm not even done training. I still have so much of that packet I didn't even read!"

"Tran, you were done training four minutes after you first started," Hades replied.

He spoke with such earnest forsooth that Tranquila's heart welled. She felt tears, tender tears, swell up in her brown eyes. She was overwhelmed by his confidence in her. She nodded her head and whispered, "Okay."

Proud Hades stuck out his hand for his progeny to grab, which she did. He was able to wrap his entire palm around her hand and Tranquila, embarrassed by her tears, did not look up as her boss said to her, "Congratulations Tranquila Obiit. Welcome to immortality."

Tranquila tried saying something; she tried moving her lips, making some use of her gaping hole of a mouth, but nothing came of it. She could only sit there, looking like an idiot with a speech impediment and a slackened jaw.

"THIS IS BULLSHIT! I CALL DIVINE BULLSHIT!" Hera roared from inside Cerberus, pounding her fists against her stomach lining. "There's no way you can make a teenager in charge of the Under—"

"Silence, you psycho!"

Everyone redirected their eyes to see it was the famous blacksmith, Hephaestus, who spoke. Suddenly, the dank, emptied lower kingdom was glutted with the presence of every god and goddess known to the universe. All stood bold and glittering; everyone but Zeus, who had been carried down to Hades by Ares, having been hog-tied by his own chiton.

On cue, Cerberus, queasy from getting inverted gut-punching, made a disgusting rasp and barfed out Hera. She summersaulted onto the Underworld ground, covered in drool, diluted vomit and half-digested pomegranate. She looked up to find herself under the collective gaze of the entire Olympus team. Zeus, bound and gagged, chuckled at his wife's appearance.

"Yeah! Why is it every time you two have marital problems, the rest of us have to deal with it?" bellowed Ares, slinging Zeus down on the ground like a sack of rapey potatoes.

"I suppose we should thank you, though," Athena mused. "After all, if you hadn't left and stolen Zeus's thunder bolts, we would never have come back to a wasteland of sex and debauchery and we would never have come to the conclusion to evict his perverted ass."

"Evict him?" Hera repeated fearfully.

"AUKTIFME?!" Zeus screamed.

"Oh, didn't we make that obvious?" Athena said to Zeus. "What, with the rebellion and the hog-tying? Nice job by the way, Aphrodite."

"Who said hair braiding had no real-world applicatory?" Aphrodite said proud.

"We took a vote. We're sick of the laziness and incest. You're out." Athena continued.

"WUT?!" Zeus cried.

"Ha!" Hera laughed, unable to contain her joy in his suffering.

"Oh, don't think this doesn't extend to you too, Hera," Aphrodite said coolly. "Where husband goes, the wife is sure to follow."

"Don't worry, Hera," reassured her sister, Hestia, goddess of family. "We figured a perfect place for you two to work out your marital and psychological woes."

The clever couple already knew to which place Hestia referred. Zeus started jerking around on the floor like a landed fish. Hera made a half-assed dash in the opposite direction but was strong-armed by Aries, holding her down, even as she raged.

Hades, smiling, held out a consecrated hand to the floor. The foundation made from ancient rock crumbled like dirt clods, and what little light the Underworld possessed fell through the ground. An unholy racket drilled through Tranquila's ears and into her teeth. She saw in the pitch-blackness that Hades rose from her side. Hades, Persephone and the others surrounded the married pair. She witnessed the gods seize Hera while the goddesses carried Zeus by the wrists and ankles, to drag them over to the terrible crevice which was blaring out—by some

unseen monsters—the same miserable, antiquated argot
Grandma Sobriquet had used in the backyard, just earlier today.
Its volume was such that if she heard it with human ears, they
would have melted upon apprehension and made her cerebral
cortex implode.

It was to this pit that Hades sat on for countless years in
order to protect his siblings from the wrath of the Titans—that
Hera and Zeus were dispelled from the Underworld—and all
other worlds. Their godly howls were drowned out by the
ungodly roars. Thus, Zeus and Hera were gone.

Hades beckoned Tranquila to come over. As she did, she
looked into the gargantuan pit and saw that two miles down
blood-soaked humanoids lurked, swarming and skidding over
and around each other like ravenous snakes. For a brief second,
she saw one of the faces more clearly. She noticed that, though
they had flesh tones and human-looking hair, their eyes were
compounded like house flies.

If she had eaten, she would have thrown up.

"Make a command," she heard Hades whisper
encouragingly into her ear. But she didn't know how. "What do
you want done?"

"I…I want this hole in the ground gone."

And so it was.

By some invisible power, the primordial foundation of
Hades regenerated on its own, patching itself up with dozens of
invisible contractors and closing itself off from the titanic prison.
Thus, the Underworld was repaired and the gods and goddesses
cheered.

"Praise for the new God of the Underworld," rang out
the bellicose voice of red-faced Ares. "All exalt the new
Olympian, Tranquila."

The Greeks erupted in jubilation: screaming, stomping,
clapping their hands all over her. Some jerk started spraying suds

everywhere. Tranquila, suffocated by the praise that she didn't understand, let out a vociferous scream until everyone backed away from her. She was able to breathe again. Panting, she cried, "BACK THE FUCK UP!"

"Hey! There's no use for such language," began Athena prudently.

"Fuck off, Athena. Let a woman speak for once," Apollo interjected.

After a slight wave of nausea that left her needing to spit up a little bit, Tranquila found strength again and demanded the burning answers: "Okay. So, I'm immortal now?"

"Right," they answered in unison.

"Just like that? Hades shakes my hand. No glowing, no burning, no magical transformation scenes? Just one minute I can die and the next minute I'm young and semi-attractive forever?"

"I'm afraid so, Tranquila," replied Hades, full of mirth. "Unfortunately, you've witnessed firsthand just how spectacular-less being a God is."

"Goddess," Persephone corrected, sweetly. "You're a goddess now. And it's a process called apotheosis by proxy."

"Apoth-what? What the hell does that even mean?" Tranquila squawked.

"It means all that time you've spent doing godly things with godly beings, facing situations and experiencing what only the gods and goddesses themselves have faced, it was elevating you," she informed. "And with Hades' blessing, his handshake and his affections, you are now ruler of the Underworld."

Somewhere, she was dimly aware of applause and some adulation and maybe even a vague catcall from Apollo, but Tranquila processed none of it. She looked over and gave Hades another dumbstruck stare. Walking over to him, she was now shamefully conscious of the resurgence of tears in her eyes.

"You gave up your job, boss," she whispered, profoundly touched and saddened all at once.

"I did," he whispered back, with a small smile that she thought meant he was sad as well. But then he put a massive hand on her shoulder and avowed, "But I had to retire at some point anyway. Opt out and give some new blood a shot."

"What are you going to do?"

Hades shrugged. "I'll figure it out."

"Boss, no—"

Hades stopped the protests by holding up his hand. "I'll be fine, Tranquila. I've served my purpose. Besides, this way I've kept my promise."

"I didn't want you to lose your job just to keep me from being bored," Tranquila said, cracking under great sadness and guilt.

"Don't think like that. Think of this as a shift in upper-level management," Hades insisted, with a smile.

With that, he broke a boundary he never had before. He leaned forward to embrace his employee—nay, coworker.

Tranquila was too stiff to do anything at first. She thought of resisting, for Persephone's sake, but she instantly forgot this thought. It was a long day. She needed a hug. Which is why she melted in his arms and hugged the god back.

Everyone 'aww'd' for them. Everyone but Persephone, who was getting stabbed in the chest by jealousy. She sprinted over and hastily broke the pair apart, urging them, "Alright, alright. That's enough. I mean, Tranquila has a ton of work to get done. We should probably leave her be."

Hades recognized the edginess in her voice but didn't get excited over it, as he would have before. Instead, he beamed at his young protégé and voiced: "Enjoy civil service, Tranquila. I'll come down and visit you."

"Oh, Boss, you don't—"

"I want to," he insisted, the gentility in his voice making Tranquila smile and Persephone scowl.

Led away by the hand of an envious deity, Hades went over to his bloodline. In one collective stroke, they became a cloud of mist, allowing themselves to be carried off by the stagnant Underworld air.

Tranquila, left alone in her newfound kingdom, found herself greatly depressed by the loneliness. That was, until she heard the familiar slushing sounds of water being pushed back. She looked over her shoulder to find Charon—hardworking Charon—back at his post, his first customer already in tow.

In the boat, looking as ugly and miserable as ever, sat Grandma Sobriquet. All the confused feelings—the guilt, the rage, the resentment—fell from Tranquila, as if they had never been there. She ran to the river bend, arms open wide, screaming, "Grandma!"

Grandma Sobriquet smiled in spite of herself. She stood on the rickety dingy, as if ready to reciprocate the hug.

"Oh, Grandma," Tranquila cried, as the boat made it to the soggy sand. "I'm so sorry I called you a salty bi—"

The expletive went unfinished. The salty bitch held up in front of her the corded phone that Charon kept in his boat. She whispered, "It's your mother."

Winded by the reminder—oh yeah she had a mother, a mortal mother, who had absolutely no idea what just happened, nor what had happened to her daughter over the last six months—Tranquila took the phone in hand. The newly dead old woman mouthed, "Good luck, Tran."

But Tranquila was too ascetic to think of what would happen. All she knew was that when she pressed the phone to her head, she was bubbling with the best news of her life.

"Mom!" she exclaimed, her girly voice and high-pitched squeals of excitement reverberating pervasively through the cavernous domain, now for the first time claimed solely by woman. "I got a job!"

EPILOGUE: LET THEM BE PETTY

Hades, ankle deep in the River Styx's muck, stood giddy and flighty, like a teenage girl who just received news that their favorite band was coming to town.

"He he he!" He giggled, addressing Tranquila, who stood beside him with a faint smile and a memo in hand. "I've been waiting for this day for years! How long ago did you say again?"

Tranquila looked at her phone. "Should be any minute now."

Hades let out another bubbly squeal. "Ahh! This is too perfect! Read the memo to me again! Read the memo to me again!"

Tranquila obliged, "'James Howard Woods, age eighty, death caused by a venomous Komodo dragon bite. Died in an illegal underground casino circuit in Las Vegas when one of the owner's prized fighting Komodo dragons escaped and bit the afflicted's foot off.'"

Hades inhaled in a satisfactory sigh. "Ah, beautiful. Thanks again for letting me do this, Tranquila."

"No problem. It'll be good practice for when I need to divinely smite somebody." She replied. She turned her attention to Persephone, who was beside her newly reconciled spouse, and inquired, "I gotta ask though. Why are you here?"

"Hey, anybody my baby hates, I hate." Persephone insisted. Then she asked Hades, "Speaking of which, what's a couple of things I need to know so I can get in the right menacing mindset to bring the holy beat down on this doomed motherfucker?"

"Well…" Hades began, contemplating. "He's white, he's rich and he voted for Trump."

"Okay, we good now." Persephone stated, cracking her knuckles in a preparatory fashion.

Tranquila turned her head to her mother, who also stood with them, and asked, "Hey mom why are you here though?"

"Oh. You see, when your father and I first got married, he used to be obsessed with becoming a card shark and one time he disappeared for three days and I found out he swiped fifthteen-hundred dollars from our joint bank account to go play in this celebrity poker tournament down in Myrtle Beach. Anyway, it turns out James Woods was the celebrity who cleaned him out so I'm here to beat his ass until I feel like I've gotten fifthteen-hundred dollars' worth. Which, back in the nineties, would have equated to two-thousand-eight-hundred-seventy-two dollars in today's economy."

Hades, Persephone and Tranquila all gave Darlene a nod of approval.

"Wow mom. I'm proud of you." Tranquila said. "Not only are you counter-transferring all your resentment for dad to a complete stranger, but you also put an empirical dollar amount on how much the other guy did you wrong."

That's when Tranquila directed her attention to another person who stood with them in the river banks. A dead man, whose name she had not learned yet.

"Hey dead guy, why are you here?"

"Oh, I'm the dead guy James Woods tried suing. I've come here to whoop his ass and to gloat about how I died before he could get any money out of me."

"Why did he sue you?" Darlene inquired curiously.

"I called him a crackhead over the internet."

"…Is he a crackhead?"

"Pfft. I don't know. But he still shouldn't've sued me for it. You know how many people I've accused of having a serious drug problem over the internet, back in the day? Besides, I don't got money. I'm a fucking dead guy. Not a fucking dead rich guy."

His reasoning was met with murmurs of overlapping assent.

"True, true," Tranquila commented before addressing yet another person on the retribution shoreline, "Hey Jane Austen, why do you wanna beat James Woods' ass?"

"Oh I'm not here for who you are all here for." She implored innocently. Then her grey eyes narrowed and her face grew bitter when she explained, "I'm here to bring the smack down on that incorrigible skeleton."

Pause. "Alright. Fair enough."

"I'm here because I think what all of you are doing is cruel. And the antithesis of what the Underworld-Afterlife stands for." Grandma Sobriquet's voice piped up, who was the last of them in the vindictive line.

Her statement garnered jeers and dissent from nearly everyone else who stood on the river bank, sans Tranquila, who didn't care enough either way. She was just a New York kid at heart, itching to watch a situation that didn't need to be escalated become reckless and unnecessarily violent.

"Oh grandma!"

"Shut up ma!"

"Hypocrite!"

"Boooo! Booooo!"

"You've gone soft Jeanette, ever since you died." Hades said, shaking his head.

"I am not soft! I'm hard as a motherfucker. Even Biggie and Oedipus said so." Grandma Sobriquet retorted before moving towards the group and snatching the memo from Tranquila's clipboard. "Besides, at least I'm not lying to you. Look! James Woods didn't die of a Komodo dragon bite. He died getting cancer, just like every other old person in America."

Grandma Sobriquet held up the memo for Hades to read. After a quick couple of glances, Hades sucked his teeth in disappointment and groaned. "Oh…I knew it was too perfect. I just wanted that to be true so badly."

"Sorry, Hades," Tranquila apologized. "I thought the real cause of death was pretty lame so I just substituted it with this reoccurring dream I keep having."

"That was very kind of you to lie to my face like that, Tranquila." Hades reassured.

Seeing the hurt and disappointment in the god's face resulted in a backlash for Jeanette. Nearly everyone in line turned to cast a glaring eye onto her fleshless form.

"Why are you adverse to our affinity for deception?" demanded Jane Austen, angrily.

"What the hell is wrong with you guys?" Grandma Sobriquet balked. "How can you allow this Catholic-like pettiness and arbitrary punishment? The Underworld doesn't torture or smite those because they are imperfect, only those who are morally repugnant."

"Ma, why are you being such a hater?" Darlene cried out.

"Because this is not how the Underworld works!" Jeanette insisted. She turned to address her granddaughter and said, "You shouldn't be instigating this kind of behavior, Tranquila. For Gods' sake you're the undying ruler of this realm! Show some class. Show some leadership."

"But I am showing leadership. Who do you think is the one who organized this one sided beat down?" Tranquila replied, cheerfully. Peering out ahead, Tranquila whipped out her phone in excitement and she announced. "OH SHIT! THERE'S CHARON'S BOAT!"

Her cry was true. There, cutting through the Underworld's dank fog and mist, shone Charon's rickety little boat, carrying two new clients.

Everyone waited in abated, but preparatory zeal, as Charon oared onto shore.

"Charon!" Hades called out in annoyance, seeing a second unwanted carrier. "I told you to only grab the old man."

"I know but they both died at the same exact time. I wasn't going to do a round trip just for that." Charon gruffed out, as the young man climbed out of the boat.

Almost immediately after the young man walked onto the river bank, effectively taking his first step in his after-life, he looked up and recognized Tranquila at once.

"Oh my god." He gasped. "Oh my god! You're the girl who saved my life!"

"*Uh...*" Tranquila droned out, unsure of what to say. How can it be called saving a life when the life you saved only lived another eleven months anyway?

Unaware of her cosmic splendor, the young man rushed over to Tranquila and beseeched, "Listen, thank you, thank you, for what you did that night. My name's Kenny and I know it doesn't seem like much now, but you changed my life that night. I swear this wasn't caused by that. I actually was on the right path for a long time after I OD'd. I enrolled into school and I reconnected with my dad and everything was going really, really good for me—"

Tranquila found his speech touching. His story was shortened by Persephone's impatience.

"Yeah, yeah, yeah. Save your speech for the rest of eternity, kido. We don't got the rest of forever like you." She interjected, pushing him forward, towards the opened Gates of Hades.

"Sorry Kenny!" Tranquila cried after the sullen man. "I promise I'll listen to your sad life story later, though!"

Finally, all attention, including Tranquila's video-recording, was back towards the white-haired dead actor, who was confronted by an intense collection of heated, unrelenting glares. None of which daunted him, though. Instead, still within the safeties of Charon's boat, James Woods' attention flicked over towards a single person. His eyes glistened with his own nasty inclinations,

"Hey Jeanette." He breathed.

Grandma Sobriquet said nothing but the change in her eyes and the shallowness of her breath was ostentatious to most of those who stood in the bellicose line.

"Jeanette?!" Tranquila parroted, unwise. "How the hell do you know him?"

Nobody answered quicker than Charon: "That's cause they fucked, boss!"

Suddenly, nobody wanted revenge anymore. Grossed out by Grandma Sobriquet's non-denial, everyone just wanted to go home for the rest of the day. Everyone except for Jane Austen who took the dispersal as an opportunity to knock James Woods into the dank River Styx and choke out Charon with her petticoat. Hades went back to Olympus with his wife. Tranquila took some personal time spending it on Earth with her mother, eating 4 different kinds of fast food and watching animal fight documentaries until she recovered from her trauma. Afterwards, she went back to her eternal servitude.

CPSIA information can be obtained
at www.ICGtesting.com
Printed in the USA
LVOW03s2249231117
557348LV00003B/282/P